MEASLE
and the
MALLOCKEE

MEASLE
and the
MALLOCKEE

IAN OGILVY

HARPERCOLLINS*PUBLISHERS*

Library of Congress Cataloging-in-Publication Data

Ogilvy, Ian, date.

Measle and the Mallockee / Ian Ogilvy.— 1st American ed.

p.   cm.

Sequel to: Measle and the dragodon.

Summary: For young Measle Stubbs, surviving a stay in a haunted castle means confronting pictures that come to life, a murderous suit of armor, and a jellybean-loving wrathmonk.

ISBN-10: 0-06-058691-5 (trade bdg.) — ISBN-13: 978-0-06-058691-1 (trade bdg.)

ISBN-10: 0-06-058692-3 (lib. bdg.) — ISBN-13: 978-0-06-058692-8 (lib. bdg.)

[1. Wizards—Fiction.   2. Magic—Fiction. 3. Castles—Fiction.]   I. Title.

PZ7.O3435Mdo 2006   2005017609
[Fic]—dc22   CIP
                                                                          AC

Typography by Amy Ryan

1 2 3 4 5 6 7 8 9 10

❖

First Edition

As ever—
Barnaby and Matilda

CONTENTS

1
MATILDA

Splat!

Something wet and warm—and very, *very* slimy—smacked against Measle's right cheek. It stuck there for a moment and then began to slide slowly down his face.

"Matilda Stubbs, you stop that this *instant*," said Nanny Flannel as firmly as she could without sounding cross.

Matilda Stubbs took no notice. She reached into the bowl in front of her and scooped up another handful.

"Tilly . . . ," said Lee Stubbs in a warning voice.

Measle noticed, much to his disgust, that his mother—sitting on the far side of the kitchen table and thus well out of range of wet, slimy stuff—was grinning openly at Matilda.

Matilda Stubbs grinned back at Lee, showing off her collection of teeth. There were six of them, all fairly new and all in the front of her mouth, and Matilda liked showing them to people whenever possible. She turned her attention back to Measle. She raised her hand above her shoulder and prepared to throw again. Tinker, Measle's little black-and-white terrier, started to edge closer and closer to Matilda's high chair. As far as Tinker was concerned, you simply couldn't have *enough* wet, warm and slimy objects whizzing about the place—and the more that came whizzing his way (and into his open mouth), the better.

"Sam, our daughter is misbehaving," said Lee. "Please do something about it."

"Hmm? What?" said Sam Stubbs. He was hidden behind his morning newspaper, and the only way to tell that he was there at all was the occasional appearance of his hand, sneaking around from behind the paper to pick up the coffee cup on the table in front of him.

"Our daughter, Sam," repeated Lee. "She's being evil again."

"Evil, eh? Oh, good for her," muttered Sam from behind the paper.

Lee sighed.

By now Matilda's arm was slowly moving backward to a spot somewhere behind her shoulder. Measle knew from experience that when the arm stopped, the missile that was clutched in her hand was only a second away from being launched in his direction.

Tinker, sensing that at any minute now a wet, slimy and very tasty thing was about to be let loose right here in the kitchen, began to wag his stumpy little tail so fast that it became a blur.

Measle sighed and put the piece of toast he'd been eating down on his plate.

"Tilly, cool it," he said, glaring at Matilda with his pretend-fierce face.

Matilda Stubbs stopped the slow backward movement of her arm and stared solemnly at Measle. Then she said, "Blobba?"

"Yes," said Measle, relaxing his face a little. "*Blobba.*

Now either put it down or eat it, Tilly. Just don't throw it at me, okay?"

"Goomba zoody gurk," said Matilda firmly, but she lowered her arm, opened her tiny fist and stared intently at the congealing lump of porridge in her hand. Then, smiling blissfully, Matilda Stubbs began to rub the porridge into her hair.

Tinker's ears drooped in disappointment. Nanny Flannel shrieked and ran for a washcloth.

With the danger past—at least for the moment—Measle felt safe enough to wipe his face with his napkin. Then he picked up his toast again and went back to his breakfast.

Matilda Stubbs had come to Merlin Manor nine months ago. She had arrived, snuggled in the arms of her mother, in a taxi that had driven them both from the local hospital. For the next nine months, she had done what all babies do. She'd slept, she'd eaten, she'd cried and—in Measle's opinion—done awful, *dreadful* things in her diapers. Sam had once said that his darling little daughter was little more than a loud noise at *one* end and an icky mess at the *other*—and

Measle thought that was exactly right. Meanwhile, Matilda Stubbs had grown steadily into a chubby little baby girl, with piercing green eyes, spiky brown hair, six small, pearly white teeth and a throwing arm of devastating accuracy.

Matilda adored her big brother. Whenever Measle was in the room, she had eyes only for him. Measle was the one she showed her teeth to most often. Measle was the one she addressed most of her remarks to, and lately—since she discovered how to throw stuff—Measle was the one she chose to throw it at.

Right now Matilda was trying to stuff as much porridge as she could into her ears before Nanny Flannel came back with the washcloth. Measle turned to his parents to tell them what Matilda was up to but, as usual, they were no good in a situation like this. Lee was too busy laughing and, as for Sam—well, he was hidden behind his newspaper and completely oblivious to everything that was going on around him.

Suddenly the newspaper started shaking as if it was going through a small earthquake.

"I don't believe it! Justin Bucket? *Justin Bucket?*"

"What about Justin Bucket?" gasped Lee, raising her

face from her hands and still trying hard to stifle her laughter.

Sam lowered his newspaper. There was a look of angry bewilderment on his face.

"The most appalling thing has happened," he announced. "You'll never believe this, but Justin Bucket is the new Prime Magus of the Wizards' Guild."

"*What?* You're not serious?" said Lee.

Sam nodded. "Quite serious. I knew the idiot was one of the candidates, but I was certain there was no way he could ever get *elected*. I was sure that Toby would win in a landslide!"

"Who's Toby?" asked Measle, taking a big bite of toast.

"Toby Jugg," said Sam, "is the fellow who should, by rights, be the new Prime Magus of the Wizards' Guild. He's the Wizard everybody *assumed* would be elected— which is why I'm finding it hard to believe how Justin the-Biggest-Fathead-in-the-Wizarding-Fraternity Bucket has managed to beat him. Poor old Toby. He must be sick as a parrot! And it gets worse. Listen to this," he muttered. "Here's a list of the new members of Justin's Advisory Board."

"Advisory Board?" said Lee. "Since when has the Prime Magus of the Wizards' Guild had an Advisory Board?"

"Never—until now, it seems. Listen—Sir Peregrine Spine, Tully Telford, Dorian Fescue, Ermintrude Bacon and Quentin Underwood."

"But Sam," said Lee, her eyes very wide, "aren't they all—"

"All Warlocks, yes." Sam lowered the paper again. He stared at his family, a worried frown creasing his forehead. "This isn't good, you know."

"Whassamatter?" mumbled Measle, through yet another mouthful of toast. (Very few things could distract Measle from his breakfast. His years of living with Basil Tramplebone—and being half starved to death by the horrible Wrathmonk—had made him determined never to go hungry again.)

"The matter is, son," said Sam, "(a) try not to talk with your mouth full; and (b) a Warlock can't be elected Prime Magus of the Wizards' Guild. It's against the rules. Warlocks like power too much, and they often reach very high levels of power in ordinary life. Sir Peregrine Spine is hugely rich, Tully Telford is a top

7

lawyer, Dorian Fescue owns a whole chain of super-markets, Ermintrude Bacon has a string of sausage fac-tories and Quentin Underwood is a junior minister in the government. Well, their hunger for power is fine in everyday life, but it's *not* fine when it comes to leading our Guild. We've always had just plain, ordinary Wizards before, who don't care about power much."

Measle swallowed his toast. "So this Bucket bloke—he isn't a Warlock, then?"

"Justin? No, he's not clever enough for that. He's just an ordinary Wizard. A pretty pathetic one, if you ask me. But—and it's a *big* but—now he's got all these very powerful, very ambitious Warlocks apparently 'advising' him. And what sort of advice do you suppose he'll be getting, eh?"

Measle—who had no idea—shook his head.

"I'll tell you, Measle," said Sam gloomily. "The *wrong* sort of advice, that's what. The sort of advice that'll make the Warlocks even stronger than they are now. The sort of advice that—if Justin Bucket listens to it (and, knowing him, he will)—could easily change the Wizards' Guild beyond recognition. I don't like it. I don't like it at all."

8

Nanny Flannel had come back into the room and was now busy cleaning the porridge out of Matilda's ear. She said, "Well, never mind what you like or what you don't like, Sam, it's time Measle and I were off." She turned to Measle and jerked her head toward the kitchen door. "Put your helmet on, dear," she said. "I'll be with you in a minute."

Measle whistled to Tinker, who scurried out from under Matilda's high chair. Then they both went out into the big hallway of Merlin Manor, where a row of brass hooks lined the wall near the heavy front door. Measle took a motorbike helmet down from a hook and jammed it on his head. The helmet was fire engine red, with orange flames painted on it. Measle swung his schoolbag over his shoulder and, with Tinker trotting beside him, went out the front door and down the wide steps that led to the drive.

The motorbike that was standing there waiting for him was big and black and shiny, and so was the sidecar attached to it. It had once belonged to the giant Wrathmonk Buford Cudgel, but now it belonged pretty much to Nanny Flannel, since she was the only one in the Stubbs family who rode it regularly. When

Buford Cudgel had owned the bike, it had been a filthy, broken-down, smoky old thing. But now it was clean and shiny and in tip-top condition, and Nanny Flannel used it to take Measle to school.

Measle and Tinker hopped into the sidecar. It was cramped and Tinker had to sit on Measle's knees—which was fine, as far as Tinker was concerned. Tinker didn't mind where he sat, or how uncomfortable it was, just as long as he got to ride in the sidecar when the old lady and the smelly kid went to school. He liked the feeling of the wind in his face and was quite proud of the way his ears flapped when the motorbike went fast.

A few moments later, Nanny Flannel bustled out the front door. She was all bundled up in a long leather coat, and a pair of leather gauntlets encased her hands. Her own helmet was already on her head. It was silver and had a sticker of a skull and crossbones stuck on the front of it.

Nanny Flannel was surprisingly agile for somebody of her great age. She hopped into the saddle and pushed the starter button. The engine rumbled into life and, with a roar, the big motorbike sped off down the long drive.

Usually Measle and Nanny Flannel didn't talk much

on the way to school. There was too much noise—
what with the thunder from the engine and the
whistling of the wind—but this time Measle had a
couple of questions that couldn't wait.

"NANNY!" he roared, shouting over the thumping
sound of the engine. "HOW COME I'M NOT A
WIZARD?"

It was a question that had been bothering Measle for
some time, but the opportunity to ask it had never
really presented itself. The whole subject of wizarding
was usually avoided in the Stubbs household and, most
of the time, Sam and Lee behaved as if they were perfectly ordinary people, so Measle had been hesitant to
bring it up. And the longer he left the question
unasked, the harder it was to ask it. But now with this
latest news and his dad's obvious anxiety about the
future of the Wizards' Guild, Measle decided it was
now or never: he *had* to ask.

"WHAT WAS THAT, DEAR?" screamed Nanny
Flannel, without taking her eyes off the road ahead.

"ME! WIZARD! WHY NOT?"

Nanny Flannel risked a quick glance down into the
sidecar.

11

"I DON'T KNOW, DEAR!" she yelled. "WHY *SHOULD* YOU BE?"

"BECAUSE I'M A WIZARD'S *SON*, NANNY!"

Nanny Flannel steered the motorbike to the side of the road, brought it to a quick stop and switched off the engine.

"Now then, why aren't you a Wizard?" she asked, pulling her helmet off her head and shaking out her gray curls. "Why are you asking me? Why not ask your father?"

Measle shrugged uncomfortably. "Well, you know, he might be disappointed that I'm *not* a Wizard."

Nanny Flannel laughed. "He's not disappointed, dear. He's relieved. So's your mum."

"Relieved? Why?"

"Because being a Wizard is not all that wonderful, dear. Being a Wizard's son or daughter does mean that there's quite a good chance of being a Wizard yourself— but it's not *guaranteed*. On the other hand, being the son or the daughter of a perfectly ordinary mother and father doesn't mean that you're *not* going to be a Wizard. There are plenty of members of the Guild whose parents have no magical qualities at all. In fact, I'm told that there are thousands of Wizards out in the world who have no idea whatsoever that they *are* Wizards!"

"Does that mean . . . that I *might* be a Wizard, then?"

Nanny Flannel shook her head. "No, dear. You're not. No more than I am. No, you're an ordinary boy."

"Oh," said Measle, disappointed.

Nanny Flannel rapped gently on the top of Measle's helmet with her gauntleted fist.

"Oh, don't sound all sad, Measle dear," she said. "There's nothing wrong with being an ordinary boy. You should be very glad you're *not* a Wizard. It isn't an easy life, you know. Wizards face dangers that ordinary people know nothing about."

"What, dangers like the ones *I've* faced?" said Measle, staring straight ahead.

There was a pause while Nanny Flannel thought about this. Then she said quietly, "Yes, dear. Just like the ones you've faced." She pressed the starter button and the big engine rumbled back to life, and they drove the rest of the way to school in silence.

When Nanny Flannel brought Measle home from school, Lee came out to meet them. She held Matilda in her arms and there was a worried look in her eyes.

"What's going on, Mum?" said Measle.

"I don't know, darling. Your dad's in his study with Mr. Needle and Mr. Bland. And they've locked the door."

"But—what do *they* want?"

"Your guess is as good as mine. They just turned up on the doorstep an hour ago and, when Dad opened the door, they barged in, waving a bunch of papers and demanding that they talk to him in private—"

Lee broke off, because here—marching out of the front door—came Mr. Needle and Mr. Bland.

Measle remembered them. They were the two representatives from the Wizards' Guild who had come to Merlin Manor when Lee had been kidnapped by the gang of Wrathmonks. The two men had been cold and unhelpful. Then, later, after Sam had trapped the last four Wrathmonks in a magical net, Mr. Needle and Mr. Bland had been the ones to take them away in a white van—although, even then, with the Stubbs family triumphant and victorious, neither of the Wizards' Guild representatives had been particularly nice about it.

Mr. Needle was tall and thin and dark. Mr. Bland

was short and round and blond. Both men wore dark suits, sunglasses and bowler hats, and each man carried a black leather briefcase and a furled umbrella. As they passed by Lee and Measle and Nanny Flannel, Mr. Needle and Mr. Bland tipped their bowler hats, then continued down the front steps of Merlin Manor, their twinkling black shoes making a sharp *tap-tapping* noise on the ancient stones.

When the white van disappeared out the distant gates at the far end of the long driveway, Measle and Nanny Flannel and Lee—with Matilda in her arms—went back into Merlin Manor and hurried to Sam's study. They found him there, sitting behind his desk, his face pale and his lips compressed. Tinker sat at his feet. In Sam's hands was a sheaf of papers. Sam looked up when they came in, and Measle saw real anger in his father's eyes.

"What was that all about?" said Lee.

"An *inquiry*," said Sam, his voice trembling with fury. "That's what it was all about. There is to be an inquiry—and we are summoned—by those two dim little office boys—to answer its questions."

"*Whose* inquiry, Sam?"

15

"The Wizards' Guild. We are summoned to appear before the Wizards' Guild! Well, by its latest committee, actually. This committee calls itself"—Sam peered at the top page of the sheaf of papers—"yes, here we are—this committee calls itself 'The Isle of Smiles Investigation Committee' and is made up of some very interesting people indeed. *Very* interesting. Guess who?"

Lee thought for a moment and then her face cleared. "Oh, dear. Quentin Underwood?"

Sam nodded. "He's one of 'em."

"Dorian Fescue?"

"Yup."

"Ermintrude Bacon?"

"Trudy will be there."

"Tully Telford?"

"He's the leading interrogator."

"Sir Peregrine Spine?"

"Every languid, lanky bone."

"And—and Justin Bucket?"

"He's the presiding chairman."

"But what do they *want*, Sam?" said Lee, shifting Matilda onto her other arm. "What's this inquiry all about?"

Sam shook his head. "Well, other than what happened on the Isle of Smiles, I have no idea, my love," he said. "And, since what happened on the Isle of Smiles turned out to be a triumph for the Wizards' Guild—not to mention for the Stubbs family, too—I can't imagine *what* they're all steamed up about. But steamed up they seem to be. All I know is, we have to be at the committee rooms, in the Wizards' Guild Building, on Sunday night at ten o'clock sharp, to answer any—and all—questions they choose to ask us."

"Us?" said Lee faintly. "Who's us?"

"The whole family."

"What, *all* of us?"

"Yup. Every single one of us. Even Tinker. Even Tilly. Don't ask me why." Sam grinned wryly. "All I can hope," he said, with as much cheerfulness as he could manage, "is that Tilly will find something nice and wet and sticky to throw at the whole lot of 'em."

2

THE
INQUIRY

The big, dark-green Stubbs car, with its dragon skull mascot gleaming white on the front of the long hood, rumbled its way down the city road. It was late on a Sunday night, and most of the city traffic had disappeared from the dark streets.

Sam Stubbs spun the wheel and the big car turned a corner.

"There it is," said Sam quietly. "The Wizards' Guild."

Measle was sitting—with Tinker perched on his knees—in the backseat behind his mother, and between Nanny Flannel and a sleeping Matilda. He stared up at the tall building with a look of intense disappointment on his face. Measle had never been here before and he didn't know quite what to expect—but the building they were approaching seemed to be just another dull pile of red bricks, exactly like all the other buildings that surrounded it.

"Oh," said Measle flatly. "I thought——"

"What did you think, son?" said Sam, over his shoulder. "That the Wizards' Guild would look all sparkly, with magical rainbows and shooting stars all over the place?"

"No, Dad, 'course not," said Measle in the sort of voice you use when a grown-up says something stupid. "But . . . well, I thought it might stand out a bit, that's all."

"It's not supposed to stand out, son. In fact, we want it to look exactly the same as all the rest of the buildings around it, if possible. That way it doesn't draw attention to itself, you see. And if you think that's boring, wait 'til you see what it's called."

Sam parked the car and everybody got out. Nanny Flannel put Matilda, still fast asleep, into her stroller, and then they all walked the short distance to the big revolving glass doors at the front of the building. As they pushed their way through them, Sam pointed to a brass plate screwed to the wall.

THE SMITH, JONES, BROWN INSTITUTE FOR THE STUDY OF CORRUGATED CARDBOARD

it read in large engraved letters.

"The dullest name they could come up with," explained Sam.

"But . . . they don't *really*, do they?" asked Measle.

"Don't what, son?"

"Study corrugated cardboard?"

"Well, er, *sort* of." Sam laughed quietly, because now they were in the grand lobby of the building and there was a big uniformed man—with a shaggy walrus moustache that straggled all the way across the bottom half of his red face—sitting behind a large desk. The man was staring at them inquiringly.

Sam bent his head and whispered in Measle's ear. "If you come here during the week and wander around all the offices we've got here, you'll find hordes of young people all peering intently at different bits of cardboard, looking like they're really busy studying the stuff. Of course, they're only *pretending* to study—just in case anybody gets too curious about us, you see. They're really apprentice Wizards, doing their six months of official corrugated-cardboard-study duty. I did it myself, years ago. I've never been so bored in all my life."

The uniformed man had stood up and was now leaning across the desk, peering at the Stubbs family with suspicion. Then, a moment later, his face cleared.

"Mr. Stubbs, is it?" he said, a grin appearing under his bushy moustache.

"Hello, Fred," said Sam, leaning over the desk and shaking the man's hand. "It's been a long time. How are you?"

"Can't complain, sir. 'Ere for the business at 'and, are we?"

"If you mean this stupid inquiry, Fred—yes, we are."

Fred's red face became a little less red and a small, worried frown appeared on his broad forehead.

"Not so loud, Mr. Stubbs," he said, looking nervously

around the lobby. "Things 'ave changed a bit around 'ere, see?"

Sam nodded gloomily. "So it would seem, Fred."

Fred tapped the side of his nose three times and nodded knowingly. Then he lowered his head toward Sam and muttered, "*And*, Mr. Stubbs, sir—walls 'ave ears, if you know what I mean." Fred straightened up and tapped his nose again. Then he glanced over Sam's shoulder and caught sight of the rest of the Stubbs family. The frown disappeared.

"'Ello, Mrs. Stubbs," he said cheerfully. "You're lookin' extremely well, if I may say so. And is this young Measle, what we've 'eard so much about?"

"That's him, Fred," said Lee, smiling at Fred. "And this is the newest addition to the family—her name's Matilda. And you know Miss Flannel, don't you?"

"Miss Flannel! A pleasure as usual!"

Nanny Flannel nodded curtly and sniffed loudly—a sure sign that, while Fred the lobby guard might consider that what was happening was a "pleasure," Nanny Flannel judged the whole business to be a thorough nuisance and certainly well past everybody's bedtime.

Fred turned his attention to somebody who seemed

a little more pleased to meet him. Tinker was wagging his tail in a friendly sort of way and Fred bent down and patted him on the head.

"And I'm guessing this is the famous Tinker?"

"You guessed right, Fred," said Sam. "Now where are we supposed to be going?"

Fred straightened up. "It's down in number thirteen, Mr. Stubbs, sir," he said, in his official lobby guard voice.

Sam led his family across the lobby to a row of elevators. One of the elevator doors was open and they all clustered inside. Among all the usual buttons on the panel by the door, there was one that was a little larger than all the others. It was bright red and had the words "For Use in Cardboard Emergency Only" engraved on its surface.

Sam pressed it.

The elevator dropped. The drop went on for quite some time and Measle began to wonder just how deep they were going. It was clear they were going a lot deeper down into the earth than any normal elevator would take them.

At last there was a hissing sound and Measle felt the

elevator slow down. A few moments later, they came to a gentle stop and the doors slid open.

There was an immensely long corridor, lit by overhead fluorescent strips, which bathed the whole area with a harsh, white light. The corridor narrowed away into the distance, its walls broken by a succession of heavy oak doors on either side.

The corridor was empty, apart from a large crowd of people about twenty yards away, who all turned their heads and stared as the Stubbs family emerged from the elevator.

"That's where we're going," muttered Sam, jerking his chin in the direction of the crowd. "Looks like we're expected, too."

The Stubbs family walked down the long corridor. When they got near the crowd, a figure detached itself and strode toward them, both hands extended in welcome. Measle saw that the man was about the same age and height as his dad, but there was something about him that made Measle a little uncomfortable. The man's face was tanned, as if he'd just come back from a sunny holiday or perhaps had spent a lot of time under a sunlamp. He had a headful of gleaming, wavy, jet-black hair. He had a broad forehead, a straight, narrow nose, a smiling mouth and a firm and jutting chin. His eyes were a dazzling sky blue and they were very bright and shiny, too. The man appeared to be smiling in the friendliest way possible, and the skin at the corner of his eyes was wrinkled in the way that showed that the smile was genuine—but there was something curiously blank about the man's eyes, as if there was little or nothing going on in the brain behind them.

"My dears!" called the man, coming up to them and taking both Lee's hands in his own. "My dears—how *lovely* to see you! Sam, old chap, you look *frightfully* well! And Lee—*lovelier* than ever! No need to ask how you both are—the very *pictures* of health!"

The man turned his empty, dazzling eyes onto Nanny Flannel.

"And *dear* Miss Flannel—it's been *too* long!"

"No, it hasn't," muttered Nanny Flannel under her breath, so that only Measle, who was standing closest to her, heard the words.

Sam Stubbs stuck out his hand. "Well, Justin," he said, "let me say congratulations on winning the election. Well done."

So this, thought Measle, *is Justin Bucket, the new Prime Magus of the Wizards' Guild. And—I don't know why—but I don't think I like him very much.*

Justin Bucket threw back his handsome head and his long, wavy black hair whipped around his face.

"Oh, goodness!" he exclaimed, just loud enough so that the small crowd of people behind him would be able to catch every word. "Thank you *so* much. And can you imagine my surprise? I was sure dear old Jugg would get it, but then I managed to *squeak* through at the last minute! I don't *deserve* it, really and truly I *don't!*"

There was a long, rather awkward pause, during which Justin Bucket slowly realized that not a single member of the Stubbs family was about to tell him that he *did* deserve it. But Sam and Lee were still smiling at him in a friendly way, so Justin decided to ignore the silence and carry on being charming.

"And this, I take it, is young Measle Stubbs?"

Measle felt his small hands being wrapped in Justin Bucket's large ones. Justin Bucket's hands were cold and limp and slightly damp.

"Well, well, young man, you've been having some *jolly* extraordinary adventures, haven't you? Eh? *Eh?*"

Measle wasn't sure whether Justin wanted an answer or whether the man was just making hearty, conversational noises, so he simply smiled and nodded and then ducked his head in an embarrassed sort of way.

"And what's *this* I see? A *baby*, I do declare!"

"This is Matilda, Justin," said Lee.

Justin bent down and put his face close to Matilda's. "Charming," he said, grinning like a crocodile with a low IQ. "Absolutely *charming!*"

Justin brought his right hand forward and tickled Matilda under her chin. Matilda ducked her head in a quick, smooth movement, opened her mouth and, using every one of her six new teeth, bit down hard on Justin's forefinger.

"Owwww!" shrieked Justin, jerking his hand away.

"Oh, Tilly—that was very, very naughty!" said Lee, in a choky, gaspy kind of voice. Measle knew she was trying hard not to laugh.

"Matilda Stubbs, you apologize to the nice Prime Magus this instant!" said Sam—and Measle heard, quite distinctly, the same suppressed laughter in his dad's voice.

"Duwwa wuwwa," said Matilda cheerfully.

"Nicely spoken, Tilly," said Sam, grinning affectionately at his daughter. "And I'm sure the nice Prime Magus forgives you now."

Nanny Flannel had other concerns. "I do hope your hands are quite *clean*, Mr. Bucket?" she said loudly—and several members of the nearby crowd snorted with poorly concealed laughter.

Justin Bucket tucked his throbbing hand into his armpit and backed away, a sickly smile plastered on his face.

"Ah, the *dear* Stubbs family," he said through gritted teeth. "As amusing as ever!"

Matilda shouted, "Gubba dubba doodoo!" and then waved her small fists in Justin's direction. Justin tried a careless chuckle, but it emerged from his mouth as a sort of choking gurgle. "Well—if you'll excuse me—" he mumbled, then he turned on his heel and marched off toward the closest door. As he neared it, a short, round, blond man detached himself from the crowd, darted forward and yanked the door open, holding it as Justin swept past and into the room beyond. Then the man approached the Stubbs family, his face twisted into what he hoped looked like a welcoming smile, and Measle saw with a start that it was Mr. Bland.

28

"Ah, Mr. Stubbs—and Mrs. Stubbs," said Mr. Bland. "Splendid, splendid—right on time, right on time. I do believe the committee is almost ready for you now, so if you'll kindly take your seats?"

Mr. Bland suddenly noticed Tinker, who was lurking by Measle's feet.

"Is that animal not on a leash?" he said, peering a little nervously at Tinker, who responded by curling one lip back from the right side of his mouth and giving Mr. Bland a quick look at some of his best teeth.

"He's very well trained, Mr. Bland," said Sam. "He'll only bite you if he thinks you're being nasty to us."

"Oh," said Mr. Bland. He took a slow, careful step backward and then, keeping an uncertain eye on Tinker, he motioned them all through the door into a huge room with a low platform at one end. Rows of chairs took up most of the rest of the large space. On the front of the platform was a long, desklike structure, with pads of paper and pencils and glasses of water on it. Behind this was a line of six chairs, all but one of them occupied at the moment. Justin Bucket was easing himself into the empty middle chair. It was just a little taller and a little wider—and a touch more ornate—than anybody else's. Measle saw, with a start of recognition, that dark, thin Mr. Needle was standing behind Justin's chair.

Measle also noticed that all six people behind the long desk were wearing black gowns of the sort that schoolmasters used to wear, and that all of them had small round black velvet caps on their heads, with little velvet flaps that covered their ears.

"Now then," said Mr. Bland, herding the Stubbs family farther into the room, "if Mr. and Mrs. Stubbs would kindly take those two chairs?" Mr. Bland pointed toward a pair of plain wooden chairs that stood, all by themselves, in the area immediately in front of the raised platform. Then Mr. Bland turned to Measle and Nanny Flannel. "And if young Master Stubbs and Miss Flannel—and the baby and the—ah—the animal—if you would all kindly find seats for yourselves up in the gallery, and hold yourselves in readiness for any questions that the committee might see fit to address you."

Mr. Bland waved his hand toward the opposite end of the long room, and Measle turned and saw that there was a sort of balcony there, high up off the floor, with a narrow staircase leading up to it on one side.

Measle turned to look at his dad, and Sam smiled

and nodded and said, "You'll get a good view from up there, son. Go on, get a seat at the front."

Measle allowed a worried look to cross his face.

Lee saw it. She bent down and kissed Measle on the cheek.

"We'll be fine, darling," she whispered. "Go on—and don't let Tilly or Tinker do anything awful, all right?"

They both glanced down at Matilda in her stroller. She had gone back to sleep.

The room was beginning to fill up now as the crowd began edging their way inside. Some took seats in the area behind the two lonely chairs, and others went to the far end and climbed the stairs to the gallery. Sam grinned encouragingly at Measle, and then he and Lee turned and sat down together in the two wooden chairs. Nanny Flannel tapped Measle on the shoulder.

"Come on, dear," she said quietly. "Let's do as we're told, shall we?"

When they reached the bottom of the narrow staircase, there was an immediate problem with Matilda's stroller. But a moment later, a man arrived at the foot of the stairs. He had a cheerful smile, a bumpy broken nose, a short beard and a great mane of curly brown hair, with little flecks of gray running through it, that fell to his shoulders. He had the broadest shoulders Measle had ever seen. Measle thought he looked like a mixture between a middle-aged rock star and a professional boxer.

"Well, hello there, Miss Flannel," the man cried in a jovial voice. "Fancy seeing you! I swear you look younger and lovelier every day!" Measle saw to his astonishment that Nanny Flannel's face was turning pink with pleasure.

"Oooh—Mr. Jugg!" stammered Nanny Flannel, smiling broadly and clasping her hands under her chin. "You are so *naughty!*"

Mr. Jugg. The name registered in Measle's mind. *Toby Jugg. The candidate who should have won the presidency of the Wizards' Guild. Mum said he was nice—*

"Now Miss Flannel," chuckled Toby Jugg, "you know you're my favorite lady in the whole wide world, don't you?"

"Oooh, Mr. *Jugg!*" Nanny Flannel's face had turned a bright red and her whole little round body was squirming with pleasure.

Measle stared—this was a Nanny Flannel he'd never

seen before. Nanny Flannel was always cool and calm and collected. She was the sensible center of the Stubbs family. She was never, *ever*, flustered by anything. . . .

Until today, it seemed.

Nanny Flannel did a little more squirming and twittering and blushing, then she glanced down at Measle and saw him looking at her with his mouth open. Nanny Flannel gave her head a little shake, as if trying to shock her brain into working normally again. She took a deep breath and became herself once more.

"Oh, Mr. Jugg, this is Measle and his sister, Matilda. Measle, say hello to Mr. Jugg."

Measle stuck out his hand and the man took it in his own. Unlike Justin Bucket's, Mr. Jugg's hand was warm and dry and hard with muscle.

"Hello, Measle," said Mr. Jugg. "Heard a lot about you. All good stuff, too. A real pleasure to meet you."

"Same here, Mr. Jugg," said Measle, feeling that he meant it.

"Oh, call me Toby," said Mr. Jugg. "Now then, let's see about this young person and her stroller, shall we?"

Toby Jugg bent down and picked up the stroller—with Matilda in it—as if the thing was a feather. He trotted up the narrow stairs with Measle and Tinker and Nanny Flannel close behind. Nanny Flannel said, "Oh, do be careful, Mr. Jugg!" but she needn't have worried. Toby Jugg seemed to be as strong as a cart horse, and Matilda remained fast asleep.

When they reached the gallery, Toby found them seats right at the front. He pulled a couple of chairs out of the way and made room for Matilda's stroller. Then Nanny Flannel, Measle, and Tinker sat down next to her, and Toby took a seat at Measle's side.

Measle couldn't see the faces of his parents or of the audience, since they were below him and all facing in the opposite direction. The only faces he could see were those of Justin Bucket and the five other members of the committee.

Measle felt a gentle nudge in his ribs.

"A pretty dim-looking lot," whispered Toby into Measle's ear, "wouldn't you agree?"

"Who are they?"

Toby snorted. "That's the Advisory Board. Ridiculous bunch! See the piggy-looking woman on the end? That's Ermintrude Bacon—a good name for her, don't you think? The glossy chap next to her, with the face like a bowl of custard, is Dorian Fescue. The little bald fellow with the bottle specs, shuffling all the papers, is Tully Telford—he's the lawyer and he'll be asking the questions. Then there's Justin Bucket himself, a fathead if ever I saw one. The boring-looking bloke next to him is Quentin Underwood, and the long piece of string on the end is Sir Peregrine Spine."

Measle found himself smiling at Toby's short but accurate descriptions. Ermintrude Bacon *did* look a bit like a pig, Dorian Fescue's face *was* exactly the color of custard, and Sir Peregrine Spine—while looking very grand and important—had the sort of long, skinny body that looked as if you *could* (if you really wanted to) tie a knot in it.

"Dad says they're all Warlocks," said Measle, bending his head close to Toby's so that they wouldn't be overheard.

Toby nodded. "Every man jack of 'em," he whispered. "Except for Justin Bucket, of course, who simply doesn't have either the brains or the power to be one."

"Dad says you should have been Prime Magus, not Justin Bucket," said Measle.

"Your dad's very kind," said Toby cheerfully. "But I lost fair and square. Mind you, if I *had* won, there wouldn't be any Advisory Board. I can't stand those ruddy Warlocks."

"How can you tell a Warlock from a Wizard?" said Measle.

Toby turned his head and stared at Measle in surprise. "You mean—you don't know?" he said, his voice registering surprise.

Measle shook his head.

"Did Sam or your lovely mum never tell you?"

"No," said Measle. "Well, I've never met any Warlocks, you see—not yet, anyway. And we don't really talk about it at home—wizarding stuff, I mean. I think it's because I'm not one."

"Well, lucky old you, that's all I can say," said Toby, gently clapping Measle on the back.

Nanny Flannel leaned around Measle and hissed, "That's what I told him, Mr. Jugg."

"Quite right, too, Miss Flannel," said Toby. Then, turning back to Measle, he said, "All the same, I think you ought to be able to tell the difference between a Wizard and a Warlock, don't you? I mean, you never know when it might come in handy."

Measle nodded and Toby went on in a low voice. "Right. Now, look over the balcony and down to the tops of everybody's heads down there."

Measle leaned forward and stared down at the sea of heads below him.

"Now," Toby's voice whispered in his ear, "have a look at the tops of their ears."

Measle peered down, looking for ears. There were plenty for him to choose from—so many, in fact, that he wondered what exactly he was supposed to be noticing. Several audience members—in particular the women— had hats or hair that covered their ears, so Measle ignored them and concentrated on only the visible ones.

"Notice anything different about any of 'em?" said Toby under his breath.

No, not particularly, thought Measle. *Ears are ears, and that's all that can be said about them—*

No! Wait a minute! Over there, by the wall—that young man's got a pair of ears that are definitely different from everybody else's! The tips are dark gray—almost black, as if somebody's taken a paintbrush, dipped it in a bottle of ink and then dabbed the very tips of his ears with the bristles. How weird! And now that Measle had seen one, he began to notice that several of the younger audience members, both men and women, had black (or *almost* black) tips to their ears.

"See anything weird?" whispered Toby.

Measle raised his hand, his finger extended. He was about to point directly at the man by the wall when Toby's hand grabbed his.

"No pointing, Measle," said Toby. "Not among Wizards and Warlocks, at least. We might think you were about to do a spell, you see, and that makes us nervous. Now then, are you looking at that chap sitting near the wall?"

"Yes," said Measle. "The tops of his ears are sort of black."

"Well spotted. The Gloomstains. All Warlocks develop them. The bigger and blacker the Gloomstains, the more powerful the Warlock. A few of the younger Warlocks quite like showing off their Gloomstains, but older, more powerful Warlocks prefer to keep 'em hidden. That's why the Advisory Board are all wearing those silly little caps, see?"

"But Justin Bucket's only a Wizard," whispered

Measle. "Why is he wearing a cap, too?"

"So that he'll look the same as the rest of 'em, of course," said Toby. "Old Justin always rather fancied himself as a Warlock, you see, but . . . Let me give you a bit of advice, Measle. Never, ever trust a person whose hairstyle covers his ears."

Measle thought about that for half a second, then whipped his head around and stared at Toby, his eyes filled with a sudden suspicion. *Toby's hair fell to his shoulders and completely covered his ears!*

Toby's face split into a wide grin. He brought both his big hands up and lifted the two curtains of hair away from his face . . . and Measle saw that Toby's ears were as pink as his own, without a trace of gray or black about them.

"All right?" said Toby.

"Sorry," muttered Measle.

"Don't be sorry," said Toby firmly. "You were quite right, Measle. That's the point I was trying to make, see? Nobody, not even me, can be trusted in this wizarding world of ours."

Measle wanted to find out more, but there was a sudden banging sound of wood on wood. Measle turned and looked down at the raised platform, where Justin Bucket, standing tall in front of his ornate chair, was whacking a small wooden mallet onto the surface of the counter in front of him. The hubbub that had filled the room died away.

"This inquiry will come to order," called Justin in a pompous voice. He glared around the room, daring anybody to make a sound. Then he sat down and turned to the tubby little man on his right. "Mr. Telford, if you please."

Tully Telford got to his feet and peered down at a sheet of paper in his hand.

"In the matter before us this evening," he began, his voice high-pitched and a little squeaky, "namely, the events that occurred at the Isle of Smiles last year—the committee is composed of myself, Tully Telford, Miss Ermintrude Bacon, Mr. Dorian Fescue, Mr. Quentin Underwood and Sir Peregrine Spine, with Prime Magus Justin Bucket in the chair. Here to furnish the committee with *their* version of the facts are Mr. and Mrs. Stubbs. I, as chief interrogator, will commence the questioning."

"Commence the *nonsense*," muttered Toby in Measle's ear.

Tully Telford leaned forward, staring fiercely down at Sam and Lee.

"Mr. Stubbs," he squeaked. "You sent a report to the Guild, describing events that you *claim* occurred both near your home of Merlin Manor and on the Isle of Smiles. In your report you *claim* that you were rendered helpless by a group of Wrathmonks and that your wife was kidnapped by them. Is that correct?"

"Yes," said Sam calmly.

"And that subsequently your wife was removed to the Isle of Smiles which, at that time, was undergoing winter maintenance and was therefore deserted, other than for the presence of a few key personnel, all of whom had been petrified, by the aforementioned Wrathmonks, by means of a Gorgon's mummified snake head?"

"Yes."

"And subsequently you stated that your wife was held prisoner by a magical being calling itself the Last of the Dragodons. . . ."

Measle found his attention drifting. All that was happening down there was a retelling of the story of the Dragodon—and he *knew* all that. He sneaked a side-

41

ways glance at Toby Jugg and whispered, "Can I ask you something?"

"Shoot," whispered Toby.

"Why don't *Wrathmonks* have black tips to their ears? Because, before they go mad, they're Warlocks, right?"

Toby smiled. "You know about Wrathmonks' rain clouds, don't you? Well, where do you suppose they come from?"

"What, you mean they come from their *ears*?"

"Well, the color does. When the madness overtakes 'em, the Gloomstains fade away and then re-form in the air, in the shape of a black Wrathmonk cloud overhead. And it's lucky for us that they do, because no amount of hair—or even the biggest hat in the world—can conceal a ruddy great rain cloud, can it?"

The voices below were becoming louder. Measle turned away from Toby and looked over the edge of the balcony. To his surprise, Sam was now on his feet, shouting and shaking a forefinger in the direction of the six robed figures on the platform. Lee was pulling gently on Sam's wrist, trying to get him to sit down again.

"Untrue!" roared Sam, his finger stabbing the air in

the direction of Tully Telford. "My son has no magical powers whatsoever! Any suggestion otherwise is a lie!"

"Then how do you explain it, Mr. Stubbs?" shouted Tully Telford, his little round face red with anger. "How do you explain the ease with which he overcame not just the Wrathmonk Basil Tramplebone, but *seven other* Wrathmonks, all equally powerful and all bent on his destruction? And not only did your son overcome them, he also—according to your report—managed to defeat and then destroy an actual living, breathing Dragodon and his actual living, breathing dragon as well! How did he manage all that, Mr. Stubbs, *without magical powers of his own?*"

"He managed it, Tully," said Sam through gritted teeth, "by being brave and resourceful and imaginative and quick thinking—and perhaps by being just a little lucky as well! Why can't you idiots accept that?"

"Insolence will get you nowhere!" snarled Tully, brandishing his papers in a shaking hand.

Lee was still pulling at Sam's sleeve, and now Measle could hear her urgent whispering. "Sit down, Sam— please sit down!"

Sam allowed himself to be pulled down into his

chair, but Measle could see that his dad was shaking his head in obvious disgust.

"May I interject for a moment, Mr. Prime Magus?" said Ermintrude Bacon in a sweet and sickly voice. It was the sort of voice you might use when talking baby talk to a toddler.

"The chair recognizes Miss Ermintrude Bacon," said Justin graciously.

"Thank you, Mr. Prime Magus. I can't help noticing that Mr. Stubbs is becoming just the *weensiest* bit *tense*, and we know what can happen when a wizard becomes tense, don't we?"

There was lot of nodding heads and rumbles of agreement. Then Ermintrude went on, "Adding to my unease is the fact that *Mrs.* Stubbs—the celebrated Manafount—is seated right next to her husband. May I remind everybody that a Manafount can produce a never-ending supply of mana to his—or, in this case, *her*—married partner! This means that Mr. Stubbs could perform an unlimited number of harmful enchantments whenever, and upon *whomever*, he chooses!"

"Oh, don't be ridiculous, Trudy," said Sam. "I'm not

going to do anything of the sort."

"In which case," said Ermintrude, ignoring Sam and now smiling sweetly at Justin Bucket, "in which case, I would feel a *tiddly-widdly* bit safer if they were separated."

There was a short, hurried consultation among the six members of the committee, and then Justin rose to his feet and banged his little hammer again.

"Mr. Bland, Mr. Needle—would you be so kind as to place the dividing screen between Mr. and Mrs. Stubbs?"

Measle watched as Mr. Bland and Mr. Needle—both of whom had been standing discreetly at either end of the platform—produced a folding wooden screen from a cupboard at the back of the room. They carried it to where Sam and Lee were sitting and slid the screen between the two chairs, so that Sam and Lee could neither touch or see each other anymore.

"Oh, thank you so much, Mr. Prime Magus," trilled Ermintrude. "I do feel a teeny-weeny bit more secure now."

"May I continue now, Mr. Prime Magus?" said Tully, rustling his papers impatiently.

"Please do, Mr. Chief Interrogator."

"Thank you. Now—leaving aside for the moment the distinct probability that Measle Stubbs does *indeed* possess magical abilities; and also leaving aside the whole question of the small dog in the case, a dog which appears to me to be an almost *unbelievably* remarkable animal—I now turn to you, Mrs. Stubbs. Would you deny, Mrs. Stubbs, that a number of illegal acts were performed by both your son Measle and by yourself?"

"Illegal acts? What are you talking about, Mr. Telford?" said Lee calmly.

Tully shuffled through his papers, picked one from the pile, and began to read.

"'Illegal act number one: unauthorized use of a Guild vehicle by a minor. Illegal act number two: breaking into an area—by both a minor and a Manafount—which had been declared off-limits by this Guild. Illegal act number three: considerable damage done, by both minor and Manafount and *dog*, to human-owned equipment on the property known as the Isle of Smiles.'"

Tully Telford took a deep breath and adjusted his

spectacles. Then he went on, "'Illegal act number four: the unwarranted—and unapproved—eradication of a Dragodon, a species of Wizard thought to be long extinct and therefore of considerable interest to this Guild. Illegal act number five: the unwarranted and unapproved eradication of an actual dragon, a species of creature also thought to be long extinct and therefore also of considerable interest to this Guild—"

"Wait a minute," came Sam's voice. "Wait just a minute! What do you mean 'unwarranted'? And what do you mean 'unapproved'? My wife and my son were about to be *eaten*! May I point out that, with only seconds before their deaths, there wasn't exactly any *time* to get Guild approval!"

"No, Mr. Stubbs, you may not point it out!" squeaked Tully fiercely. "This court—I mean, this *inquiry*—is concerned only with the breaking of a number of laws of the Wizards' Guild, all of which infractions you and your family are shown to be clearly guilty . . ."

Tully Telford's voice began to trail away, because he was slowly becoming aware of the sudden gasps of astonishment—and the stifled sounds of choked-back laughter—that were starting to come from every member of the audience in that great room. At exactly the same moment that he noticed the change in behavior in the audience, he also started to feel a strange sensation in the area of his ears. There was a sort of gentle flapping, a kind of soft fluttering, as if a little bird was trying out its new wings—a soft, velvety little bird, flapping its baby wings, trying to take off for the very first time from its nest . . . a nest that just happened to be *on top of the chief interrogator's head*!

3

DISORDER
IN THE COURT

Tully Telford raised both hands and grabbed the pair of soft velvet folds that hung from the little black cap on his head. They were moving! Moving up and down! Fluttering and flapping against his ears!

The laughter from the audience became louder and less stifled. Tully glanced to either side and saw that all the other members of the committee also had their hands raised, their fingers clutching at the velvet flaps on their caps, and every little flap was moving up and down, up and down.

"Whoever is responsible for this childish behavior," said Tully loudly, his eyes glaring around the room, "whoever is responsible for this, would he or she kindly desist? This is a serious matter, and this court—I mean, this *inquiry*—will be not be trifled with!"

But if anything, the ear coverings on every little cap began to flap faster and with greater strength and, try as they might, the committee members found themselves unable to keep them under control. Faster and faster they flapped, and now the committee members could actually feel a breeze on their cheeks, as the beating of the little cloth wings became more and more powerful.

It was Ermintrude Bacon's cap that was the first to leave her head and fly around the great room. Ermintrude had dropped both her hands for a moment, letting go of her cap, and the little thing seemed to jump at this opportunity for escape, because it did literally that—it jumped off her head and soared up toward the high ceiling. *It looked*, thought Measle, staring up at it with astonished eyes, *just like a small black bat*.

"My cap!" wailed Ermintrude.

"This tomfoolery must stop immediately!" thundered Tully. "Mr. Prime Magus, if you would kindly bring this court—I mean, this *inquiry*—to order!"

Justin Bucket rose to his feet and picked up his little wooden mallet. In doing so, he let go of one side of his own cap. The flaps over his ears blurred in a sudden powerful effort, and his cap wrenched itself from his head and darted up to join its fellow that was hovering near the ceiling.

The laughter from the audience was getting out of hand. Adding to the din was Justin Bucket. He was now whacking the desk in front of him as hard as he could with his little mallet and shouting, "Order! *Order! ORDER!*" at the top of his voice, but nobody seemed to be paying him any attention. Sir Peregrine Spine—with a look of despair—gave up the battle to keep his cap on his head and let go of the wildly beating flaps. Instantly his cap zoomed up to join its two companions.

The remaining caps began to beat their wings even more powerfully now, and it became harder and harder for the rest of the committee to hang on to them. Tully Telford let his go when he began to feel himself literally being lifted off his feet. With his ears revealed, it was obvious that Tully Telford's Gloomstains were bigger and blacker than anybody else's in that great room.

Dorian Fescue and Quentin Underwood quickly surrendered, too, letting their caps fly from their heads and join the little group of fluttering objects high above them.

Most of the audience members were howling with unsuppressed laughter now, tears running down their cheeks, neighbor clutching neighbor, fingers pointing, feet stamping, while up on the platform Justin was pounding his little hammer and screaming, "Order! ORDER! *ORDER!*"

Tully Telford was on his feet, screeching, "This is intolerable! THIS IS *INTOLERABLE!*" Ermintrude Bacon, looking bewildered, was trying to pat her disarrayed curls back into place. Dorian Fescue was staring up at the ceiling with his mouth wide open. Quentin Underwood was smiling vacantly, like a person who's been told a joke he doesn't understand but pretends he does. And Sir Peregrine Spine was shaking his head angrily and drumming his fingernails on the desk in front of him.

Tully Telford pointed a shaking finger down at Sam Stubbs. "It's you!" he shrieked. "You're doing this, aren't you?"

"Not me!" shouted Sam, his voice raised over the hubbub of laughter that roared from behind him. "Nothing to do with me!"

"If it isn't you," screamed Tully, "then who is it?"

"You tell me!" yelled Sam. "You're the Warlock, Tully! I'm just a lowly Wizard—what do *I* know?"

Tully Telford's stout body seemed to swell and his face grew very red. He raised his eyes to the fluttering caps high above and yelled, "I have had quite enough of this nonsense! *Incognate encanto negatobile!*"

The flaps on the small round hats suddenly stopped fluttering and, a second later, all six caps fell back toward the floor. They landed, with soft, lifeless little plops, in the area exactly between Sam's and Lee's chairs and the front of the platform.

Tully Telford sat down. "Mr. Bland. Mr. Needle," he said quietly, "would you kindly retrieve our head coverings and return them to their respective owners?"

Mr. Needle and Mr. Bland stepped forward and advanced toward where the six caps lay still. When they reached the spot, Mr. Bland and Mr. Needle bent over and reached for the caps—and, as they did so, the flaps started moving again. But this time, instead of fluttering like wings, the flaps acted like little pairs of legs, lifting the caps off the floor and balancing them there. Mr. Bland made a grab for the nearest cap, which suddenly moved, the two flaps waddling it away from his outstretched hands. Mr. Needle reached for the next cap—and it, too, scurried away, out of his reach.

There was no laughter now in the great room. Instead, a wondering hush fell over everybody. Every person there was realizing the same disturbing fact. Turning the caps into little flying objects had been *one* spell; giving them legs was—without a doubt—a *second* enchantment. And that meant that there was more than one practical joker in the room, because Wizards and Warlocks (and even Wrathmonks) can perform only one major spell in twenty-four hours, and the flying hats—and now the *walking* hats—were both quite major enchantments, even if both examples were, in the infuriated eyes of Tully Telford, thoroughly childish.

"Mr. Needle—Mr. Bland—we are *waiting!*"

Mr. Bland stayed where he was while Mr. Needle began to walk slowly around to the other side of the collection of caps. When he'd arrived at the opposite side from Mr. Bland, he nodded at his companion and both men began to advance on the waiting hats. When they got as close as they dared, they paused.

"On three, Needle?" said Mr. Bland.

"On three, Bland."

"One—two—*three!*"

Mr. Needle and Mr. Bland jumped forward, both men diving toward the caps with arms outstretched—

And the caps scattered in all directions, looking like a nest of tarantulas that had been suddenly disturbed. Mr. Needle and Mr. Bland landed, together, with a thump, on the bare and empty floor.

"Mr. Needle, Mr. Bland, if you would both kindly stop wasting this court's time!" shouted Tully Telford.

Justin Bucket tapped Tully on the arm. "I say, Tully," he said, "it seems to me that there must be more than *one* rascal doing this."

"Of *course* there is more than one, you *idiot!*" squeaked Tully, pulling his arm away from Justin's hand. Then, realizing that, perhaps, this wasn't the way the audience expected a member of an Advisory Board to address the Prime Magus of the Wizards' Guild, he changed the tone of his voice to one of oily politeness. "And, Mr. Prime Magus, rest assured we shall of course get to the bottom of this nonsense and, when we do, the two troublemakers will be severely—"

Tully broke off, because what was happening on the floor of the great room now bordered on pandemonium. Mr. Needle and Mr. Bland were running this way and that, each man frantically trying to snatch at least one of the scurrying caps. The caps were doing an efficient job of keeping themselves from being snatched, and several had taken to slithering under the seats of the audience members, some of whom found the scuttling black things so disturbing that they had climbed to safety up onto the seats of their chairs.

There was a sudden rustling, scuttling movement as the six little caps emerged from their various hiding places and ran together into the middle of the floor. Once again Mr. Needle and Mr. Bland advanced toward them, arms outstretched. . . .

And all six little caps turned a bright, brilliant— almost luminous—*pink*.

Ermintrude Bacon screamed.

"So!" shrieked Tully Telford. "*Three* of you, are there? Three childish hooligans! I demand that you all put a stop to this tomfoolery this *instant!*"

Tully's words had no effect whatsoever. The little flaps on the caps began to flutter like wings again, lifting them off the floor and raising them steadily up toward the ceiling. But this time, instead of flying wherever they wanted, the six pink caps formed in a line, marshaled like a row of soldiers. The line rose slowly and, as it climbed through the still air, it moved toward the front row of the gallery. When the line reached the level of Measle's nose, it stopped—and the six little caps hovered there in front of him.

Tinker, sitting close by Measle's side, cocked his head to one side and let out a short, sharp bark.

"*Proof!*" screamed Tully Telford, on his feet again, one trembling finger pointed up at Measle. "*Proof* that the boy has powers! See how he controls them? Undoubtedly with the help of his unnatural dog! And the Flannel woman is probably one of his accomplices!"

Sam and Lee twisted around in their chairs and stared up at Measle with their mouths open. Measle shook his head furiously at them. He wanted to shout, to yell, "It isn't me! I'm not doing anything!" but the words wouldn't come. He looked wildly around him and saw that everybody up there in the gallery, including Nanny Flannel and Toby Jugg, were staring at him with wonder and fear in their eyes.

And then, quite suddenly, Measle knew.

At first glance, it looked as if the line of little pink caps was hovering directly in front of Measle. But they weren't.

They were hovering directly in front of Matilda's stroller.

And Matilda was awake.

4

THE
MALLOCKEE

Matilda's bright green eyes were fixed on the line
of caps. She smiled happily at them, showing all
six of her little pearly teeth. Her chubby arms waved
and her feet kicked and . . .

The caps began to dance up and down. As they did
so, a bouncy little tune began to play, the individual
notes apparently coming from each cap as it bobbed in
the air. Measle recognized the tune at once. It was
Matilda's favorite song, "The Whistling Pony."

And, because Measle was now staring, wide-eyed

and openmouthed, at his sister, all the eyes that had been on Measle began to shift—slowly—from him to Matilda. A deep silence fell over the great room.

"Tilly!" hissed Measle, and Matilda turned her head and gazed at him.

"Tilly! Cool it!"

"Googa?"

"Yes! *Googa!* Stop it, Tilly! Stop it now!"

Matilda grinned, showing all her teeth. Then she turned back to the line of caps and waved her hands. The caps stopped bobbing up and down and "The Whistling Pony" died away. The pinkness faded to black and, a moment later, all six caps floated slowly down toward the floor. At the last minute, they veered toward the platform and settled themselves in a row, each cap resting on the counter in front of its respective owner.

The silence was profound. Nobody in that great room moved so much as a muscle. Finally Justin Bucket broke the silence.

"I say, everybody," he said, his voice echoing in the hush, "what—um—what on earth is going on?"

Tully Telford turned his head and glared hard at Justin. "What is going on, Mr. Prime Magus? *What is going on?* Surely it's painfully obvious! The Stubbs family has trained a magus infantum, which is against every rule, ancient and modern, in the book!"

"A what?" said Justin blankly.

"A *magus infantum*! An infant Wizard! A most dangerous creature! And not only have the Stubbses produced this—this—*appalling* thing, but they also seem determined to make a mockery of these proceedings! No doubt Mr. Stubbs began it, then Mrs. Stubbs took over—"

"I'm not a Wizard, Mr. Telford!" said Lee.

Tully Telford waved a dismissive hand. "The idiotic prank was continued by the Flannel woman—"

"You silly little man!" shouted Nanny Flannel furiously. "How dare you call me 'the Flannel Woman'! And anyway, I haven't got an ounce of magic in me!"

Tully ignored the interruption. "And the vulgar performance was then taken over by young Measle Stubbs and his canine accomplice, and then finally by his magus infantum sister! This sort of behavior will not be tolerated by this court! I demand that this court be respected! I demand that the Stubbs family be punished! I further demand that—"

A steady banging sound—of wood on wood—started from somewhere at the very back of the room. As Tully Telford's voice died away, Measle leaned forward over the edge of the balcony. Emerging from the shadows came the figure of a little old man. He was small and thin and bent, his gnarled right hand clasping a knobbly walking stick which he was banging rhythmically on the wooden floor. From his vantage point, above, Measle could see that the old man's white hair was cropped short and that his ears were free of Gloomstains. He shuffled forward slowly and all the eyes in the room followed the little man's progress.

It took a while, but at last the old man reached the front of the platform. Tully Telford stood up and leaned over the front of the counter, and the little old man muttered a couple of sentences up at him, too quietly for anybody but Tully to hear. Tully's eyebrows shot to the top of his forehead, then he nodded in a respectful way. Tully straightened up, stared out at the audience and announced, "The committee recognizes His Worship, Supreme Justice Lord Octavo, who wishes to address a few remarks to this court. I mean, this inquiry."

Lord Octavo turned and faced the audience, and now Measle could at last see the old man's face. It was deeply wrinkled. The nose was a sharp and bony beak, and the beady black eyes beneath the heavy white eyebrows shone with intelligence. Measle watched as the old man surveyed the audience in front of him. Then Lord Octavo lifted his gaze to the gallery and, a moment later, those clever old eyes fastened on Measle's face.

"Ah, there you are." His voice was quiet and friendly. "May I ask, young man, if I am addressing Master Measle Stubbs?"

Measle nodded nervously, aware that every eye in that great room was now fixed on him.

"A pleasure to make your acquaintance, Master Stubbs. My name is Lord Octavo. I'm the Supreme Justice of the Wizards' Guild. It sounds a very grand job, doesn't it? And I suppose it *is* quite grand. I help to decide what's right and wrong, you see. Not here— this is just an inquiry into some rather strange recent events—but when somebody has done something really wicked, I'm one of the people who decides what to do about it. That's why they're letting me interrupt, you see. Now then, would you mind answering a couple of questions?"

Measle nodded again. He had no idea whether this little old man meant him harm or good, but, so far, Measle rather liked what he saw.

"Thank you, Master Stubbs. Now the small child next to you, in the stroller? She is your sister?"

"Yes, sir."

"And what is her name, Master Stubbs?"

"M-Matilda, sir."

"And can you tell me, Master Stubbs—it's a little hard for me to see from down here—is young Matilda asleep at the moment?"

Measle glanced down at Matilda. Her eyes were closed, her head was lolling to one side and she was breathing steadily, her little chest moving gently up and down.

"Yes, sir."

"I am glad to hear it, Master Stubbs. She must be quite tired after all her exertions. For an adult Wizard, casting spells can be a grueling business. For a child, it must be truly exhausting."

"A magus infantum!" said Tully loudly.

"Now that, Mr. Telford, is where you're wrong," said Lord Octavo quietly. "Miss Matilda Stubbs is not a magus infantum. What Miss Matilda Stubbs is—well, she's something a great deal more *extraordinary* than a magus infantum. And a great deal more dangerous, too. I wonder if any of you can guess what she is?"

The six members of the inquiry committee bent their heads toward each other and held a hurried, whispered discussion. There was a lot of nodding of heads and an equal amount of shaking of heads as well. Then Tully Telford said, "Ah—well—we admit that we have no idea what you're talking about, Lord Octavo. Would you be so kind as to tell us?"

Lord Octavo smiled a wintry smile.

"Fellow Wizards and Warlocks. Please listen very carefully. What I have to tell you is profoundly disturbing, but I must ask that you all remain very calm and, above all, very *quiet*. There must be no shouting, no panic, no rush to the exits. Do you all understand?"

There was a nervous murmuring from the audience and a general nodding of heads.

"Thank you. Now then, unlike all these clever Warlocks on the platform here behind me, I am nothing more than a simple Wizard. Well, perhaps not altogether *simple*, because there is one thing I can do that they cannot. I can detect the origins of concealed spells. I can *sense* where they come from. Today this small talent of mine has revealed something truly extraordinary. Today, my fellow Wizards and Warlocks, we are in the presence of something wonderful and unique, something that has not been seen in a very, very long time."

Lord Octavo paused again. There was an impatient rustling in the audience, and Justin Bucket leaned forward and said, "*Frightfully* sorry, Lord Octavo, to be so dim—but what exactly hasn't been seen in a very, very long time? And where is it?"

Lord Octavo slowly raised one hand and pointed his gnarled old finger up at the gallery.

"It is there, Mr. Bucket. Up there in the gallery. At present, it is asleep in its stroller and therefore—for the moment, at least—relatively harmless. I can only hope it stays that way."

"What, you mean the Stubbs baby?" said Justin, absentmindedly rubbing the finger that Matilda had bitten earlier.

"The same," said Lord Octavo.

"The magus infantum?" said Tully.

Lord Octavo turned a small, weary smile on Tully Telford. "Mr. Telford, I have already informed you that little Miss Stubbs is *not* a magus infantum."

"Then what *is* she?" said Tully, irritably tapping the desk in front of him with a pencil.

"Miss Matilda Stubbs is a very terrible creature. She is—and I am quite sure of this—she is a *Mallockee*."

A mumbling, rumbling muttering went around the great room as the audience tried out the word.

"What did he say?" "Mallockee?" "What's a Mallockee?" "Never heard of a Mallockee . . ." "Any idea what the old chap's talking about?" "Mallockee?" "Mallockee?" "Mallockee?"

Lord Octavo held up two wrinkled hands and the muttering died away. Then Lord Octavo looked up toward the gallery, caught Measle's eye, and smiled at him.

"See what being very old and reading lots of books does for you, Master Stubbs?" he called. "I know things that nobody else here knows!"

Lord Octavo dropped his gaze from the gallery and swept his eyes around the room.

"Is this, in fact, the case?" he demanded. "Am I the only one here who knows of the Mallockee?"

An uncomfortable silence fell over the great room. Nobody wanted to be the first to admit his ignorance, so they all held their tongues, hoping somebody else would be the first to speak. When no one did, Lord Octavo shook his head sorrowfully.

"Scholarship—and the love of learning—are disappearing so fast. Such a pity. In my young day, education was something we all yearned after—"

"Excuse me, Lord Octavo," said Sam, twisting around in his seat to see the old man, "excuse me, but my wife and I are understandably anxious to learn what exactly you are accusing our daughter of being?"

Lord Octavo made a small bow in Sam and Lee's direction. "My apologies, Mr. Stubbs," he said gently. "You're quite right. I have a tendency to ramble. So, to the point. As we all know, Wizards and Warlocks—and even those contemptible Wrathmonks—can perform only one major spell in a twenty-four-hour period. But the Mallockee has no such limitations. The Mallockee can perform spells without stopping, until he or she becomes too exhausted to continue. Also—and this is most interesting—a Mallockee doesn't need incantations for its spells. All a Mallockee has to do is *think* the spell, and it's done! This is what I detected a few moments ago. All those spells—those *silent* spells involving those little hats of yours—they all emanated from one source. *One source only.* They emanated from that little girl up there in the stroller, currently sleeping the sleep of the exhausted. And it occurs to me that we are extremely lucky."

"Lucky, Lord Octavo?" whispered Ermintrude Bacon.

"Yes, indeed, Miss Bacon. Extremely lucky. So far the child seems to possess a charming and playful personality. Can you imagine what might have happened if she was a poisonous brat?"

Tully Telford leaped to his feet again. "Lord Octavo!" he cried, "are you seriously asking us to believe in a magical entity with no boundaries to its powers?"

"Yes, I am, Mr. Telford," said Lord Octavo.

"Impossible! For a start, where does it obtain an endless supply of mana?"

"From *itself*, Mr. Telford. You don't seem to understand—a Mallockee is both a Wizard *and a Manafount*!"

Tully gulped. "But . . . such a being would have powers beyond reason!"

Lord Octavo nodded. "Indeed he—or she—*would*, Mr. Telford. And may I remind you to speak as quietly as possible, since a Mallockee *asleep* is considerably less dangerous than one which is awake."

Tully took a deep breath and shook his head angrily, but when he spoke, it was in little more than a whisper. "Lord Octavo, this Mallockee creature . . . why have none of us *heard* of such a thing?"

"Because, Mr. Telford—first, nobody reads books anymore; and second, there hasn't *been* such a thing for several thousand years. Indeed, such a thing has been impossible for several thousand years. In fact, it was thought that such a thing could never occur again. And yet it has. This is no random event, you understand. A Mallockee does not simply come by chance—it is *created*."

"You mean this was done on *purpose?*"

Lord Octavo turned and looked at Sam and Lee. He stared at them for several seconds, with a quizzical expression on his lined old face. Then he seemed to make up his mind about them and, abruptly, shook his head.

"In this case, I believe not, Mr. Telford. In the distant past, it's true to say that the very few Mallockees that appeared were made on purpose. But I believe that in *this* case, there was a series of catastrophic accidents, nothing more. However, these accidents have led to the appearance among us of a genuine Mallockee."

"But—but—how did this happen, Lord Octavo?" stammered Tully.

"A Mallockee is created when a female Manafount is to become a mother. The female Manafount simply bathes herself in the blood of a dragon. She absorbs a vast amount of mana from the dragon's blood, which overloads her *own* mana production. This enormous volume of mana in her system has to go somewhere. It goes to the unborn baby. When the baby later arrives into the world, it is a Mallockee."

A nervous muttering rose up in the room. Lord Octavo took a few shuffling steps toward Lee, who was staring at him in astonishment.

"My dear Mrs. Stubbs," he said, not unkindly, "none of this is your fault. You and your son were in great peril from a gigantic dragon. When the seawater came rushing into that great cave, it killed the dragon—and you were forced to swim for your lives. You can hardly be blamed for the fact that much of what you were swimming in was dragon's *blood*. And in doing so—and without meaning any harm—you have produced a Mallockee, an extraordinary magical being, not seen on earth for several thousand years, simply because of a— how shall I put it?—a general scarcity of Manafounts and an even greater, and worldwide, *shortage of dragons!*"

There was a very long silence while everybody in the great room thought about what Lord Octavo had said. The silence was broken by Sam. He stood up abruptly, the legs of his wooden chair scraping on the bare floor.

"Well," he said, all business, "now that all this has been cleared up, we'll be off, I think. It's *very* late— well past my children's bedtime, in fact—and since we've got a long drive ahead of us, I reckon we ought to make a start. Thanks so much for having us. Come on, my love—"

Sam began to step out from behind the screen that separated him from Lee, and Lee herself was starting to rise out of her chair—

"Wait!"

The sharp, almost-shouted word had come from the distinguished-looking silver-haired man at the far end of the platform. He leaned forward on the counter, his long, thin hands clasped under his chin.

"Please, Mr. Stubbs, Mrs. Stubbs, please sit down," said Sir Peregrine Spine, his voice smooth and soft and polished. "Much as I understand your urge to leave, I'm afraid that this inquiry is far from over, particularly in light of these recent revelations."

Sam and Lee glanced at each other over the top of the dividing screen. Sam gave a small shrug, winked at his wife and then slowly settled back in his chair. Lee did the same. Sir Peregrine Spine said, "Thank you so much, Mr. Stubbs, Mrs. Stubbs." Then he turned and looked down at the small, bent figure in front of him.

"Lord Octavo."

"Sir Peregrine?"

"Are you quite positive about all this?"

"There really is no other explanation."

Sir Peregrine raised his noble head and looked out at the packed room.

"If I could ask you all to bear with us for a few moments? I request that this court will allow the committee a moment of consultation?"

Nobody raised any objection, so for the next few minutes, all six members of the committee leaned toward each other and whispered intently.

Up in the gallery, Measle did a bit of whispering of his own.

"What's happening, Nanny?"

Nanny Flannel shrugged her shoulders. "I don't know, dear. But don't worry. Your mum and dad will sort it out."

But will they be allowed to? thought Measle. *I don't like the look of those whispering faces down there.* He glanced down at his sister. Matilda was fast asleep, and from the look of her, Measle guessed that she wouldn't wake up for several hours.

Measle looked at Toby. "Did you know about Mallockees?" he said. "I mean, before?"

"Never heard of 'em. Mind you, if Lord Octavo says they exist, then I for one believe him. He's read more books than me, and your dad, and your mum, and half a dozen other Wizards put together."

There was some movement down below. The committee members were settling back into their chairs.

Justin Bucket beckoned to Mr. Needle and Mr. Bland. Both men hurried to Justin's side, bent their heads and listened. Then they nodded sharply, straightened up and marched briskly out of the room. Justin Bucket waited until both men had disappeared. Then he turned and addressed the room.

"Thank you all *so* much," he said, nodding his handsome head in a friendly way. "If you would all be *terribly* kind and remain in your seats for a few more minutes, we'd all be *terrifically* grateful. The secretaries won't be gone for long—they are simply consulting a reference book on our behalf, to help us *verify*, as it were, all these remarkable theories. So interesting, isn't it?"

Moments later the door to the corridor burst open with a crash. Six big figures, dressed in black uniforms, strode into the room. They wore jet-black helmets and jet-black boots and their eyes were obscured behind darkened visors. Behind them came Mr. Needle and Mr. Bland. Mr. Needle pointed at Lee, and Mr. Bland pointed at Sam. Two of the burly figures marched silently up to the two wooden chairs. One man grabbed Lee by an arm and dragged her out of her chair. Sam jumped to his feet, swept the dividing screen to one side and reached for Lee—but he was too late. The second figure wrapped a pair of massive arms around Sam and pinned his arms to his sides. A third man approached the struggling figures. He had something in his hands—no, *two* somethings, Measle saw with horror. They were a pair of neck-sized rings, like dog collars, made of some sort of dull gray metal, with a hinge set in the outer circle. When this third man reached Sam, he lifted one of the rings, pulled it open and snapped it around Sam's neck. Then he turned and did the same to Lee. Sam and Lee were pushed roughly back into their chairs. Nobody bothered to pick up the dividing screen that now lay flat on the floor, and Measle watched as Sam reached out his hand toward Lee, who reached out *her* hand and grasped Sam's.

"*Stasimus exertico fortegilimus!*" yelled Sam—

And nothing happened.

The only effect of Sam's shouted spell was a dim flash of blue light that traveled from Sam's fingertip. But instead of zipping away from him, the light traveled in the opposite direction, up Sam's arm and then disappeared—as if it had somehow been swallowed up into the metal ring around his neck.

By this time there was panic in the great room. Half the audience seemed desperate to get out of there and streamed out of the rows of chairs, heading fast for the door. Lord Octavo himself shuffled forward toward Sam and Lee, his lined old face creased with concern. But when he got within a couple of yards, one of the uniformed men stepped forward and pushed him back with such sudden force that the old man staggered and almost fell.

Measle was out of his chair, standing with both hands on the rail in front of him and staring with horror at what was going on down below. Out of the corner of his eye, he saw two more of the black-uniformed men start toward the foot of the stairs. One of the men held three metal hoops in his gloved hands. . . .

Measle turned back and saw that Toby Jugg was bending over Matilda's stroller and undoing the buckles that held the little girl in place. He lifted the still-sleeping Matilda out of her seat. With his free hand, he clicked the catch that held the stroller open. The chair folded and Toby scooped it up—

"What are you *doing?*" blurted Measle.

Toby threw a hurried look in Measle's direction. "We've got to get her out of here! And you, too, come to think of it!"

"But what about Dad?" blurted Measle. "And Mum?"

"I can't help them, Measle! But I can help you and your sister! Now come on!"

Toby turned to Nanny Flannel. "Miss Flannel—I can get them away, but we've got to move fast and I can't manage you as well. Trust me, I'll keep 'em safe for a couple of days. I'll sort it out, but right now there's no time for anything but getting them away, all right?"

Nanny Flannel began to shake her head, but then she seemed to change her mind. She looked at Measle, then at Matilda nestled in Toby's strong arms, and then she started making shooing gestures with both hands.

"Go on, Measle dear!" yelled Nanny Flannel. "Go with Mr. Jugg!"

"But—"

"Go on! It'll be all right! Look after Tilly! Oh—wait!"

Nanny Flannel reached into her old black handbag. She pulled out a small plastic bag and tossed it to

Measle. Measle caught it and felt the hard little oval shapes inside. . . .

Jelly beans!

"Just in case you get hungry, dear!" shouted Nanny Flannel.

The two men with the metal rings were halfway up the stairs of the gallery now.

"Come on, Measle old son," muttered Toby, tucking Matilda and her stroller under one muscular arm and grabbing Measle by the other. "No time to lose!"

Measle felt himself being hustled against the flow of people, all of whom were pressing forward to get to the top of the stairs. Toby dragged him through the mob, heading as fast as possible toward the wall farthest away from the stairs. It looked like a perfectly blank wall, but a moment later Measle saw a door there—a hard-to-see, flat-faced door that was painted the exact same color as the wall that surrounded it.

Measle and Toby pushed clear of the last of the people streaming in the other direction, and Toby reached out, grabbed the door handle and yanked it open. Glancing back, Measle saw the two uniformed men standing over Nanny Flannel—they seemed to be barking questions at her. Then one of them looked up and saw Measle and Toby.

Measle felt a strong hand pull him through the opening.

Toby slammed the door shut. He was just reaching for the heavy iron bolt at the top when suddenly there came a frantic scratching from the other side. Before Toby had time to drive the bolt home—and without bothering to ask if this was a good idea—Measle pulled open the door and a small, black-and-white, fuzzy bullet shot through the opening.

"Not the dog, Measle!" said Toby, his voice filled with exasperation. "We can't take the dog as well!"

Measle felt a sudden welling of anger. *All these people, telling my family what we can do and what we can't do—I've had enough!*

"I'm not going without him," said Measle.

Toby growled like an angry old lion and then, a moment later, grinned in surrender. He pushed the bolt into its socket with a thud.

"All right," he said. "That should hold them for a bit. Just make sure the little guy doesn't slow us down, okay?"

"Slow us down?" said Measle. "Have you seen him run? It's more likely he'll speed us up!"

Toby laughed. He looked upward and said, "Come on, now, Measle old son, we've got a bit of a climb ahead of us. And we'd better get started. That bolt won't hold them for long."

Measle and Toby were at the bottom of a deep well. There was a cast-iron spiral staircase set in the middle of the well and, when Measle tilted his head backward and looked up, he saw that the staircase was immensely tall. Far, far above him, the column of winding iron steps narrowed to a point and then disappeared altogether in the far-off darkness.

"We've got to get to the top of that," said Toby cheerfully. "Think you can manage it?"

"But where are we going?" said Measle.

Toby seemed to read his thoughts because he said, quickly, "Look, Measle, your mum and dad will be all right. But it seems to me that the Guild might come down a bit hard on you and the baby."

"B-but why? What did we do?"

"Between the two of you, an awful lot, old son. They already think you're a secret Wizard. They now believe your sister is that thing old Octavo said—"

"A Mallockee."

"Right. There are a bunch of tests they can do—none of them very pleasant, I'm afraid. I think we ought to keep you both clear of all that. And once I've got you to safety, then I can work on getting your mum and dad out of there as well. Okay?"

Measle nodded slowly. He was terribly confused. Everything had happened so fast, he hadn't had time to stop and think.

There was a pounding on the door and muffled shouts from the room beyond. Toby grabbed Measle's arm.

"Come on, Measle. Run now, talk later!"

Toby led the way to the first step on the towering spiral staircase, and they began to climb.

5

ESCAPE!

By the time Measle had climbed the first two hundred iron steps, his legs were trembling, his lungs bursting and his heart was pounding so hard in his chest that it felt as if it might, at any moment, jump clean out of his body.

He had to rest. Measle paused, panting. He closed his eyes, bent over and pressed his burning forehead to the cold iron of the handrail.

Far below there was a heavy crash and the sound of splintering wood.

Tinker growled.

Toby's footsteps came back down the stairs and, a

second later, Measle felt Toby's strong hand on his arm.

"Come on, Measle," Toby whispered, "we can't stop now. They're through the door. We've got to keep going. I'll give you a hand." He looped his arm through the stroller's frame and reached out. "Come on."

Measle felt Toby's hand grab onto his own and start to pull him upward, and with Toby taking at least some of Measle's weight, the endless placing of one foot above the other became a little less difficult. Tinker scurried upward, close by Measle's dragging feet. He didn't seem to be tired at all.

The sounds of their pursuers far below certainly helped to speed the three of them up and up and up, higher and higher and higher. Measle began to wonder just how high this staircase was because, along with the trembling legs and the burning lungs and the pounding heart, now he was getting really rather dizzy from the continuous circular movement of climbing the endless spiral.

The sounds of pursuit continued, not getting any louder but not getting any quieter, either—just a steady pounding of boots on metal.

Clang—thump—clang—thump—clang—thump.

Measle felt as if he'd been climbing forever—for all of his life, in fact—and, quite probably, that's all he'd be doing for the *rest* of his life, too. . . .

Just climbing. Around and around and around.

Up.

And up.

And up.

And up.

And then, quite suddenly, they were at the top.

They had reached a small iron platform. There was a concrete ceiling two yards above their heads and, in front of them, a heavy iron door, with the sort of horizontal bar at waist height that you push to open.

Toby slammed his free hand against the bar. The door sprang wide and he pulled Measle out into a dark, narrow alley, bounded on both sides by high brick walls. Tinker slipped through and Toby pushed the door shut. Then he glanced left and right and, panting hard, said, "Looks like the coast is clear, Measle. But it won't be for long. Come on."

Measle's legs felt as if they were made of hot marshmallows, but he managed to stumble along, close behind Toby's stocky figure. There was a dim light at the far end of the alley and, when they neared it, Toby slowed down and motioned to Measle to do the same. They both shrank against the rough brick of the high wall, and Toby inched forward and peered around the corner. He reached back and took Measle's hand again.

"Okay, Measle. My car's just down the street. Think you can make it?"

From behind them came the sound of the iron door being smashed open, and a gruff voice yelled, "Oy! You! Stop right there!"

But they were already at the car.

Toby pulled open the door and bundled Measle inside. Tinker jumped in and dropped down into the shadows by Measle's feet. Toby threw the stroller into the backseat and thrust the sleeping Matilda into Measle's arms. Then, in one fluid movement, he slid into the driver's seat and slammed his door shut.

Measle glanced back through the car's rear window. The owner of the gruff voice was just emerging from the alley—a huge man, encased in black, his hands holding a smaller metal hoop that looked just about the right size for Measle's neck.

Toby jabbed his thumb against a big red button in

the middle of the dashboard and the car's engine rumbled to life.

The car jumped forward, its tires squealing. They roared off down the dark street and Measle, looking backward, saw the black-uniformed figure get smaller and smaller and smaller.

Toby drove fast—*Just like Dad,* thought Measle—through the dark city streets. Soon they were in the suburbs and, twenty minutes later, they were racing through the open countryside.

"Where are we going?" said Measle, staring out into the darkness.

"Somewhere safe," said Toby. "Somewhere far away." There was a short silence and then Toby said, "I'm sorry about what happened back there, Measle—I mean, I couldn't have done anything about Sam and Lee—but I'm sorry about not being able to get Miss Flannel out of there, too."

"I don't think we could've done anything," said Measle glumly, picturing Nanny Flannel trying to drag herself up that endless staircase.

"Probably not, but I'm afraid it means you're going to have to look after your sister all by yourself."

After a while, as they were racing up a freeway, Toby glanced across to Measle and said, "We've got a long way to go, Measle old son. There's a freeway café up ahead. Do you fancy something to eat? I could murder a cup of coffee myself. I think it's safe to stop now."

"Sure. Thanks."

The café was bright and cheerful and—so late at night—fairly empty of customers. Measle found a table and, with Matilda sleeping peacefully in her stroller beside him, sat down at it. Toby went to the counter and bought a Coke and a ham sandwich for Measle, and a big mug of black coffee for himself.

Measle ate his sandwich and drank his Coke, but they didn't make him feel any better. Instead, he felt tired and depressed. If he could only get those images out of his head—those disturbing images of black-uniformed men roughly grabbing his mother and father. . . .

"Mr. Jugg?"

"Toby, Measle—call me Toby."

"Oh, right. Toby. What were those ring things the men had?"

Toby sniffed in disgust. "Those are wrathrings. They use 'em on beastly Wrathmonks—to restrain 'em. The rings absorb spells, you see—a captured Wrathmonk with a wrathring around its neck can't cast magic. I must say, I never thought I'd live to see the day they were used on innocent *Wizards!*"

"They were going to put one of them on me, weren't they? And on Tilly, too?"

Toby nodded seriously. "Looked that way, didn't it?"

"Would it work on a Mallockee, though? If she's so powerful, I mean?"

"I don't see why not, old son. The principle's the same, no matter how powerful you are."

Five minutes later they were back in the big black car and heading up the freeway again. After a few miles, Measle began to feel quite sleepy—it was very late, long past his bedtime, and it had been an exhausting and emotional day—so, holding tight to Matilda and with the comforting feeling of Tinker's compact little body between his feet, Measle lay back against the car's soft leather upholstery and closed his eyes. He felt himself beginning to drift away. . . .

There was just one more question.

"Where are we going, Mr. Jugg—I mean, Toby?"

"We're going to one of my homes, Measle. It's way

out in the wilds, about as far away from everything as you can get. There isn't another house for a good five miles around. It's called Caltrop Castle."

"You've got a *castle?*"

"Yup. I hope you like it, because you'll be staying there while I sort out this mess. Now we've got a long way to go, Measle. See if you can get some rest."

And with the thought that he was going to be staying in a real castle floating about in his head and the steady, muffled roar of the big engine in his ears, Measle quite soon fell fast asleep.

6

CALTROP CASTLE

For Measle, waking up in the morning was usually a swift affair. One minute he would be asleep, the next he'd be wide awake and ready for whatever the day had in store for him.

But not this time.

This time waking up was like floating slowly upward from the bottom of a lake. At first there was nothing but a soft, velvety blackness. Then a gentle light began to press against his closed eyes, and the soft light got brighter and brighter and brighter—and now he could feel the touch of some sort of material against his fingertips—a smooth, fine-textured cloth of some kind—it smelled fresh, as if it had come straight from a laundry (*sheets, perhaps?*)—his head seemed to be resting on something soft and squashy (*a pillow!*) and there was a weight on his legs, a warm weight that felt familiar—and now the weight was moving, as if it had a life of its own—the weight shifted off his legs and moved up toward his head—there was a snuffling sound in his ear—then something warm and wet flapped against the side of his face and a breath—a very *doggy* sort of breath—wafted over his nostrils.

Measle's eyes opened a crack.

Tinker was standing over him, staring down into Measle's face, his fuzzy head cocked to one side and his stumpy little tail a wagging blur.

"Hello, Tink," muttered Measle. He felt a little groggy. Rubbing the sleep from his eyes, he pulled himself up against the pillows and stared around him in wonder.

He was in a big, airy room, full of light that streamed in through a tall window set in the far wall. The glass in the window was made up of small, diamond-shaped panes that were held in place with lead strips, just the kind of window you'd expect to see in a very grand old house. There were heavy, dark-green velvet curtains on either side of the window, and the window frame wasn't made of wood—it was arched at the top and made of a warm, sand-colored stone.

Whether the rest of the walls were also made of stone, Measle couldn't be sure, because they were completely covered, from floor to ceiling, by dark wood paneling. On the right hand wall, set into the paneling, was a huge fireplace. A couple of comfortable-looking chairs and a big squashy sofa stood near the fireplace, on either side of which were bookshelves that reached to the high ceiling. Several of the bookshelves on one side of the fireplace had been removed to make room for a large television set. The bed itself, where Measle lay propped up against the pillows, was a wonder. It was huge, with four carved wooden posts, one at each corner. When Measle raised his eyes and looked over-head, he saw that the four posts held up a sort of canopy, made of the same dark-green velvet that framed the window. Hanging from the supporting canopy were a pair of green velvet drapes that reached to the floor on either side of the bed. These drapes were held back by a pair of heavy brass hooks, but Measle saw that, if you unhooked the curtains, you could draw them all the way around the bed, enclosing yourself completely in a little private room of your own.

Where on earth am I? thought Measle. And then slowly the memories began to filter back into his brain.

Caltrop. Caltrop Castle! He was safe in Caltrop Castle! He and Tinker—and Tilly! Where was Tilly?

Measle looked frantically around the huge room. He saw Matilda's stroller first—and there, next to it, was a high-railed wooden crib. Matilda was standing up inside it, peering at him with a serious look on her face. Matilda was still in the clothes she'd been wearing yesterday.

Oh, no, thought Measle, *she's going to be all stinky and I'm going to have to change her diapers. . . .*

But when he picked her up, he realized that Matilda's diaper was as fresh and clean and dry as if she'd just put it on.

"Ah," said Measle slowly. "How did you manage that, Tilly?"

How Matilda had managed it was quite simple, in a magical sort of way. She had woken up in this strange crib, in this strange room, with that familiar damp and uncomfortable feeling that meant she needed changing. When nobody came anywhere near her, she'd pulled herself upright and, holding tight to the crib rail, had looked around the room. She'd seen her big brother sleeping soundly in the enormous bed. She'd seen Tinker, curled up at Measle's feet. She'd said, "Brocka-brocka-brocka!" quite loudly, several times, but Measle didn't wake up, and Tinker had simply lifted his head, glanced at her and then gone back to sleep. Matilda had tried the crying trick next—a bit of "Waaah! Waaah! Waah!" usually worked and got everybody's attention—but not this time. Measle hadn't moved a muscle, and the damp, uncomfortable feeling was getting worse, and where was Mum when she needed her?

And then, since nobody was taking any notice of her at all, Matilda had simply decided to stop the nasty, damp feeling all by herself. She decided to *make it go away*.

And it did.

She'd felt a little sleepy after making it go away, so

she lay back in the crib and had a nap. An hour later she'd woken up again and pulled herself up and had stood there in her crib, waiting patiently for somebody to come and take care of her.

Measle set Matilda on the floor. He glanced quickly around the room to make sure there was nothing there that could hurt her. Then, satisfied that there wasn't, he went to the window. The first thing Measle noticed about the window was that it didn't open. There were no catches, no hinges—it was just a tall expanse of lead strips and diamond-shaped pieces of glass. Measle thought about this for a moment and then decided that perhaps windows in old castles weren't supposed to open. He peered out through one of the diamond-shaped panes. There was a flower bed under the window, a broad gravel drive, and beyond that a sweeping lawn that ended, a hundred yards away, in a dark, glassy lake. On the far side of the lake, distant pine trees lined the horizon.

There seemed to be no sign of life out there, so Measle turned his attention back to the room. On the wall opposite the fireplace was a door. Measle padded across and opened it—beyond was a bathroom, bigger by far than any at home, tiled in dark-green marble. Measle crossed to the washbasin and found a brand-new battery-operated electric toothbrush, just like the one he had at home, propped up in a glass and, next to it, a tube of toothpaste—and the toothpaste was the same brand he used at home, too.

Measle brushed his teeth and washed his face and hands and then dressed himself in yesterday's clothes and jammed his feet into his old sneakers. He checked to see that Matilda was all right—she seemed quite happy, busily trying to see if Tinker's tail was properly attached to Tinker's body, and Tinker was letting her do it, because having his tail pulled by Matilda usually meant that he was given a tasty treat later.

As Measle was shrugging on his leather jacket, there was a knock on the door. Toby was there, a friendly smile under his broken nose.

"Hi, Measle old son," he said. "Did you all sleep okay?"

"Yes, thanks," said Measle, holding the door half closed because Tinker was right behind him and wanting to get out.

"Um—I think Tinker needs to go outside. Can

we go out into your garden?"

Toby rubbed his beard and said, "Ah—well, the thing is, Measle, I don't want you wandering around outside. Caltrop Castle is a funny place. Those woods—well, let's just say there are things out there you wouldn't want to meet. But there's a solution, old son. We've got an *inside* garden here at Caltrop, and that's perfectly safe. Come on, I'll show you. Bring your sister, too."

Measle lifted Matilda into her stroller and, pushing her in front of him, followed Toby out into the corridor. Tinker trotted at their heels. They walked down a long passage, all paneled in the same dark wood that was in Measle's bedroom. There were various doors leading off the passage, all closed and, around one corner, Measle spotted an enormous suit of jet-black armor, complete with a sword held upright in its gauntleted hands. The armor stood on a black marble plinth and was so huge that Measle guessed that it must have been made for a real giant of a man.

The passage twisted and turned—left, then right, then left again—and Toby stopped abruptly outside a door that looked just like all the others, except that it had the word "Jardin" painted on it in small gold letters.

"That's French for 'garden,'" said Toby. "This place was built a long time ago by a very famous French Wizard, the Duke of Touffou. That's him up there."

Toby pointed to an enormous oil painting. It was a portrait of a tall dark man with long, straight black hair that framed a pale, narrow face. The man's eyes were dark and piercing and, wherever you stood, his eyes seemed to follow you. He was dressed in a long crimson robe and stood by a twisted tree, one hand resting on a crooked branch. Beyond him, in the background, a herd of cows grazed in a distant field.

"The Duke of Touffou was a very early Prime Magus back when the Wizards' Guild was just beginning," said Toby. "The story is that he discovered that this area was full of natural magic, and so he built Caltrop Castle on this very spot. And there's something else in the painting, too—I wonder if you can find it?"

Measle looked more closely at the picture. He saw the Duke, the twisted tree, the fields stretching away into the distance, the herd of cows in the background. . . .

"Look for a cave, Measle."

Measle's eyes flickered all over the great expanse of painted canvas—until he spotted the entrance to the cave. It was dark, but something even darker seemed to be lurking in its depths. Measle could just make out a vague shape that was a shade blacker than the shadows that surrounded it. And in the blackness were twin points of light, set close together, slanting upward at the edges—

They looked like the eyes of a cat.

"What is it?" said Measle, gazing up at the picture.

"That was the Duke's murderer," said Toby. "A very nasty and dangerous denizen of the local woods. People called him Gobbin Good."

"Called him *what?*" said Measle, trying not to smile. "Gobbin Good sounds like Robin Hood. . . ."

"I'm afraid he wasn't like Robin Hood at all. Quite the opposite, in fact. For a start he was always spitting, which was why he was called 'Gobbin,' you see. I don't think Robin Hood did all that much spitting, do you? And, while Robin Hood was an exiled nobleman who stole from the rich and gave to the poor, Gobbin Good was a murderous creature called a grimling, who stole

100

from the poor and kept it all for himself. Not only that, he always killed his victims after he'd robbed them by shooting them with a powerful crossbow, usually from a long way off. That's how he got the Duke. Shot him in the back, which was the only way he could have got the better of such a powerful Wizard, of course."

"What did he look like?" said Measle, squinting up at the painting and trying to see more detail in the dark shape in the cave.

"Horrible, so they say," said Toby. "All bent and twisted, with a face that would give you nightmares. Not something you'd want to meet down a dark alley, that's for sure. Now come on, old son—let's see about this garden, shall we?"

Toby twisted the handle and threw the door wide open.

The little garden was perfect. It was about twenty yards by twenty yards, with shrubs and flower beds and little pebbled paths all surrounding a small, perfectly manicured lawn with a stone fountain in its center. Water tinkled in the fountain. High overhead was a frosted glass ceiling, through which soft sunlight filtered down. Matilda expressed her approval of the place by making crowing noises, like a rooster.

"It's not very big, I'm afraid," said Toby. "But then, neither is your dog. Perhaps he won't mind too much, eh?"

Tinker didn't seem to mind at all. After the usual sniffing around to find exactly the right spot, the little dog did his business and then trotted back to Measle.

"You can come here whenever you like," said Toby. "Just remember the word 'Jardin' and you'll have no trouble finding it."

As they walked back to Measle's room, Toby said, "Now, I'm afraid I'm going to leave you for a while, Measle old son. I've got to get back to town and see what I can do about this mess. I can't do it from here, you see. No phone, no fax, no e-mail at Caltrop. They don't work here. It's all the magic around us—it acts like some sort of interference. So I'll be gone for a couple of days. Just make yourself at home. Read a book. Watch TV. Wander about as much as you like . . . but don't go outside. Okay?"

"Okay. Thanks, Toby."

They reached the door to Measle's room. Toby clapped Measle gently on the back and said, "Right—

well, I'd better make a start, eh? Enjoy yourself, and I'll see you in a couple of days."

Toby waved his hand cheerily, marched quickly off down the long passage, turned a corner and was gone.

Measle sat on the edge of the four-poster bed, rocking Matilda gently back and forth in her stroller. He stared out of the tall window, trying hard not to think about the terrible situation that he and his family were in. The whole business of his parents' capture was so scary, and he hadn't been able to do anything to help them. He had no idea where they were and, come to that, he had no idea where *he* was, either. And now he had the huge responsibility of looking after Matilda, too.

Miserable and frightened as he was, Measle couldn't help feeling a little hungry. And then he realized that, if *he* felt hungry, so would Matilda. What could he feed her? All he had were his jelly beans—he could feel the lumpy plastic bag in his trouser pocket pressing against his thigh. He didn't take the bag out of his pocket, though. Measle didn't want Matilda to see it, because then she'd want some, and Measle knew that you didn't feed a nine-month-old baby jelly beans. They could choke her to death.

And Tinker was hungry, too. He was sitting on the floor at Measle's feet, looking up at him expectantly. *Oy! Smelly kid! What about a little dog, then? What about a poor, hungry little dog, what has had nothing to eat forever and ever and ever? What is starving to death down here!*

Both Tinker's and Measle's thoughts were interrupted by a strange scratching, scrabbling, tapping sound from the other side of the bedroom door. It was the sort of sound that made you wonder *what* exactly could make such a sound—and whatever it was—what did it want?

"Come in," called Measle, and Tinker stopped pretending he was a starving dog and concentrated on being a fierce watchdog instead. He flattened his ears against his head and began a low growling in the back of his throat.

For a moment the scratching, scrabbling, tapping sound stopped. Then it started up again—*scratchscratch, scrabblescrabble, taptap* . . .

"Come *in*!" shouted Measle. Tinker curled one side of his lip, exposing two of his best teeth.

Scratchscratch, scrabblescrabble, taptap . . .

Measle got off the bed and crossed over to the door.

He put his ear against it and listened. Now, in addition to the scratching and the scrabbling and the tapping, he could hear something else: heavy breathing.

Measle reached for the doorknob, twisted it and pulled the door wide open.

Standing there in the passage—and glaring at him with a pair of cold, round, fishy eyes—was a very small, very skinny, and very damp little Wrathmonk.

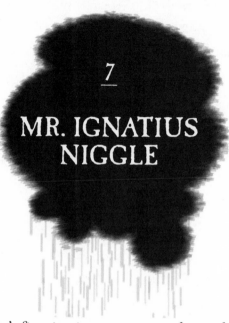

7

MR. IGNATIUS NIGGLE

Measle's first instinct was to reach into his pocket and find a yellow jelly bean. Ever since Nanny Flannel had taught him how, Measle had known that biting down on his least favorite jelly bean (lemon, in Measle's case) was probably the best thing to do when faced with a Wrathmonk. But there wasn't time to *find* a yellow one—and anyway, invisibility for thirty seconds wasn't much good right now since he had Matilda to think of, too.

The little creature standing in the passage was no

taller than Measle and appeared just as skinny, but he had the bone-white face of a real Wrathmonk and a pair of eyes that looked like they should belong to some-thing lying on ice in a fishmonger's shop. And when his thin lips parted in a humorless grin, he exposed—on either side of his mouth—his pointed yellow teeth.

The rest of the creature was Wrathmonkish, too. He wore a shabby black suit that was several sizes too small, and his limp hair was a mousy color and stuck flat to his head. His ears were pointed, his nose was thin and hooked and his eyes were rimmed with red, which made him look as if he'd been crying.

The oddest thing about him was his rain cloud. All the Wrathmonks that Measle had come across so far in his short life had black rain clouds hovering over their heads. A black rain cloud was the sign of a Wrathmonk, but these rain clouds never came indoors. They were always too big to fit inside a house. So when a Wrathmonk entered a building, his rain cloud stayed outside, dribbling its rain down onto the building's roof and not onto its Wrathmonk owner's head.

This little creature was less fortunate. His rain cloud was very small—no larger than a man's fist—and it hovered over the Wrathmonk's head and drizzled a constant stream of very small raindrops down onto his head and shoulders. The tiny cloud didn't produce enough water to *soak* the Wrathmonk beneath it, but it generated enough to make the creature's hair permanently wet and the whole top half of its body very damp. In fact, when Measle looked a little closer, he saw that there was actual moss growing on the shoulders of the shabby black suit and that the collar was streaked with a bright green slime.

Measle saw all this in a horrified fraction of a second, and he was about to slam the door in the little Wrathmonk's face when the creature opened its thin gash of a mouth and said, "Mumpsss?"

Measle stopped his hand from hurling the door shut. "What?"

The Wrathmonk sighed irritably. *"Mumpsss?"* he repeated. "Is dat your name—'Mumpsss'?"

"No—it's Measle."

"Funny. I fot Mr. Jugg sssaid it was Mumpsss."

"No. Measle."

The Wrathmonk frowned crossly. "Well, I don't care. I'm going to call you Mumpsss. Dey is both nasssty diseases, ain't dey? Huh? Jussst like *you*, huh?"

Measle nodded politely, being careful not to anger the creature.

The Wrathmonk sniffed. "Mr. Jugg sssaid I got to do wot you tells me to do."

"What?"

"Wosssamatter? You deaf or sssumfing? MR. JUGG—SSSAID—I GOT TO DO—WOT YOU TELLS ME."

The little Wrathmonk was interrupted by Tinker. Having given the nasty-looking creature out in the passage a long, hard stare, Tinker made up his mind that the occasion called for some serious protest, and so he let loose a succession of furious, teeth-baring, lip-curling snarls and barks.

The Wrathmonk cocked his head to one side and peered around Measle and down at Tinker.

"I don't like dat, Mumpsss," he said nervously. "You better ssstop it doing dat, or I'll breave on it, sssee if I don't."

To Measle, there was something oddly un-frightening about this little creature. He was so small and so damp and so wretched—and his rain cloud was so ridiculously tiny—that Measle felt brave enough to step out into the passage and close the door behind him. The sounds of Tinker's fury diminished by half.

"Who are you?" said Measle, watching the creature warily.

The Wrathmonk stood up straight and puffed out his narrow chest. "I am Missster Niggle," he said haughtily. "Missster Ignatiusss Niggle."

"What are you doing here?"

The Wrathmonk blinked several times in bewildered outrage. "Wot am I doing 'ere? WOT AM I DOING 'ERE?" Mr. Niggle's eyebrows had shot up to the top of his head and he stared at Measle with a look of huge superiority. "I shall tell you wot I am doing 'ere! Disss is my 'ome! I live 'ere!"

"I thought it belonged to Mr. Jugg?" said Measle.

For a moment Mr. Niggle looked a bit uncomfortable. Then he shook his head irritably and several drops of rainwater flew off and spattered against Measle's face.

"Well, yesss," said the little Wrathmonk, "it belongs to Mr. Jugg all right—but dat don't ssstop it being my 'ome, does it? Dat don't ssstop me living 'ere, does it?

Dat don't ssstop me working 'ere, does it?"

"You *work* here?"

A sort of panic seemed to seize Mr. Niggle. His thin white face twisted fantastically, all of his features looking as if they were trying very hard to put themselves somewhere else.

"Never sssaid dat," he muttered.

"Yes you did. You said that it belongs to Mr. Jugg, but that didn't stop you working here."

Mr. Niggle stared at Measle, his fishy eyes blinking slowly. It was obvious he had no idea what to say next. The seconds ticked by.

"You *watch* it, Mumpsss," whispered Mr. Niggle at last. "Jussst you *watch* it. I'll *breave* on you, sssee if I don't. I'll breave on both of you!"

Mr. Niggle and Measle glared at each other for several seconds. Then Measle said, in his most reasonable voice, "Well, if Mr. Jugg says you've got to do what I tell you to do, then I'm telling you *not* to breathe on us."

Mr. Niggle's face twisted into another variety of fantastic contortions while he thought about this. Then his round eyes narrowed and he said, "Right—but, if I *did*—coo! Den you'd sssee sssumfing!"

Measle decided that silence was the best answer to this, so the pair of them stared at each other for another ten seconds without saying a word. Mr. Niggle appeared to take Measle's silence as a sign that he wasn't very impressed, because he said, "I 'ssspect you'd like to know what 'appens when I breave on you, eh?"

Measle shrugged, trying to look as if he didn't really care.

Mr. Niggle frowned irritably. Then he leaned forward and put his face close to Measle's.

"Deaf. Dat's what 'appens. Deaf!"

"You make people go deaf?"

"No! No! Not 'deaf'! Deaf! When I breave on dem, dey die!"

"Oh, you mean 'death'?"

"Yeah, dat'sss what I *sssaid*! *DEAF*! Wosssamatter wiv you? You deaf or sssumfing?"

Measle felt a little laugh trying to bubble its way to the surface, so he put on his most serious and respectful face and said, in an awed voice, "You mean, when you breathe on people, they die?"

Mr. Niggle shook his head, sending several drops of rainwater into Measle's face.

"No, no, no—not *peoples!* You get into 'orrible trouble if you kill peoples! I don't kill *peoples!*"

Mr. Niggle bent close to Measle, and when he spoke, Measle could smell the faint but familiar smell of old mattresses, dead fish and the insides of ancient sneakers on the Wrathmonk's breath.

"Bugs!" hissed Mr. Niggle. "I can kill bugs wiv my breaving!"

"Bugs?"

Mr. Niggle nodded proudly. "Billions! Dat'sss 'ow many I've killed! Billions and sssquillions of bugs! All dead, 'coz of me!"

Mr. Niggle sighed a long, satisfied sigh. Then he seemed to have another thought, because he glanced down the passage and said, abruptly, "You comin' den?"

"Er, where to?"

Mr. Niggle snorted crossly. "De kitchen, o' course! Mr. Jugg sssaid I 'ad to make you breakfassst. Come on!"

Tinker was scratching hard at the door, so Measle opened it and Tinker burst out. He peered suspiciously at Mr. Niggle and then opened his mouth and started to bark at him, as if he was challenging the nasty creature to a fight. Measle bent down and put his hand on

Tinker's neck and the little dog stopped barking at once.

"It's okay, Tink," said Measle. "We're going to have *breakfast*."

Tinker knew a few words. He knew *sit* and he knew *stay* and he knew *be quiet, Tink*. There were several others, too, and one of them was *breakfast*—which was why his ears pricked up immediately and his tail started flipping from side to side. Measle went back into the bedroom and collected Matilda and her stroller.

"Breakfast, Tilly!" he announced, and Matilda clapped her hands together and showed him her six teeth. Measle pushed her out into the corridor—and when Mr. Niggle saw her, he screwed up his face into a look of extreme bewilderment.

"Wot is dat fing?" he muttered out of the corner of his mouth.

"This is my sister, Matilda. I call her Tilly."

Mr. Niggle goggled at Matilda for several seconds, and Matilda looked back at him. Then Matilda decided the little man looked quite funny, so she opened her mouth and grinned at him. Mr. Niggle jumped backward.

"Wot did it do dat for?" he asked suspiciously.

"I think she likes you," said Measle.

This idea seemed to puzzle Mr. Niggle. His face muscles started wriggling about again and he began to say something—then obviously decided against it, because he turned on his heel and, with a grumpy-looking wave of his hand, motioned at them to follow. So, in a little procession, Measle and Matilda and Tinker set off, close on Mr. Ignatius Niggle's heels.

The passage twisted and turned, zigzagging this way and that. Several times Measle got the impression that they had turned around and were walking back the way they had come. They went along another corridor—around a corner—under a stone archway—around several more corners—through a swinging door that was covered with green baize material—and down several more dim passages before arriving, at last, at a heavy wooden door studded all over with large square iron nail heads. The door stood open and Measle, Tinker and Matilda stepped into a room with a high, vaulted stone ceiling. There was a big black old-fashioned cooking range along one wall. In the middle of the room was an ancient pine table, scarred and gouged and scrubbed, its worn surface showing many years of use. There were several old pine chairs set around the table. Copper pots and pans hung from hooks on the stone walls, and there was a big white sink, rust stains streaking its sides.

Mr. Ignatius Niggle went and stood by the stove, his arms folded across his narrow chest, glowering at Measle and Matilda and Tinker as they entered his domain.

"Right," said the little Wrathmonk, peering sourly at them. "Wodja want?"

"Er, can I have some toast, please?" said Measle. "And marmalade? And a glass of milk? And Tilly likes cereal and milk."

Mr. Niggle sniffed and said nothing.

"And Tinker likes dog biscuits," said Measle. "If you've got any. And some water for him, please."

Mr. Niggle sniffed again. He gestured Measle toward the old pine table and Measle sat down, pulling Matilda's stroller next to him. Tinker squatted at their feet, looking expectantly at the little Wrathmonk. Mr. Niggle glared back. Then, abruptly, he turned on his heel and marched out through a small door on the other side of the room. By leaning sideways, Measle could see through a crack in the door. There were shelves stacked with stuff in there, and Measle guessed that the room was a sort of pantry. There was a sound of banging pots and pans, then Mr. Niggle reappeared, carrying a wooden tray. On the tray were two plates together with a couple of glasses and a pair of metal bowls.

Mr. Niggle dumped one of the plates and a glass in front of Measle. He did the same for Matilda. Then he bent and placed the two tin bowls on the floor in front of Tinker's nose.

With a sly and nasty little smile on his mouth, he straightened up and glared at Measle and Matilda.

"Your breakfassst," he announced.

Measle looked down. On his plate was a dusty old brick, with bits of cement still stuck to it. His glass was filled to the brim with a clear liquid that looked like water. It didn't smell like water, though—even from a foot away, Measle could detect the strong, chemical stink of the stuff. It smelled familiar. . . .

"Er, what's this?" asked Measle, pointing at his glass.

"Dat is purplepine," said Mr. Niggle smugly. "Lovely,

lovely purplepine. Drink up."

"Purplepine?" said Measle. "What's purplepine?"

Mr. Niggle rolled his eyes impatiently. "Purplepine! Dat is de ssstuff wot you clean paintbrushes wiv!"

"Oh, you mean *turpentine*," said Measle.

"Dat'sss what I sssaid," muttered Mr. Niggle. *"Purple-pine."*

Measle knew what turpentine was, because one of the things his mother liked doing in her spare time was oil painting. Lee wasn't very good at it, but that didn't matter. She *liked* doing it, and Measle liked to watch her, and sometimes he helped to clean her brushes— and that was why the smell of the liquid in his glass was so familiar. The trouble was, turpentine was pretty poisonous stuff, and Matilda was reaching out one chubby hand toward her glass. . . .

Measle shoved the glass out of Matilda's reach.

Tinker whined softly. Measle looked down at the little dog. In front of Tinker's nose was his plate. There was a brick in it, too—and the tin bowl next to it was full of turpentine.

Mr. Niggle sniggered.

"Eat up," he said. "Eat up your lovely breakfasssts."

Measle's mind was racing. This was such typical Wrathmonk behavior—nasty and spiteful and point-less—only, in Mr. Niggle's case, it was nasty and spite-ful and pointless in a not-too-terribly-dangerous way. He was remembering all the other Wrathmonks he'd dealt with before—Griswold Gristle and Judge Cedric Hardscrabble, Scab Draggle, Buford Cudgel, Frognell Flabbit and the Zagreb couple—and everything they had tried to do to him had been *extremely* dangerous. Life threatening, in fact. And then there was Basil Tramplebone, his horrible old guardian, who had tried to turn him into a cockroach.

All those Wrathmonks had something in common.

They weren't very bright.

"Mmm! Yummy!" said Measle, licking his finger and then dabbing it against the dusty old brick. He lifted his finger, stuck it in his mouth and sucked it loudly. He could taste the cement dust. "Really delicious!"

Mr. Niggle looked puzzled. "Huh?" he said doubt-fully.

"The best breakfast ever! Thanks a ton for not bring-ing me toast and marmalade and milk! That's what they make me eat at home—and I hate it! I only asked for it because that's what I'm *supposed* to have. But I think it's really disgusting! So does Tilly! Horrible, icky stuff! Eeeuuugh! And Tinker really hates dog biscuits, too! But bricks and turpentine—wow! Thank you very much! Thanks from *all* of us!"

Mr. Niggle's expression changed from bewilderment to a look of crafty cunning. He rubbed his pale hands together and his fishy eyes darted around the big room. Measle guessed that the little Wrathmonk was trying to use his brain to its fullest capacity. Measle hoped that the capacity of Mr. Niggle's brain was very, very small.

Without a word, Mr. Niggle collected the plates and glasses and put them back on his tray. He picked up Tinker's metal bowls. Then he scurried off to the pantry. Measle listened to the sounds of cupboards opening, packages being unwrapped, cartons being opened, lids being twisted off. . . .

Five minutes later Mr. Niggle returned. He carried his wooden tray, which was again filled with dishes and bowls and cups and glasses, and he marched up to the kitchen table with an air of triumph and dumped everything down in front of Measle and Matilda.

"Dere!" he exclaimed, loudly. "Eat dat if you dare!"

On the table in front of Measle was a plate piled high with perfectly toasted toast. There was a dish of marmalade, another of butter, and a tall glass of milk. Matilda had a bowl of cereal and her own bottle of milk, and on the floor at their feet, Tinker was looking with interest at a metal bowl filled to the brim with dog biscuits.

"Eeeuuugh!" said Measle, making a disgusted face. "Are you trying to make me sick?"

Mr. Niggle grinned delightedly, clasped his hands under his chin and did a strange little hopping, shuffling dance.

"Ho, yesss!" he squealed. "And you will eat every bit of it! Or elssse I shall just 'ave to breave on you! Eat! Eat!"

Measle sighed and tried to look depressed. He sneaked a sideways look at Matilda and saw with relief that his sister was doing what she usually did with food when it was first presented to her—she was sloshing it around with her hands and not actually putting anything in her mouth. Now all that was left to hope for was that Tinker would do what Tinker usually did with a bowl of dog biscuits.

To Measle's relief, Tinker did. He took a quick sniff at the bowl—and then he turned his face up, cocked his head to one side and stared up at Measle with his *look-at-me-I'm-a-poor-little-starving-orphan-doggy-what-needs-real-human-food* expression.

"Poor Tinker," said Measle, dejectedly buttering a piece of toast. "He hates those things just as much as I hate this stuff."

Mr. Niggle peered down at Tinker and frowned angrily.

"Well, 'e'sss being a wicked dog, isn't 'e?" he announced. "Not eatin' nuffing. A very wicked dog indeed. I shall jussst 'ave to breave on 'im, won't I?"

And before Measle could do anything to stop him, Mr. Niggle took a deep breath, bent over and puffed hard in Tinker's face.

Interesting, thought Tinker. *Very interesting. I've smelled that smell before, lots of times. Usually a bit stronger than this— Hello? Where's my tickle gone?*

Tinker's tickle was a semipermanent itch, usually located behind his right ear. Sometimes the itch went down his neck and occasionally he had to sit down and scratch his stomach as hard as he could because the itch had traveled down there. But mostly the itch stayed behind his right ear and that's where it had been all morning.

And now, quite suddenly, it was gone.

(And the flea—which had been living for some time very comfortably behind Tinker's right ear—dropped dead as a doornail, and fell out of Tinker's wiry fur and onto the stone floor at his feet. Several thousand other tiny parasites—all too small to see with the naked eye—also fell dead from Mr. Niggle's poisonous breath and, for the first time in his doggy life, Tinker found himself entirely free from tiny hitchhikers.) He let out a little yelp of pleasure, and Measle, who knew Tinker's barks and yelps well, heaved a quiet sigh of relief. Obviously Mr. Niggle's breath had had no ill effects at all.

Mr. Niggle, on the other hand, took Tinker's yelp as a sign that the little dog had suffered something nasty. "That'll teach 'im," muttered Mr. Niggle. To the little Wrathmonk's satisfaction, Tinker gave up waiting for a bit of toast and wandered instead back to his bowl of biscuits. He sniffed them again, sighed, and then he picked out a single biscuit and began to crunch it thoughtfully.

Measle ate steadily through his pile of toast, carefully keeping up a series of little grunts designed to make Mr. Niggle think that he was having a hard time eating this disgusting stuff. All the while Measle watched the little Wrathmonk out of the corner of his eye. Measle decided that Mr. Niggle didn't pose much of a threat. If the Wrathmonk's spell-casting abilities were as pathetic as his breathing magic, then Ignatius Niggle wasn't going to be too much of a problem. *But it might be a good idea to find out exactly* what *he can do.*

"Can I ask——(Eeeugh! This toast is horrible!)——can I ask you something?"

"Don't sssee why not," said Mr. Niggle, looking pleased with himself.

"Well——(Oh, yuck! Disgusting marmalade!)——I was wondering what spells you can do? Apart from the breathing one, I mean?"

Mr. Niggle stopped looking pleased with himself and, instead, adopted a look of deep sadness.

"Can't do any," he muttered. "Not anymore. Dey won't let me do it, sssee?"

Mr. Niggle lifted both hands to his neck and pulled apart the wet collar of his grubby shirt. There was a ring around his scrawny throat—a ring made out of a dull, silvery metal.

A wrathring!

Which means that Mr. Niggle can't hurt me with magic, even if he wants to!

Measle decided to ask some more questions.

"Um, when you *could* do spells, what sort were they?"

Mr. Niggle looked a little embarrassed. He sniffed nervously and rubbed his nose with the back of his hand. Then he said, in a low, sad voice, "I could only do one."

"And what was that?"

Mr. Niggle stared at the floor and mumbled something under his breath.

"Sorry?" said Measle. "I didn't quite catch that."

"I sssaid . . . I could open fings. Doors and fings."

Measle thought about this for a second and then he said, "But I can do that. All you've got to do is turn the handle, see—"

"I *know* dat, Mumpsss," said Mr. Niggle, shaking his head irritably. "De point is, I could open dem when dey was *locked*, sssee?"

"Oh, I see. That's very clever."

"Ho, yesss. Dat is what I am—very clever *indeed*. Wot elssse do you want to know?"

"I was wondering . . . how you came to be living here?"

Everybody likes being asked to talk about themselves and Mr. Niggle was no exception. "Ho! Well, it all come about after I was 'appily ended, sssee—"

Happily ended? Measle didn't think that Mr. Niggle's end was particularly happy looking, so he said, "Happily ended? (Ugh! I hate milk!) What's 'happily ended' mean?"

Mr. Niggle didn't look very pleased at being interrupted.

" 'Appily ended? Wosssit mean? It means—well—it means—er—when you've done sssumfing bad, sssee and den you get arresssted, sssee?"

"Oh—you mean 'apprehended'?" said Measle.

"Dat'sss wot I sssaid," muttered Mr. Niggle irritably. " ' 'Appily ended.' Kindly do not interrubble me again—"

" 'Interrubble?' What's 'interrubble' mean?"

Mr. Niggle banged both his bony white hands down

hard on the kitchen table. Obviously he did it a little bit too hard, because he said, "Ow!" quite loudly. Then he swiveled his big, fishy eyes around and glared angrily at Measle.

"You're doin' it again!" he hissed. "Interrubbling! 'Ow can I tell you my ssstory if you keep on interrubbling?"

Measle found himself actually feeling a bit sorry for the creature—*and how can I feel sorry for a Wrathmonk? Well—it's weird—but I do!*

"I'm sorry," said Measle in a humble little voice. "I won't inter—um—I won't interrubble again."

"Sssee dat you don't," said Mr. Niggle severely. "Now den, where was I? Ho, yesss—I was happily ended, 'coz I done sssumfing bad, sssee? Wot I was doin' was—I was burglariding disss old Wizard's houssse. You know what burglariding is, do you?"

Measle shook his head, trying hard to keep a straight face.

"Coo—you don't know *nuffing*, do you? It's when you take ssstuff wot ain't yours, sssee? Dat'sss burglariding. Dat'sss wot I was, sssee? A burglarider!"

Measle nodded slowly, but his mind was racing. *So,*

poor Mr. Niggle must have started out as a pathetic little one-spell Wizard—a spell that he'd used to help him steal stuff—and being a petty thief would pretty soon have turned him into a pathetic little one-spell Warlock—and, with a brain as hopeless as Mr. Niggle's, it wouldn't have taken long before the strain of being a Warlock burglar proved too much for his sanity—turning him into this pathetic little excuse for a Wrathmonk!

"Ssso," Mr. Niggle went on, "dere I was, busy burglariding, when I got caught, sssee? Disss old Wizard, he come down de ssstairs in his jimmy-jammies and he putsss a big ssspell on me wot completely paraglides me—wot? Wot's ssso funny?"

"Nothing," gasped Measle, hurriedly wiping away a tear of laughter from the corner of his eye. "I wasn't laughing, honestly I wasn't. I got some of this horrible toast stuck in my throat. Please—go on."

"Right—well, dere I was, completely paraglided. I couldn't move nuffing, except for my mouf. Den de old Wizard, he goes and makes a fellytone call—'ere, you're doing it again! You ought to learn 'ow to eat dat toassst ssstuff wivout choking to deaf!"

"Sorry."

"Right. Jussst you be careful. Well, after de fellytone call, we sssits about and waits and disss old Wizard, he tells me his name is Lord Octopusss—"

Measle sat up straight. "Lord Octavo?" he blurted.

"Dat's wot I *sssaid*, Mumps," said Mr. Niggle. "Lord *Octopusss*. Anyway, he was quite nice. Made me a cup of tea, gave me a cookie. Den, after a bit, disss uvver Wizard come in and he had disss lady wiv 'im. Dey was quite young, not like Lord Octopusss. Now, disss *young* Wizard asssked me a whole lot of quessstions and den he sssaid he was going to—wot was 'is exact words, now? Ho yess, he sssaid he was going to 'ricky-bend leaningsssea.' Dat'sss what he sssaid to me. 'I'm going to ricky-bend leaningsssea,' he sssaid."

Even after several moments of intense thought, Measle couldn't work out what "ricky-bend leaningsea" could possibly mean. But Mr. Niggle didn't look too upset about what had happened to him, so . . .

"That was very—er—nice of him. Ricky-bending leaningsea, I mean."

"Yeah, well, I wasn't burglariding *'im*, was I? I was burglariding Lord Octopusss. I even remember 'is name. It was Mr. Sssam Ssstubbs—"

129

"That's my dad!" yelled Measle, jumping up out of his chair.

"Your dad?"

"Yes! And the lady with him—that must have been my mum!"

"Your mum?"

"Yes!"

Mr. Niggle, frowning with terrific concentration, let his small brain absorb this new information. Then, at last, his face cleared.

"Ho!" he said, excitedly, "ssso dat means your name is Mumpsss *Ssstubbs*!"

"Well, *Measle* Stubbs, actually," said Measle.

Mr. Niggle waved a hand carelessly in the air. "Measles, mumpsss—sssame fing! But dat'sss not de point! De point *is*—Mr. Sssam Ssstubbs is your dad! And dat changes *everyfing*!"

"It does?" said Measle, wondering what, exactly, was going to change.

"Yesss!" shouted Mr. Niggle, grinning widely and showing all his pointed teeth. "Dat means I *like* you now! 'Coz your dad was nice to me, sssee, and he *ricky-bended leaningsssea*! Dat'sss why I'm working here, and

130

not"—Mr. Niggle ducked his head, looked suspiciously from side to side and then whispered hoarsely into Measle's ear—"and not ssstuck in de uvver place!"

"What other place?"

Mr. Niggle didn't reply straightaway. Instead, he just shook his head very hard, scattering droplets of water all over Measle and the remains of the toast. Then, looking very mysterious, he winked, tapped the side of his nose with a long, bony finger and muttered, "Asssk no quessstions, tell no fibby-dibs."

"Oh, right," said Measle, trying to look wise.

Quite suddenly Mr. Niggle swooped forward and gathered up Measle's and Matilda's now nearly empty plates and glasses. He clattered them down onto his tin tray and then bent and picked up Tinker's bowl from right under the little dog's nose.

"You won't be wantin' disss nasssty ssstuff no more," he said, sounding just a little bit apologetic. "You can 'ave your nice brick and your lovely purplepine back."

Measle did some very fast thinking and—hoping that Mr. Niggle had meant what he'd said about liking him now—decided to come clean.

"Well, actually, I was only joking. I don't really like

131

bricks and turpentine, you see. Neither does Tilly. Not even Tinker."

Mr. Niggle considered this for several seconds. He beamed and said, "Dat was a *joke*? Dat's *funny*! Hahahahahahahahaha! Hoohoohoohoohoohoo!" Mr. Niggle bent over and laughed like a mad hyena. Wiping his streaming eyes, he straightened up and said, "I likesss you. I do. Ssso, now you can call me Iggy."

"Iggy?"

"Iggy. Dat's short for Ignatiusss, sssee? Okeydokey?"

"Okeydokey, Iggy."

It was a new sensation for Measle, having a Wrathmonk be friendly to him. He decided to make the most of it while the friendship lasted. In Measle's experience, Wrathmonks' madness made them horribly unpredictable and likely to change their minds in an instant, so he kept himself alert and ready for anything. For instance, how would Iggy react to his next request . . . ?

"Um—could you show me around the castle, Iggy?" he asked.

"Sssee around *my* cassstle?"

"If you don't mind."

It was obvious that nobody had ever asked Iggy

such a thing before, because once again the little Wrathmonk's face screwed itself up in whole succession of wild grimaces as he tried to work out what his answer should be. Then, at last, the wriggling of his facial muscles settled down.

"Yesss," he said firmly. "Dat would be all right. But only de *inssside*. Not de *outssside*. We can't go outsssside, sssee? Dat's not allowed."

For the next half hour, Measle and Matilda—with Tinker trotting at their heels—followed Iggy Niggle all over the inside of Caltrop Castle. It was a vast place. There were endless corridors that twisted this way and that, sometimes doubling back on themselves, then turning again and resuming their original direction. They all looked pretty much the same, too, with their dark paneling and stone floors. Measle thought it was like being in a sort of maze, and as in a maze, he never had any idea where he was.

At one point, near the end of the tour, Iggy Niggle threw open a door and said, "Dese is Missster Juggs's rooms."

Toby's rooms weren't very interesting. There was a small bedroom and an even smaller bathroom. In the bathroom were all the things you'd expect to find in a bathroom—and Iggy seemed to want to show Measle every single one of them.

"Disss is Mr. Juggs's bath, and disss is Mr. Juggs's toilet—and disss is Mr. Juggs's basin, and disss is Mr. Juggs's washcloth, and disss is Mr. Juggs's sssoap. . . ." And on and on went Iggy, detailing everything down to the smallest item in a droning voice, as if he were reciting a shopping list.

A couple of objects caught Measle's eye. There was a little, flat, round silver case, full of what looked like compressed face powder, and a small brush, which looked like something an artist would use. Measle recognized it immediately—his mother Lee had several on her dressing table in Merlin Manor, and on the rare occasions when she put on makeup, she used the brushes to smooth the color onto her cheek.

I wonder who that belongs to? thought Measle. *Perhaps Toby's got a girlfriend?*

There was nothing more to see in Toby's bare rooms, so Measle and Matilda and Tinker followed Iggy back out to the corridor. Iggy paused and said, "Now den, wot elssse do you wanna sssee?"

"What about where you sleep, Iggy?" The idea of sleeping in the same building with a Wrathmonk—even one as simple and unthreatening as Iggy—was a little unsettling, and Measle simply wanted to know just how close Iggy's quarters were to his own room.

Iggy's face brightened.

"You wanna sssee where I sssleep?" he said delightedly. "Come on, den!"

Iggy waved one bony hand and set off at a terrific pace, making Measle and Tinker break into a trot just to keep up with him. Matilda, who liked it when somebody pushed her along really fast, squealed with delight and kicked her legs. They went along a dark passageway, around several corners, through a succession of doors, left and right and right and left. Measle noticed that their surroundings were growing shabbier and shabbier. Patches of damp appeared on the ceilings and ancient, dusty spiderwebs hung in the corners. The stone flooring ended after they passed through one door and became old and dirty planks of wood, cracked and splintered with age. These dark and dingy corridors seemed to Measle to go on and on, twisting and turning and getting progressively more and more run down. And, quite suddenly, Measle realized, with a start of fear, that he had no idea how to retrace his steps to anywhere in this vast castle, let alone back to his bedroom. He caught up with Iggy and tapped him on a wet shoulder.

"Is it much farther, Iggy?"

Iggy shook his head and pointed down the passage.

They were approaching a dead end. The passage simply stopped, about twenty yards away, in a brick wall. At the foot of the wall, set tight up against it, was an old plywood tea chest, turned on its side. As they got closer, Measle saw that there was a puddle of water all the way around the tea chest, like a little moat—and that the brick wall next to it was wet and mossy and green with slime.

"Dere," said Iggy proudly. "Dat'sss where I sssleep."

"You sleep in a *box*?" said Measle.

"Yesss, I do," said Iggy. "'Ere, I'll show you."

Iggy stepped forward and then bent in half and wriggled himself into the box. He fitted so tightly that his head was twisted over to one side and he had to talk out of the side of his mouth.

"Sssee?" he said proudly.

Now Measle saw why Mr. Ignatius Niggle slept in an old tea chest. The rain cloud couldn't follow him into the confined space and, unable to drop its constant load onto Iggy's head, was now forced to drift over the tea chest and dribble on the top of the box instead.

"Very nice, Iggy," said Measle.

Iggy tried to nod, but he was squashed so tightly into his tea chest that the only movement he could make was blinking his fishy eyes.

"It *is* nice, innit?" He blinked. "Nice and dry, too. I'm ever ssso lucky, ain't I?"

Iggy blinked several more times, and then his eyelids slid down and stayed there.

"Iggy?" said Measle, wondering what was happening.

Iggy's eyes stayed tightly shut, but he waved one limp hand in a dismissive sort of gesture.

"Go away, Mumpsss," he said, in a sleepy voice. "I'm all tired now, ain't I? All disss runnin' around. I'm goin' to 'ave a little nap."

"But how do I get back to my room?" said Measle.

Iggy opened one eye.

"You lift up one of your footsss, den you make it go forward and den you put it down. Den you do de

137

sssame fing wiv de uvver foot. Den de sssame fing wiv de uvver foot—den de sssame fing wiv de uvver foot—and you go on doin' dat until you get dere."

"But I don't think I can remember the way, Iggy."

Iggy hissed impatiently. "You go de sssame way dat you came!" he said. "Now go away!"

Iggy closed his eye and started to make snoring noises. They weren't very convincing snoring noises, so he was obviously just pretending to be asleep, but Measle realized that Iggy was determined to be no help at all.

"Come on, Tink," he said. "Let's see if we can get back, shall we?"

Within five minutes Measle realized that they were hopelessly lost. He looked down at Tinker, who was staring up at him with his fuzzy head cocked to one side.

Then Measle had one of his ideas. It was a small one compared to some of his others, but it might just work. . . .

"Tink, you want to go outside? Huh? You want to go outside?"

Going outside was one of the things that Tinker

understood. Back at home it meant fresh air, open skies and grass under his paws. Here, in this shadowy place, it could mean only one place—

"Outside, Tink? Wanna go outside?"

The smelly kid was smiling and nodding his head in an encouraging sort of way, so Tinker stretched, yawned and then set off briskly back the way they had come. Measle, pushing Matilda in front of him, followed, hoping for the best.

For Tinker, the problem of getting lost simply didn't exist. All you had to do was keep your nose fairly near to the ground and smell the scent you'd left behind on your way here, and soon enough you'd arrive back at your starting point. So with his nose half an inch off the floor, Tinker led Measle and Matilda with perfect accuracy right to the little indoor garden. From there it was an easy walk back to their bedroom.

The next few hours passed slowly and Measle was terribly bored. Matilda was happy playing with Tinker on the floor, so Measle turned on the television, but it showed nothing but news. The books on the shelves were equally dull. They were leather bound and dusty and had titles like *Accountancy for Warlocks* and *Cobbett's*

Property Laws as Pertaining to Wizards' Estates.

Measle sat by the big window and stared out at the sweeping lawn and the glassy lake and the dark forest beyond.

Not a leaf stirred, not a branch waved.

It's very quiet out there, thought Measle. *Not even a tiny breeze.*

At home in Merlin Manor, even at the dead of night, there were always sounds—the gentle sighing of the wind in the treetops, the distant barking of a dog, the soft hooting of an owl. . . .

Noise.

But not here. Caltrop Castle was silent. As silent as—well, as silent as a *grave.*

But, outside the bedroom door, things were happening.

Things were changing.

Things were being—*rearranged.*

Silently.

8

A CHANGE
FOR THE WORSE

The morning drifted into afternoon.

Measle came out of a daydream—in which he
was rescuing his parents from an entire army of fire-
breathing dragons—and noticed that Tinker had left
Matilda's side and was standing hopefully by the door.

"Come on then, Tink," said Measle, "let's go to the
garden again, shall we?"

Measle put Matilda into her stroller.

He opened the door . . .

. . . and then he stood there, very still, his feet frozen

141

to the floor, his eyes wide and staring and his mouth gaping open.

The passage outside his bedroom door was—well, it was utterly *different*. The color and texture of the walls were the same, the floor was still made of worn old flagstones, but there was one extraordinary and—to Measle—utterly mind-boggling alteration. Where, yesterday, the passage outside the bedroom door had stretched out to the left and the right, so that he could pick which direction to go in, now there was no left or right. Now the corridor stretched out in *front* of the bedroom door, making Measle's room the last door in a dead end.

"What's going on, Tink?" whispered Measle, staring in bewilderment at the corridor in front of him. A moment later Tinker started to move. The little dog, with his nose half an inch from the stone floor, started to trot off down the corridor—and Measle, with no choice in the matter, started to follow.

None of this seemed to bother Tinker in the least. He kept his nose down close to the floor and simply followed the distinctive smells of his own—and Measle's—footsteps. The scent of his own paws—and the scent of the soles of Measle's sneakers—were two things that hadn't changed, and as far as Tinker was concerned, the fact that everything *else* had altered didn't matter in the least.

But to Measle it was one of the most unsettling feelings he'd ever experienced. Yesterday that massive, towering suit of black armor had been on the right side of an arched door. But now there was no arched door, and the armor was positioned on the other side of the passage—and the passage itself turned sharply right, and Measle remembered distinctly turning sharply *left* earlier that morning.

They turned another unfamiliar corner and then stopped dead outside a door. The door was the same familiar garden door, with "Jardin" painted on it in small gold letters—only instead of being on the right-hand side of the corridor, it was on the left, next to a sharp bend in the passage, which Measle knew had not been there the previous day. And the great portrait of the Duke of Touffou was now positioned right next to the garden door, instead of hanging on the opposite wall.

But it wasn't just the location of the portrait that had changed.

Something had changed in the painting itself.

The Duke of Touffou wasn't in it.

Where the tall figure of the Duke had once stood, close by the twisted tree, now there was just a smudge—as if somebody had come and wiped the figure off the canvas, leaving only a smear of dark base paint behind.

There was another, smaller smudge in the background of the painting. In the distant fields—where once had stood a herd of cows—there was nothing but a faint outline.

And in the far-off cave entrance, the twin points of light that looked like a pair of slanted eyes were no longer there, either.

Measle stared up at the ruined painting, wondering who could possibly have done this—and why? There seemed to be no point to it at all.

He felt a nudge against his ankle. He looked down. Tinker was staring up at him, his tail wagging fast, the expression in his eyes quite plainly saying, *C'mon, smelly kid! It's the garden, isn't it? Open the door and let me in!*

Measle opened the door and Tinker darted inside. Measle followed and was vastly relieved to see that the garden itself appeared to be unaltered. He pushed Matilda over to a stone bench and sat down. His mind was in a whirl. How could a building as solid and as ancient as Castle Caltrop suddenly change its entire geography? Why would somebody rub a figure out of an old oil painting? Or was he simply going mad?

No, I'm not mad, thought Measle. *I've seen lots of weird things in my life, like dragons and giant cockroaches and flying hats, and this is just another weird thing.*

Measle got up, and he and Matilda and Tinker went back into the unfamiliar corridor. Measle looked down at Tinker and said, "I hope you can find your way back, Tink, because I don't think I can, and Tilly *certainly* can't."

That was when they heard the first scream.

The scream was faint and a long way off, but Measle could still hear the terror and the panic and the desperation in it. A moment later the scream came again.

Another scream—

Tinker growled softly and turned his head in the direction of the sound.

Another scream—

The screams had a familiar tone to them. They were

145

the kinds of screams you might expect to come from the scraggy, scrawny throat of a terrified little Mr. Ignatius Niggle.

"It's Iggy, Tink! Come on—let's find Iggy!"

They were forced to search for him using only their ears.

"He could be anywhere, Tink," said Measle as they stood at the start of yet another unfamiliar corridor and waited for the next faint, panic-filled scream.

It came all too soon. . . .

"Come on, Tink—this way!"

When they found him at last, Iggy was in a doorway, curled up on the floor, his head buried in his arms. His tiny rain cloud hovered a few inches over his prostrate body, dribbling its load down onto the little Wrathmonk. Iggy was moaning in terror, and as Measle and Matilda and Tinker rounded the corner and saw him for the first time, Iggy raised his head from the protection of his arms, opened his mouth and let out another piercing shriek.

Measle ran to Iggy's side. He knelt down and put his hand on Iggy's damp shoulder, and Iggy screamed again and pulled away, burying his head even deeper in his arms.

"Iggy! It's me!" yelled Measle.

Iggy raised his head and opened one fishy eye.

"Mu-Mu-Mumpsss?" he whispered, his voice shaking with fear. "Is dat you, Mumpsss?"

"Yes, Iggy, it's me."

Iggy grabbed Measle's hand, wrapping it in his own damp and bony one. His long, clawlike fingernails dug into Measle's palm.

"Sssumfing's 'appened, Mumpsss," he muttered. "Sssumfing awful! I don't know where I am, I don't know where I'm going and I don't know how to come back again! I woked up and it was all 'orrible and I ssstarted to run and now I can't find my box, can't find my kitchen, can't find *nuffing*! Wot 'appened, Mumpsss?"

Measle tried gently to pull his hand out of Iggy's grasp, but the little Wrathmonk held on tight.

"I don't know, Iggy," he said. "But everything's— well, it's all sort of *rearranged*."

"Re-a-wot?"

"It's sort of changed itself around, Iggy. It's a kind of magic, I think. All the passages and the doors and things are in different places."

147

Iggy's eyes opened very wide and two big tears welled out of them and trickled down his cheeks.

"Oooh!" he moaned, softly. "It'sss never done dat before! Not never!"

From behind Measle, still sitting in her stroller, Matilda said, "Cubba doogy wump."

Measle looked over his shoulder and saw Matilda kick her feet and hold out her arms, ready to make a lot more noise if somebody didn't pay her some attention pretty soon and do exactly what she wanted.

Measle knew what the kicking and arm stretching meant. Matilda wanted a cuddle. He went over and unbuckled the straps that held her in place.

"Come on then, Tilly—upsy daisy."

He lifted Matilda out of her chair, expecting her arms to curl around his neck as they usually did when he picked her up. But her arms remained stiffly outstretched, both of them rigidly pointing at something down the passage. Matilda wasn't looking at him, either—she was staring fixedly down the corridor, her feet still kicking—

"What is it, Tilly?" said Measle, and Matilda said, "Cubba doogy *wump*!" again, only more firmly this time.

Measle turned to see what she was looking at. There was only Iggy Niggle, sitting there in a sniveling heap on the floor, his back against the wall.

Matilda's kicking was growing more desperate, so Measle carried her over to Iggy and squatted down next to him. Iggy looked up, his eyes pink with tears—and he saw this strange little creature stretching her arms out toward him, her feet kicking, her mouth smiling, lips parted, revealing six pearly little teeth.

"Wosssit want?" said Iggy, shrinking back against the wall.

"I think she likes you, Iggy."

"*Likes* me?" Iggy's eyes were even rounder than usual. His mouth was gaping open. "Wosssit like me for?"

"I don't know, Iggy," said Measle. "But when Tilly likes somebody, she always wants to give them a hug. That's what she wants to do now. And you'd better let her, otherwise she'll start making a horrible noise, and believe me, you don't want her to do that, because it hurts your ears really badly."

Slowly and cautiously, Iggy edged forward until he was within reach of Matilda's hands. Matilda lunged forward and threw both arms around Iggy's neck, and Measle let go, releasing her into Iggy's nervously clutching little claws.

Matilda liked people who took no notice of her. All too often, when she was introduced to strangers, they would want to cuddle her and kiss her and coo in her face, and most of the time, Matilda didn't want them to do that.

But Iggy had never done any of those things. In fact, Iggy had made a point of not even *looking* at her, if he could possibly help it. So Matilda decided that she liked him. Matilda also was very fond of wet things. She liked baths and paddling pools and porridge and cereal and she liked getting her hands into them all and having a good splash around . . . so Iggy, with his own personal rain cloud, was something special. The first thing she did with him—after the hug—was to scrumple her hands around in his wet hair, until every sodden strand was standing up on end.

"Wosssit doing?" whispered Iggy, holding Matilda as if she was made of the most fragile glass in the world.

"Messing up your hair, Iggy," said Measle. "Oh, she *really* likes you."

Matilda *did* like Iggy—she liked him a lot. He looked so funny and she admired his cloud enormously. But there were one or two little things wrong with him. His breath wasn't very nice—so Matilda *changed* it. She waved her hands and the smell went away. Nobody noticed—certainly not Iggy—but now his breath no longer smelled of dead fish, old mattresses and the insides of ancient sneakers. Now it didn't smell of anything at all.

The other thing about Iggy that Matilda changed was the color of his teeth. Matilda was very proud of her own—so, with a wave, she took the yellow stains away from Iggy's teeth and made them the same color as hers. Nobody noticed Iggy's new pearly-white teeth, either.

Matilda, having performed two little spells, felt the tiredness sweep over her. She put her head on Iggy's damp shoulder and, within five seconds, fell fast asleep.

"Is—is it dead?" said Iggy, his voice quavering with terror.

"No, Iggy. She's just asleep," said Measle. He looked at his sister thoughtfully. "She's been doing a lot of that lately."

"Wot should I do wiv it?" said Iggy, squinting down at Matilda's head resting on his shoulder.

"You could carry her for a bit," said Measle. "She loves being carried by somebody she likes."

A slow grin spread across Iggy's face. Nobody had ever liked him before. In fact, everybody he'd ever come into contact with had tried to get away from him as fast as possible. Certainly nobody had ever hugged him. Nobody had ever messed with his hair. Nobody had ever fallen asleep on his shoulder. . . .

And, in that moment, Iggy felt—for the first time in his miserable little life—actual love for another living being.

"You *sssure* it'sss not dead, Mumpsss?"

"I'm quite sure, Iggy. Look, you can see her breathing."

"Does it want sssumfing to eat?"

"Well, she might when she wakes up."

Iggy's face fell. "But—we is lossst, Mumpsss," he muttered sadly. "How is we going to find de kitchen? If we can't find de kitchen, it'sss going to ssstarve to deaf!" And he started to snivel again.

"No, Iggy," said Measle gently. "I think we're going

to be fine." He pointed at Tinker. "Tinker can find the kitchen. He can smell it."

Iggy stopped sniveling almost as quickly as he'd started. The corners of his lips drew themselves up in a cautious little grin, exposing Iggy's newly whitened teeth.

And now, Measle noticed Iggy's teeth. For a moment he was puzzled. Then he realized what must have happened. Obviously this was Matilda's doing—and here she was, asleep again, and this seemed to happen immediately after his sister had performed some magic, which was rather interesting—

His thoughts were interrupted by Iggy tugging at his sleeve.

"Can we go to de kitchen now, Mumpsss?" he asked. "'Coz it might wake up sssoon and be 'ungry, and den it might make de 'orrible noise, mightn't it?"

Measle clicked his fingers and Tinker's ears pricked up.

"Dinner, Tink! Want some dinner?"

Tinker never turned down an offer of food. He wagged his tail twice, then raised his nose in the still air and sniffed—*There! A long way off . . . a definite smell of toast! Right—follow me!*—and Tinker set off briskly down the corridor, his nose twitching all the way.

"Come on, Iggy!" said Measle. He folded Matilda's stroller and, trailing it behind him, set off after Tinker. Iggy, holding Matilda carefully as if she was a glass of water from which not a single drop must be spilled, brought up the rear.

They threaded their way through the endless maze of corridors.

Left, right—

Right, left—

On and on and on—

And then Tinker stopped so abruptly that Iggy almost tripped over him.

"Go on den, doggie," muttered Iggy, prodding Tinker on the rump with the toe of one scuffed old shoe.

Tinker's legs didn't move. In fact, the only thing that moved on Tinker's body was the ridge of fur that ran all the way from his neck to the base of his tail. This line of coarse hairs rose and stood upright, so that it looked like a little Mohawk haircut. At the same time, Tinker curled back his lips and, exposing his teeth, began a low growling.

"Wot'sss de matter wiv it?" whispered Iggy.

"I don't know, Iggy," said Measle. "But I think there's something up ahead that Tinker doesn't like."

They were almost at the end of a corridor. Ahead of them was a **T** junction, giving them the choice of turning either left or right. There was nothing to be seen at the junction itself, so Measle guessed that whatever Tinker was sensing, it must be lurking a few yards down one side or the other. Very cautiously he crept past Iggy and Matilda, then past the rigid, quivering Tinker. He reached the junction and poked his head forward. He looked first to the left—

Nothing there.

Then to the right—

Something there.

Something tall and thin and dark. Very tall, very thin, very dark, with a pair of piercing black eyes that gleamed in the gloom.

The figure stepped forward.

And Measle's jaw dropped.

It was the man from the painting—the Duke of Touffou—brought somehow to life! That alone was startling enough, but the most unsettling thing to Measle was that the Duke was quite obviously made out of *paint*. Measle could see fine cracks crisscrossing the Duke's face and clothes. On an old painting, the cracks simply indicate the painting's age, but on the Duke those same cracks gave his face the look of a long-dead corpse.

Slowly, Measle backed away—and the Duke smiled uncertainly and moved forward equally slowly, until he was standing in the center of the T junction.

"What have we here?" said the Duke, in a thick accent that Measle guessed was French. "A small boy, a small dog, and a small peasant—wiz a *very* small person in his arms! And what are zey doing here? Here in my château?"

The Duke frowned. Then, quite suddenly every muscle in his body jerked spasmodically. He opened his eyes wide, as though astonished beyond belief at what he was seeing. Then, slowly, he lowered his eyes and stared down at his own chest. Measle—who had never seen anybody behave like this before—also lowered his gaze to the Duke's chest.

A short, gleaming spike of metal was sticking out of the front of the Wizard's crimson robe.

The Duke brought one hand up and touched the tip

of the spike. Then he raised his dark eyes and stared—with an expression of deep bewilderment—at Measle. Slowly he shook his head. Then he took one staggering pace forward and, without warning, fell forward. He didn't bend in the middle as he fell—he toppled over, as straight as a tree that had just been cut down. He hit the ground with a thump and lay still.

Sticking out of the Duke's back was a short wooden rod. At the end of the rod were three black feathers.

For several moments it seemed to Measle that the world was standing still. Nothing happened, nothing moved, and—apart from his own breathing—Measle didn't hear a sound. Then in the shadows far down the passage appeared two points of light. The points slanted up at the outer edges. . . .

And they were moving, coming closer and closer, and soon Measle could see a bent and shambling shape accelerating toward him. He took another step backward—

The shape came into the light.

Measle gasped, because here—it could be nobody and nothing else!—was Gobbin Good.

Gobbin Good had a head. The head had two eyes,

two ears and a mouth. Gobbin Good also had two arms and two legs and, in between, a body of sorts—but even though the number of limbs and organs was perfectly correct, any resemblance to a human being stopped right there. The grimling looked as if he had been stitched together from bits and pieces, collected from a whole lot of people of completely different sizes. His painted skin was cracked—just like the Duke's had been—but it was also lumpy and colored a sickly shade of green, like a toad. His head was small, not much bigger than a grapefruit, and came to a point at the top. A few strands of greasy hair hung around the thing's face—a face that Measle would remember for the rest of his life. The grimling had no nose, just warty green skin where his nose should have been. His mouth was lipless and the lower jaw jutted forward like a bulldog's. The teeth in this bottom jaw were jagged and stained, and they overlapped the creature's upper lip, like a row of crooked tombstones. Gobbin Good's eyes were yellow and slanted. He had no neck—at least as far as Measle could see—and his shoulders sloped down to a pair of long and powerful arms. The hands were huge, far bigger than they should have been, and the fingers were gnarled, with long, curved fingernails that were black with dirt. The creature's feet were huge, too, although his legs were short and bowed. Covering the grimling's misshapen body were layers upon layers of tattered, filthy black rags, and in his enormous hands he carried a massive crossbow made of iron and wood.

Gobbin Good came level with the still body of the Duke of Touffou. He nudged the corpse with one booted foot, and satisfied that the Duke was dead, he spat disgustingly, sending a glob of greenish slime to splatter against the crimson robe. Then he bent over and, with his powerful hands, reset the string on the crossbow. Once the string was taut again, the grimling looked up, concentrating his yellow eyes on Measle. He grinned cruelly, exposing even more stained and crooked teeth. Without a word, he reached into a quiver that was slung on his back, pulled out a short arrow and placed it into the slot on the crossbow.

Measle didn't need to be told what was likely to happen next. He looked around him for some means of escape. Iggy had shrunk back against the wall and was clutching Matilda protectively. Tinker was, as usual, standing his ground, his head cocked to one side and his tail tucked down between his back legs.

And then Measle saw that the herd of cows—which had stood in the distant background of the painting—was now shuffling forward out of the shadows behind the grimling.

Cows are clumsy creatures—and very curious, too. They like to see what's going on, and the ones at the back of the herd have a tendency to shove and push at the ones in front of them.

The cows jostled forward and one of them nudged against the grimling's right arm. Instinctively Gobbin Good tightened his grip on the crossbow. Without meaning to, he also tightened the tension of his index finger on the bow's trigger—

TWANG!

An arrow whistled across the corridor, missing Measle's nose by an inch before thudding against the stone wall. Gobbin Good's lips twisted in a snarl and he spat again. He pushed the nearest cow away and bent down to reset the crossbow.

Measle backed slowly away . . . until he saw something that made his heart beat even faster.

One of the cows was much bigger than the rest. It stepped forward, lowered its massive head and glared at Measle through small, reddened eyes.

It wasn't a cow at all.

It was a bull.

It had a brass ring in its nose, and a wide pair of wicked-looking horns on its head. The bull shook its head from side to side, pawed and scraped across the stone floor with a hoof, then lowered its horns and snorted loudly.

Measle dropped the folded stroller and screamed, "*RUN!*" at the top of his voice.

The bull was the first to obey. It bunched the muscles in its powerful legs and leaped forward.

Fear can make a person do extraordinary things. In this case it made Measle run faster than he'd ever run before—and it seemed to do the same thing for Iggy, too, even with the weight of Matilda in his arms. Tinker had always been a fast dog, so he had no trouble keeping up with their racing feet as they tore away down the corridor.

Behind them came an angry snorting and heavy, pounding hooves.

Left, right—right, left—on and on they ran.

Slowly the sounds of the pursuing bull began to diminish. The animal was simply too huge and heavy to handle all the twists and turns that the corridors of Caltrop Castle presented, so a couple of lightweight humans and a small terrier had all the advantages. But the sounds of the bull's massive body thudding against the castle walls—and the sounds of its hooves and its snorting breath—never quite died away altogether, which kept Measle and Iggy and Tinker running for all they were worth.

Once again Measle had no idea where they were. From the look on Iggy's face, neither did he. But they had to be aiming for *somewhere*—and it might as well be the kitchen. Tinker's nose should still be able to lead them there.

Panting hard, Measle shouted, "Tink, dinner! Dinner!"

As he ran, Tinker lifted his nose and sniffed, and once again he caught the distant scent of toast and dog biscuits. Off he galloped, and Measle saw, to his relief, that Tinker wasn't simply doubling back the way they had come but, instead, was setting off down yet another unfamiliar passage, which must mean that they would now approach the kitchen from an entirely new direction.

Quite suddenly the heavy, open wooden door to the kitchen loomed. They dashed through the gap and Measle turned back and threw his weight against the door, swinging it shut with a ground-shaking crash. There was a heavy iron bolt next to the handle and Measle slid that home into its hasp. Then, panting for breath, he pressed his ear against the door's rough wooden surface.

In the distance was the faint sound of thudding hooves.

The sound grew steadily louder.

And Measle heard something else, too—the sound of distant mooing—which could mean only one thing: the cows had left Gobbin Good and had caught up with their leader and were joining him in the hunt.

Nearer and nearer they came—

Then the mooing stopped. There was the sudden sound of skidding, of hooves on stone, and a hard thump that rattled the hinges of the great wooden door.

Measle stepped hurriedly away from the door.

"I—I think it's going to charge," he said, and ran back into the great kitchen to join Iggy and Matilda on the far side of the massive pine table. Tinker ran with him.

Behind him came an earsplitting *CRASH!* of bull against door. Measle threw a look over his shoulder and saw, in that instant, that the door had lost the encounter. Standing in the splintered wreckage was the great beast. Its sides were heaving, its eyes glowing red, its breath came snorting out of its flaring nostrils—and behind it, clustered in the corridor, was the rest of the herd, milling about and waiting for their leader to make his next move.

Measle grabbed Iggy's hand and dragged him to the storeroom door. He seized the door handle and twisted it hard, but the door didn't budge.

"It's locked, Iggy!" hissed Measle. "Where's the key?"

Iggy, wide-eyed with fear, could only point a trembling finger at the far side of the great kitchen. Beside the shattered remains of the door, an iron hook was fastened to the wall. Hanging from the hook was a rusty key.

Measle felt his heart sink. An enraged bull stood between them and the key.

The bull snorted and pawed angrily at the ground. Then it lowered its head, took three shambling steps forward and smashed its horns against the table.

The table slid with a grating sound over the stone floor. The bull, in a fury, bunched the massive muscles in its neck and tossed its head upward with a jerk, sending the table flying end over end across the room. It landed with a crash on its side, only a yard away from where Measle and Iggy were huddled, and it landed in such a way as to form a kind of barrier, behind which Measle and Iggy, who was carrying the sleeping Matilda, could hide. Measle and Iggy and Tinker hunkered down behind the table, out of the bull's view.

Bulls have bad tempers and poor eyes. Once it lost sight of its quarry, the bull looked around for something else to attack. All it could see was the room.

So it attacked the room.

Behind the table, Measle and Iggy and Tinker listened to the sorts of sounds you might expect when a herd of cows, led by a very angry bull, invades a kitchen. There were crashings and bangings and the splintering sounds of breaking wood, the clanging of copper saucepans on stone floors, the thudding of heavy bodies against walls—and, above it all, a steady, fear-filled mooing from the cows, mixed together with furious snorting from the bull.

It was very noisy. It was so noisy that it woke up Matilda.

Held tightly in Iggy's arms—and hunched together with her brother and Tinker behind a kitchen table— there wasn't much for Matilda to see. But it happened that her eyes were exactly level with a long crack that ran down the length of the table's pine boards. She leaned forward in Iggy's arms and peered through the narrow gap.

Cows.

Matilda liked cows. She especially liked the little plastic cow Measle had found at the bottom of a box of cornflakes and given her. She had also seen the cows in the big painting near the garden door. Matilda hadn't been particularly impressed by the tall dark man in the foreground, but she had noticed and admired the cows in the background. And *because* they were set in the far distance in the painting, those cows had appeared to

Matilda to be very small. As small as her plastic cow, in fact.

But *these* cows here in the kitchen weren't little. These cows were big. And Matilda really only liked little cows. . . .

Suddenly all the sounds stopped. One minute it had been all crashings and bashings and clangings and snortings and stampings and mooings—and the next, dead silence. It was as if the herd had simply disappeared.

"Wot'sss 'appening, Mumpsss?" hissed Iggy into Measle's ear.

"I don't know, Iggy. I think they might've gone."

Very carefully, very slowly, Measle rose and peeped over the side of the table.

The kitchen looked as if ten hand grenades had exploded in it. Apart from the massive table, there wasn't a stick of furniture left in one piece. The chairs were just scattered piles of kindling wood. Most of the pots and pans lay on the floor and were little more than dented, twisted heaps of scrap metal. A couple of the iron doors from the kitchen range had been torn off their hinges, and the floor itself was dusty with great chunks of plaster that had been gouged from the walls by the horns of the herd.

But the herd that had done all this damage was nowhere to be seen.

Measle gingerly stepped out from behind the table and Iggy followed, holding Matilda in his arms. Matilda yawned. Tinker trotted to Measle's side—and then his small, wiry body stiffened and, staring hard at the far corner of the kitchen, he started to growl.

"What is it, Tink?" said Measle, looking in the same direction.

A tiny flicker of movement caught Measle's eye. In the shadow of a splintered chair seat that leaned up against the wall . . .

The herd of cows hadn't gone anywhere. The herd of cows was still in the kitchen.

But now they were as small as they had been in the picture. They milled around on the floor, like little guinea pigs, mooing faintly in obvious distress. The tiny bull stood apart from the rest, breathing heavily. Its head swung uncertainly from side to side. It looked utterly bewildered.

There could be only one explanation. Measle

glanced at his little sister. She was resting her head on Iggy's shoulder and her eyes were drooping.

I didn't see her wake up, thought Measle. *And I didn't see her wave her hands, either.*

Measle's thoughts were interrupted by Tinker, who growled again, more fiercely this time. Tinker strutted toward the milling cattle. The bull stopped swaying its head from side to side. It stared up at the huge, hairy monster in front of it, and the rest of the herd crowded in behind their leader.

The bull's bewilderment turned to rage again. It didn't matter that the creature in front of it was the size of a barn—the intruder was standing its ground and challenging the bull and, under these circumstances, the bull did what bulls will do. It lowered its head and pawed at the ground, then shook its quarter-inch-long horns. It bunched the muscles of its haunches and leaped forward in a charge. The herd lowered their heads and started forward after their leader, the hooves of each tiny cow scrabbling for a grip on the stone floor.

Tinker barked once, very loudly.

The bull planted both its forefeet straight out in

front of itself and skidded to a stop. Behind it the cows jumbled and bumped and slipped to a clumsy halt.

Tinker took another step forward, pushed his nose close to the panting bull, curled his lips back and displayed every one of his sharpest teeth—and then barked again.

There was a moment of frozen stillness. Then the bull gave a tiny, shrill squeak of terror. It heaved its body around and charged off in the opposite direction. Then the cows, too, turned tail and stampeded after their leader. They ran along the wall until, quite suddenly, the bull veered and disappeared into a small black hole. A moment later the cows did the same.

Tinker pushed his nose down into the hole and sniffed loudly. Measle ran to his side and knelt down, staring in wonder at the little hole in the wooden wainscoting. It was an obvious mouse hole, its edges gnawed smooth by little mouse teeth. Measle bent further, and pushing Tinker gently to one side, he put his ear close to the hole and heard a distant mooing. The sound got fainter and fainter until it disappeared altogether.

"Coo—wot a messs!" said Iggy. He trotted over to the shattered door and lifted the key off the iron hook.

"I gotta clean all disss up before Missster Jugg sssees it, or elssse 'e is goin' to be ssso *crosss!*"

Iggy scuttled over to the storeroom. He put the key in the lock and twisted it. The door opened and Iggy, still clutching tight to Matilda, disappeared inside.

Measle got to his feet and was just brushing the plaster dust from his knees and thinking how lucky they all were to have escaped this particular danger—when Gobbin Good stepped out of the shadows of the corridor and into the kitchen.

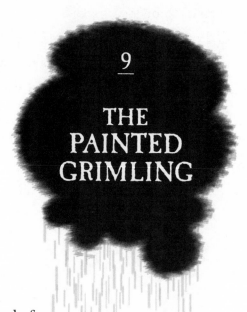

9

THE PAINTED GRIMLING

Measle froze.

Gobbin Good spat onto the dusty floor. Then he lifted one side of his mouth and sneered. He pointed a gnarled finger at Measle and said, "Gotcha! Now gimme all your money!" His voice sounded like sandpaper rubbed across gravel.

He stepped forward, lifting his crossbow and aiming it at Measle's head. Measle put his hands up and stammered, "I—I'm sorry, b-but I haven't g-got any money."

"Too bad," snarled Gobbin Good. "Too bad for *you*, I mean."

Measle slowly retreated toward the storeroom door. His feet stumbled over something that made a clanging sound as his heel caught it. He risked a quick glance downward. By his foot was a battered iron frying pan. It looked pretty heavy. . . .

Measle bent down and grabbed it. Then he held it out in front of him, like a weapon.

Gobbin Good laughed contemptuously.

"Ha! What are you going to do with that?" he rasped. "*Bat* my arrows away?"

Measle didn't answer. Instead, he kept walking steadily backward, hoping desperately that he wouldn't trip. Gobbin Good sauntered casually after him.

Measle felt his back bump into the frame of a door, then a hand grab at the collar of his jacket and drag him roughly backward into the narrow confines of the storeroom.

Measle's head whipped around and saw Iggy right behind him. Iggy was holding an old dustpan and brush in one hand. Matilda was nestled in the little Wrathmonk's free arm.

Measle tried to smile in a reassuring way, but all he could manage was a sickly grin, because Measle realized that perhaps the narrow storeroom wasn't the best place to make a last stand. In fact, it was the worst place to be, because there was no room in here to dodge a speeding arrow.

It was too late now. Measle and Iggy went on backing up, until Iggy's shoulder blades touched the rear wall of the storeroom. Then they both stopped, facing the open door.

Gobbin Good was stepping through the opening. He looked around at his surroundings and then spat contemptuously on the floor.

"No sport here!" he muttered. "It'll be like shooting fish in a barrel!"

The grimling raised the crossbow and sighted down its length at Measle's head. Measle didn't know what to do, other than hold his battered frying pan in front of his face. The only trouble with that idea was that Gobbin Good could just as easily shift his aim and shoot him in the chest.

Besides, Measle's frying pan was shaking like a leaf in a high wind.

The grimling lowered his crossbow, threw back his head and laughed at the ceiling.

"Stupid boy—put that down, before I kill you!"

The crossbow came back up. There was only one thing left for Measle to do: he threw the heavy frying pan with all his might straight at Gobbin Good's head.

Gobbin Good saw the pan flying toward him and, with amazing agility for one so misshapen, neatly side-stepped. The frying pan zipped past the grimling's head and crashed to the floor.

Gobbin Good lowered his crossbow again, grinned and spat.

"Missed!" he snarled. "What are you going to do now?"

Measle didn't know what he was going to do now. There wasn't anything he *could* do.

But Iggy, half hidden behind Measle—and feeling a little brave—had an idea. Mumps might not have anything left to throw, but *he* did. Iggy lifted his old dustpan and brush and hurled them past Measle's shoulder at the hulking grimling.

Once again Gobbin Good stepped smartly to one side, and the dustpan and brush clattered harmlessly to the floor.

Gobbin Good spat. "Got anything else you wanna throw?" he growled. When neither Measle nor Iggy replied, he slowly raised the crossbow again and took aim at Measle's head. He paused.

"You know what I reckon?" said the grimling, cocking his small head to one side. "I reckon that if I get you three lined up nice and proper, I could get you all with just one arrow! Yeah—I reckon that would work!"

Gobbin Good took a small sideways step and sighted down his crossbow, this time aiming for Measle's chest. Then he nodded to himself and muttered, "Perfect!"

His finger tightened on the crossbow trigger.

Measle winced, waiting for the impact of an arrow stabbing through his ribcage. . . .

Then something fluid zipped over Measle's shoulder. It glittered in the dim light of the storeroom as it sailed past his eyes—a clear liquid, which splashed over the crossbow and its arrow.

A familiar chemical smell hung in the air.

Nobody moved or said anything while Gobbin Good stared down at his crossbow, a puzzled frown creasing his lumpy green forehead.

Measle watched in astonishment as the massive crossbow started to melt. The arrow dissolved first, then the string and then the actual body of the crossbow itself, all flowing together in a mess of different colors. The gooey stuff dripped down onto the floor at Gobbin Good's enormous feet, until all that was left of the crossbow was a stump of black wood in the grimling's right hand.

Gobbin Good looked a little nervous.

"What—what happened to my crossbow?" he said.

Measle pointed to the puddle at Gobbin Good's feet. "It's on the floor," he said politely.

The chemical stink explained what had happened, but what Measle didn't understand was how the chemical smell had got there in the first place. He turned around and saw Matilda, still in Iggy's arms, wide awake and glaring at Gobbin Good. In one little hand, she held an empty glass.

Iggy had his shoulders pressed against the back wall, right by a wide shelf. On the shelf were the remains of Iggy's first attempt at breakfast—the plates of dusty bricks, the glasses and bowls of—

Turpentine.

Then Measle understood. Matilda had seen the ugly creature. She'd seen him threaten her brother with his crossbow. She had watched first Measle and then her wet friend throw things at the nasty man. They had

177

both missed. Then it was her turn. Matilda had reached for the nearest object—which just happened to be her brother's breakfast glass, still filled to the brim with turpentine. Then she had hurled the contents of the glass at the grimling.

The turpentine had fallen a little short, splashing not over the grimling but across the creature's crossbow instead. And the turpentine had thinned and softened and weakened the paint that made up the crossbow, dissolving it all until it was nothing more than a little puddle on the floor.

Gobbin Good snarled in fury and threw the useless stump of wood to one side. Then he glared at Measle with his yellow eyes and said, with a sneer, "Well, it don't matter. I don't need no crossbow to kill you all. I can kill you just as good with these!"

Gobbin Good raised his huge, gnarled hands and stepped forward. Measle tried to take a step back, but he was already pressed so close to Iggy that he found himself forced sideways instead—right within arm's length of the shelf.

The grimling's huge, bony green claws reached toward Measle's throat.

In one smooth movement, Measle dragged Tinker's

bowl of turpentine off the shelf and flung the contents at Gobbin Good.

It wasn't a very good throw. Instead of hitting the grimling full in the face, as Measle had intended, the splash of turpentine struck Gobbin Good across the knees and then dripped down his shins, forming a puddle on the floor.

For a moment the grimling simply looked a little surprised. Then the realization of what was happening to him struck him like a blow to the head. He looked down at his feet. . . .

They were no longer there. They had dissolved in the turpentine, and Gobbin Good himself now appeared to be steadily sinking into the puddle as, slowly but surely, the turpentine softened and dissolved the paint of his ankles, then his calves, then his thighs, then his middle . . . and now the grimling was no taller than Measle, because all that was left of him was his upper half.

To Measle's great relief, Gobbin Good didn't seem to be experiencing any pain. The only expression on his face was one of horrified surprise.

"I—I—I got a horrible sinking feeling!" he exclaimed. "What have you done to me?"

"I'm very sorry," said Measle, "but you shouldn't go around killing people. Not when you're made of paint and there's turpentine around, you shouldn't."

By now Gobbin Good had sunk into the turpentine puddle right up to his chin, so all that remained was his little pointed head.

"Hah!" screamed Gobbin Good's head. "Never mind! I don't need legs to kill you! Or arms, come to that! I can *bite* you to death!"

Gobbin Good bared his cracked, painted mouth, revealing his stained and jagged teeth. But a moment later, those teeth were gone as well, and all that was left was a pair of startled and angry yellow eyes. Then they, too, sank down into the turpentine puddle, followed by the lumpy green forehead, and lastly the wisps of greasy hair that grew from the very top of the pointed head. The strands of hair floated for a few seconds on the surface of the oily liquid and then dissolved away into nothing.

There was a deep hush in the little storeroom for several moments. Finally Iggy broke the silence.

"Coo. Dat is ssstrong ssstuff, dat purplepine."

"It certainly is," said Measle. "And, in case there are any more of those things, I think we need a plan."

10

THE
IRON MAN

The plan they came up with was this: they would go back to the bedroom and hole up there—the bedroom door had looked pretty solid and there was a big iron bolt up near the top. Iggy produced three bottles of turpentine, in case they met any more paintings that had come to life, and also a box of Matilda's cereal—"In case it gets 'ungry and makes de 'orrible noise, Mumpsss." Measle retrieved the battered frying pan from the floor of the storeroom. He liked the heavy feel of it in his hand and—well—it seemed as good a weapon as anything else.

181

The next problem was finding their way back to the bedroom, but Measle solved it by getting Tinker to lead them first to the little garden. Once there, Measle hoped that, by carefully backtracking the route they had taken earlier they'd be able to get back to the relative safety of the bedroom. With the loss of the stroller, Iggy had taken the responsibility of carrying Matilda, which was lucky for Measle, because Iggy was much stronger than he was. Iggy didn't *look* particularly strong, with his weedy little body and skinny little arms, but there were real, wiry muscles under Iggy's damp black coat and he never seemed to get tired. In fact, even if Iggy *was* tired, Measle doubted that he would have stopped carrying Matilda. Iggy appeared to like carrying Matilda as much as Matilda liked being carried by Iggy and, every time Measle turned and looked at them both, Matilda—now wide awake—had given Iggy yet another wild and wonderful hairdo.

They were about halfway there when a familiar sound reached their ears. First there was the distant sound of cracking, splintering, smashing wood, followed by a series of desperate mooing noises and, a moment later, the bellow from a furious bull. A very *large* and furious-sounding bull.

"Wosssat, Mumpsss?" whispered Iggy, clutching nervously at Measle's arm.

"I think it's the cows, Iggy. And the bull, bursting out from behind the paneling. They must be back to full size again."

They hurried on, and slowly the sounds of the herd diminished behind them. As they walked down the endless passages Measle was thinking hard. *Tilly made the cows small—now they're big again. And she didn't do that second spell, because she's still wide awake and busy playing with Iggy's hair. Which means—which means Tilly's first spell must have worn off! Maybe—maybe they all wear off after a little time?*

"Iggy, I want to see your teeth!"

"You wot?"

"Show me your teeth!"

"Why?"

"Because—because—because I really like them, Iggy! I wish I had teeth like yours! Especially the pointed ones! Please, Iggy—show me your teeth!"

Flattery worked wonders with Iggy. Looking pleased with himself, he opened his mouth and bared his teeth at Measle—and Measle saw in an instant that Iggy's teeth were no longer that attractive pearly-white color* that Matilda had turned them. Iggy's teeth were back to their ugly shade of yellow.

So, Tilly's spells do *wear off. . . .*

At last they reached the bedroom. Once inside, with the door bolted firmly shut, Measle felt more secure. Iggy put Matilda down on the floor, where she crawled about, chasing Tinker's tail. Outside the tall window, it was getting dark. The distant trees of the park were shrouded in shadows, the lake was a sheet of blackness, and the wide, sweeping lawn had lost its color and was now a dull and gloomy gray.

There was the question of where Iggy was to sleep. Measle suggested one of the armchairs, but Iggy shook his head firmly.

"No, Mumpsss—I can't do dat."

"Why not, Iggy?"

"I can't go in dose sssquashy chairs. After I been in dem for a bit, dey sssmell all funny."

Iggy found the perfect place all by himself. He dragged Measle into the bathroom and pointed excitedly at the big gleaming bath.

"Dere, Mumpsss! I could sssleep in dere! Sssee— dere'sss even a little hole where de water can go down!"

It was a good idea—and then Measle had one of his own. He went into the bedroom and pulled open the big wardrobe. The bottom half of the wardrobe was made up of three large drawers. They were all empty. Measle dragged the top drawer wide open, and then went on pulling at it until the whole thing slid free from its runners. He half carried, half dragged the empty drawer into the bathroom and laid it upside down, across one end of the bath, making a sort of roof.

"There, Iggy," said Measle. "That's nearly as good as your box, isn't it?"

Iggy squeaked with delight and crawled into the bath and under the drawer. To Measle's satisfaction, the little rain cloud stayed outside the makeshift shelter and dribbled its drops down onto the underside of the drawer, leaving Iggy relatively dry inside.

"Dat is *better* dan my box, Mumpsss," said Iggy from inside his shelter. He sounded happier than Measle had ever heard him sound before.

185

Measle left Iggy in his new shelter and went back into the bedroom. There was nothing to do, other than watch Matilda play with Tinker—and Measle found his mind wandering down paths that grew more and more miserable with every passing thought. He missed his mum and dad terribly. Where were they? What had happened to them? Would he ever see them again? And how long was he going to be stuck here in this weird place, with this silly little Wrathmonk, where the geography changed at will and where pictures came horribly to life? And how could he look after Matilda all by himself? When was Toby coming back? And what would he think when he saw what had happened to his castle? What to do? How to get home? *What to do?*

Measle's increasingly despondent thoughts were interrupted by a chomping sound in his right ear. He turned around—Iggy was there. Iggy was chewing something. His jaws were going up and down and he had a look of rapture on his face.

Iggy swallowed—then he brought up his hand and Measle saw, to his horror, that Iggy was holding the little plastic bag of jelly beans.

"Where did you get those, Iggy?" said Measle.

"Out of your pocket, Mumpsss," said Iggy carelessly. He reached into the bag, took out another jelly bean and popped it into his mouth.

"My *pocket?*" said Measle, incredulously. "When?"

"When we was in de ssstoreroom," said Iggy, chewing greedily. "When you was busy killing dat nasssty green fing."

"How?"

"How, Mumpsss? *How?* I jussst reached in your pocket and took dem, dat'sss how."

"But—I never felt you do it, Iggy."

Iggy smiled a superior smile. "Well, you wouldn't *feel* it, Mumpsss," he said proudly. "You wouldn't feel it because I am not jussst a brilliant burglarider. I am *alssso* a brilliant picklepocket. I am one of de bessst picklepocketsss you will ever meet. Dere isn't a pocket I can't pickle."

"You mean you're a *pickpocket,* too, Iggy?"

"Dat's what I *sssaid,* Mumpsss," said Iggy, rolling his eyes with impatience. "A *picklepocket.*"

"But—but why, Iggy? Why did you pick my pocket?"

" 'Coz I *like* dese fings, dat'sss why. Dey is very nice, dese sssweeties."

Measle frowned at Iggy, trying to look fierce. "But they don't belong to you, Iggy. They're mine, not yours. And I thought we were friends. Friends don't do that, Iggy—they don't pick each other's pockets."

A look of wonder swept across Iggy's face. "Dey don't?" he said, surprised.

"No, Iggy. They don't. Now can I have my bag back, please?"

Measle held out his hand and glared firmly, and Iggy sighed and slowly passed the bag over. "I only eated a few of dem, Mumps," he muttered.

Measle took the bag. It felt very light. He looked inside it and saw that there were very few jelly beans left. Frantically he poked a forefinger into the bag and stirred the few remaining beans—there! Right at the bottom—two lonely little yellow jelly ones!

"I like de yellow ones bessst, Mumpsss," said Iggy.

"Really?" said Measle sourly. "I'd never have guessed."

A thought crossed Measle's mind. Without appearing to be too interested in the answer, he said, "What's your *least* favorite jelly bean, Iggy?"

"De green ones, Mumpsss. I don't like dem at *all*."

"And—er—what happened when you ate a green one, Iggy?"

"I *didn't* eat a green one, Mumps," said Iggy, rolling his eyes with impatience at Measle's stupidity. "I told you—I don't *like* de green ones."

Measle wondered whether he should ask how, if Iggy hadn't actually eaten a green jelly bean, he knew he didn't like them, but then Iggy distracted him by rummaging in one of the pockets of his damp and shabby old coat. He pulled out Measle's battery-operated toothbrush. He held it up in front of Measle's face and said, "Wot'sss disss, Mumpsss?"

"That's my toothbrush, Iggy."

"Dat'sss a funny lookin' toofypeg brush, if you asssk me," said Iggy, peering critically at the toothbrush.

Measle was about to say that Iggy really ought to stop taking other people's belongings and would he *please* give him back his toothbrush before he got it all dirty, when he heard a sound from beyond the closed bedroom door. It was a distant sound, at least two or three corridors away—and it reminded Measle of the noise that Matilda sometimes made when she was allowed to bang her cereal spoon against one of Lee's saucepans.

Clang. Clang. Clang.

Measle forgot about the toothbrush. He turned

away from Iggy, crossed over to the door, unbolted it and carefully cracked it open. There was nothing to be seen in the passage—but now the sound was just a little louder. . . .

And it seemed to be getting closer, too.

Clang. Clang. Clang.

"Wosssat noise, Mumpsss?"

Iggy pressed against him and stuck his face out into the corridor. Measle felt the little drops of rain from Iggy's cloud spatter against the top of his head.

"I don't know, Iggy," he muttered. "But I don't think it's the cows."

Clang. Clang. Clang.

Whatever it was, it was definitely getting closer, because now Measle could hear another sound—

A measured, heavy tread.

Clang. Thump. Clang. Thump. Clang. Thump.

"Iggy," said Measle nervously. "Maybe we ought to shut the door."

"Hah!" said Iggy scornfully. "Don't worry, Mumpsss. Wotever dat fing is, I will sssave you—again!"

Measle was about to object and point out that Iggy hadn't saved him *once* yet—while he, Measle, had actually saved Iggy several times already—but Iggy had turned back and disappeared into the bedroom again and anyway, the clangs and the thumps were now so loud that Measle realized he was going to have to *shout* his objections.

CLANG! THUMP! CLANG! THUMP!

And then Measle saw what was making all these deafening sounds. In an instant he realized that he and Iggy and Matilda and Tinker were suddenly in a world of trouble.

Terrible trouble—because rounding the corner of the passage came a figure out of a nightmare. It filled the passage—a great, massive, hulking black shape that swayed from side to side as it approached.

And then the thing came into a pool of light—one of the regular pools of light that was thrown onto the floor and walls by the succession of dim lightbulbs that hung from the ceiling—and Measle saw what the thing was.

It was the huge, jet-black suit of armor. And it was alive.

Next to Gobbin Good, it was one of the most awful things that Measle had ever seen. With every lurching step, the sword swung from side to side in great sweeps, the wind whistling as the blade sliced through the air, and each sweep of the sword brought the gleaming blade into shattering contact with the walls on either side.

CLANG! CLANG! CLANG! CLANG!

And then Iggy was back at his side.

"Oo-er," muttered Iggy. Measle could hear the uncertainty in the little Wrathmonk's voice. "Coo—dat is big, innit? But I—Mr. Ignatiusss Niggle—will sssave you!"

Iggy elbowed Measle aside and stood in front of him, facing the approaching horror. Two bottles of turpentine were tucked under his arm, and he held the third bottle in his right hand.

"Take dat, you 'orrible fing!" screamed Iggy. At the same moment, he hurled a bottle of turpentine directly at the lurching suit of armor.

The bottle sailed through the air and smashed against the iron chest. Shards of glass flew everywhere and the turpentine splashed and dribbled down the breastplate . . . and the iron thing took no notice at all and simply continued in its swaying, lurching way.

CLANG! CLANG! CLANG! CLANG!

Iggy screamed, "Ho—you want anuvver one, do you?" and he hurled a second bottle. It, too, struck the armor—this time on the crest of its enormous black helmet. There was another splintering crash as the bottle exploded—the turpentine splashed across the thing's lowered visor—and had no more effect on the iron creature than if a fly had landed on it.

"It'sss not meltin', Mumpsss!" yelped Iggy over his shoulder. "Why ain't it meltin'?"

"Because it's not made of *paint*, Iggy!" shouted Measle over the deafening clanging of the thing's huge sword. Measle grabbed at Iggy's shoulder and tried to pull him backward, but Iggy didn't budge. Instead, he threw the third bottle, which smashed against the armor's knees.

And still the monster advanced.

Measle had seen enough. He grabbed Iggy with both hands and pulled him quickly back into the bedroom, slammed the door shut, then reached up and smacked the bolt hard—and it slid, with a grating sound of metal on metal, into the hasp that was screwed to the frame of the door.

Tinker was where he always was whenever there was danger—standing by Measle's side, growling softly deep in his throat. Tinker was uncertain about what, exactly, he was growling at. He'd caught a whiff of the noisy thing just before Measle had slammed the door in its face. It had smelled of metal—in fact, it smelled exactly like the iron poker that stood by the fireplace in the living room of Merlin Manor. And that was fine, except Tinker couldn't remember a time when the iron poker had ever—well—had ever *moved*.

The moment the bolt slid home, the entire door shook under a furious attack. Whatever was inside the suit of armor was using its great, iron-gauntleted fists to pound against the door panels. Measle backed away slowly, wondering how long the door would stand before giving way under this heavy assault.

He didn't have to wonder for long.

Measle watched in horror as the tip of the great black sword suddenly stabbed its way through one of the door panels. There was a wrenching noise and the tip disappeared. A moment later came another splintering *crash!* and the whole blade was thrust through the heavy oak, right up to its hilt. The blade twisted violently, slicing through the splintered wood and widening the hole by several inches, so that Measle could suddenly glimpse the massive iron fist wielding the sword.

Measle eyed the window. He knew it didn't open, so he grabbed his battered frying pan from where he'd dropped it on the bed and swung it hard against the glass. Some of the diamond panes shattered and the lead strips holding them bent outward.

Measle swung again.

And again.

"Wot is you *doin'*, Mumpsss?" screamed Iggy.

Measle turned away from the smashed window and saw Iggy crouching on the floor next to Matilda. They were both staring at him with horror plastered all over their faces.

"We've got to get out, Iggy!" yelled Measle, turning back to the job of breaking through the window. It was easier said than done. The trouble wasn't with the glass panes. The trouble was with the lead strips, which bent but didn't break. Try as he might, Measle hadn't been able to do anything other than make them bulge outward.

"You mustn't break de window, Mumps!" screamed Iggy. "Mr. Jugg will get fuming mad! *Ssstop* it! Ssstop it disss *inssstant!*"

All this noise was too much for Matilda. There was a nasty noise from the door, and a nasty noise from the window, and nasty yelling noises from her brother and from her new wet friend—so Matilda did what all babies do when they're upset. She screwed up her face and began to scream at the top of her voice. Iggy looked at her in horrified amazement.

"It'sss 'ungry, Mumpsss!" he yelled, diving for the box of cereal. He ripped it open, plunged one clawlike little hand inside, scooped up a fistful of dry flakes and pushed them under Matilda's nose. " 'Ere!" he shouted. "Eat disss, baby!"

Matilda screamed louder and batted his hand away. The last thing she wanted at that moment was a handful of cereal. What she wanted was the noise to go away. . . .

The worst noise was coming from the door. She looked over toward it and saw that the door was breaking. . . .

Matilda didn't like things being broken.

196

So she waved her hands and *mended* the door.

One second the panels were a splintered mess; the next, the hole filled itself in, replacing the jagged splinters with a smooth panel of unbroken wood.

Measle stared in amazement at the mended door, then threw a quick glance over to where Matilda was gulping back her tears. But a moment later the attack from the suit of armor started up once more, and the door began again to shake under a second wave of heavy blows.

Measle didn't waste any more time. Using all the power in his arms, he smashed away at the lead strips. One wild whack of his frying pan succeeded in ripping a strip out of the corner of the window's stone frame and, with that single piece free and dangling, his next three blows tore out a man-sized hole.

Once again the sounds of splintering wood made Measle whip his head around. There was a sizeable hole in the door. This time a huge iron fist came through the ragged fissure. The massive fingers opened and the hand grasped the edge of the broken panel and gave it a great wrench. A section of oak broke off as if it was no stronger than a cracker.

The fist was about to push through again when the hole once more filled itself in. The door was solid as it ever had been. Matilda's head began to droop into sleep—and Measle knew immediately what that meant. Her two mending spells had utterly exhausted her and this brief moment was the last breathing space they were likely to get. There wasn't much time.

Measle yelled, "Tink! Come here!" and the dog instantly scampered across the floor to Measle's side. Measle didn't hesitate. He scooped Tinker up and pushed him through the ragged hole. Tinker fell the short distance to the ground outside, landing with a rattling of leaves and twigs right in the middle of a small bush that grew below the window.

Measle turned back.

Iggy had disappeared.

No, there—poking out from under the hanging ruffle of the bed frame—a foot! Measle ran to the bed, bent down, grabbed Iggy's foot and pulled hard. The little Wrathmonk slid out from under the bed, both hands pressed tightly over his ears.

Measle dragged Iggy to his feet. He could feel Iggy's thin, damp frame quivering with terror and see his fishy eyes swiveling madly in their sockets, so he didn't bother trying to reason with him. Measle simply grabbed Iggy by one hand and pulled him across the room to the smashed window. He shoved Iggy's head into the opening and, ignoring Iggy's wails of terror, bent down, grabbed both of Iggy's skinny ankles and heaved him bodily out of the window.

There was a short scream, followed instantly by a solid thump as Iggy landed on the ground outside.

Measle raced to Matilda. Her eyes were closed and she was slowly slipping over sideways, into another deep sleep. Grabbing her as gently as he could, he lifted her off the floor and carried her to the window.

"Iggy!" he yelled. "I'm going to drop Tilly down to you! You've got to catch her, Iggy!"

Measle poked his head through the opening and saw Iggy staring up at him with fear-filled eyes.

"Do you understand, Iggy? I want you to catch her! Okay?"

Iggy nodded dumbly and extended his arms. Measle gently pushed the sleeping Matilda over the threshold of the window, held her there for a moment and then let go.

There was a sudden grinding, grating, tearing sound from the other side of the room. Measle turned and saw that the suit of armor had managed to hack his way through the broken door and was now standing inside the bedroom, with the remains of the door—still in its frame—hung around his enormous black metal body like a necklace.

"Who are you?" whispered Measle, his voice shaking with fear.

Slowly the iron man raised one huge fist. When the fist reached the visor of the helmet, the iron man extended a forefinger. He touched the tip of his finger to the peak of the visor—and then, very slowly, he pushed the visor up, revealing . . .

Nothing.

There was no face inside the helmet.

There was nothing but blackness there.

The suit of armor was empty.

The visor dropped shut with a clang, and the iron monster raised its great sword and, with a thump that shook the room, stepped forward.

11

THE
PARK

Measle watched in dread as the suit of armor tramped toward him. The floor shook under its huge weight, and then the creature began to sweep its great black sword from side to side, the blade whistling though the air.

Time to go.

With a quick twist—like a fish changing direction in a stream—Measle turned and dived through the opening in the window. By now it was so dark outside that it seemed like he was diving into a bottomless abyss.

But he was in the air and falling for only a second before he landed, with a bone-shaking thump, onto the hard ground. For a moment he lay there, gathering his breath. Then he felt Tinker push his cold nose against his cheek, and a spattering of raindrops splashed against his face.

"You pushed me out of de window!" said Iggy. "You didn't ought to do dat, Mumpsss—dat'sss not very polite, pushing people out of windowsss."

Measle looked up. He could see, dimly in the darkness, Iggy's form looming over him. Measle was relieved to see the little lump that was Matilda nestled safely in Iggy's arms, and he could just make out the fuzzy shape of Tinker standing by his side. A little light filtered out of the bedroom—just enough to see by, once his eyes had adjusted to the gloom.

And then the light dimmed. From above his head, there came the sound of metal grating against stone. Measle struggled to his feet.

There, filling the whole window was the outline of the suit of armor. The thing seemed to be trying to push its way through the remains of the window. Glass cracked and lead strips popped apart and—

"Let's go, quick!" shouted Measle. "It's coming through the window!"

They pounded across the gravel drive, their feet crunching on the stones. It was very dark and difficult to see where they were going. . . .

Then, directly in front of Measle there was a sudden thud, followed by a sharp squeal of pain. A second later Measle himself ran hard into something soft and damp that smelled strongly of wet clothes and mildew.

"Owww!" squealed Iggy again. Measle felt the little Wrathmonk slide to the ground at his feet, so he too squatted down in the near pitch darkness, straining his eyes to see.

Iggy rubbed the top of his head with his free hand. "Oooh—dat 'urtsss, Mumpsss!" he moaned.

"What's the matter, Iggy?" whispered Measle.

"Wot's de matter? Wot's de *matter*? I'll tell you wot's de matter, Mumpsss—a big bump on de 'ead, *dat'sss* what de matter is!"

Measle peered past Iggy; there didn't seem to be anything there. The park stretched out in front of them—a sweeping lawn, leading the eye down to a dark lake, a line of trees beyond. . . .

And then, as his eyes grew more accustomed to the dark, Measle saw what it was that Iggy had bumped into.

It was a wall.

A very high and very wide one that disappeared into the darkness above and to both sides.

The extraordinary thing about the wall was that it was only obviously a wall in *close-up*. From a few yards away, it looked as if there was nothing there—just the sweeping lawn and the distant lake. But when you were a few inches away, it was possible to see that what appeared to be a sweeping lawn, a distant lake, a line of trees, etc., was, in fact, the most brilliantly realistic of paintings.

A vast, almost photographic painting that stretched up and out as far as the eye could see.

A painting of a park.

"It's a wall, Iggy," whispered Measle. "You ran into a wall."

"Wot?" said Iggy, irritably. "Wot is you talking about, Mumpsss?"

"You're leaning against it, Iggy. Turn around and look."

Iggy sighed—one of those long, impatient sighs people give when they think somebody has said something really stupid—and then he turned his head and looked at the wall he'd been leaning against.

Iggy looked for quite a long time, blinking slowly at the smooth, solid surface only a few inches from his nose. Then, without any warning, he burst into tears. It was all too much for his little brain to handle. His beloved Caltrop Castle had turned against him! Kitchens weren't where they were supposed to be! Cows had smashed his pots and pans! A suit of armor was trying to kill him! And the lovely park wasn't a park at all!

"Boohoohooo!" He wailed.

From the direction of the castle, there was the noise of metal grating and screeching against stone—then, the sound of huge iron boots crushing broken glass underfoot.

Measle grabbed Iggy's trembling shoulders. "Come on, Iggy!"

Measle struggled to his feet and, using all his strength, dragged Iggy upright. Together Measle and Iggy staggered along the base of the wall. Tinker gave a couple of aggressive little barks in the direction of the iron man—*just to show him who's the boss*—and then, tail tucked tightly between his legs, ran to join Measle and Iggy.

But where were they going? It was now very dark, but Measle had a sense that, by following the course of the wall, they were traveling in a steady curve. The wall that surrounded Caltrop Castle seemed a perfect circle of stone—which meant that, sooner or later, they would arrive back where they had started.

But there, ahead—a little gleam of light!

It must be coming from a window in the castle's wall, Measle decided. A light—any light—would be better than this darkness.

As they drew near, the point of light grew into the small rectangle of a window, lit from within. By the time they reached the wall beneath the window, their breathing was ragged, and they were exhausted. Only Matilda's breathing was slow and steady—she was deep asleep on Iggy's shoulder.

Measle looked up at the window. It was about eight yards above his head. The walls that surrounded it were heavy with ivy, the leaves as black as night. The ivy grew from a bed a bed right at Measle's feet and he saw that the trunk and the branches that supported the ivy were thick and strong.

"Quick, Iggy!" he said. "We're going to climb! You first!"

"You want me to climb up dere?" said Iggy, staring up at the window.

"Yes, Iggy! And you'll still have to carry Tilly, too. Can you do it?"

Iggy turned and glared at Measle. "Of *coursse* I can do it," he said grandly. "I was a burglarider, wasn't I? All burglariders can climb, *and* dey can carry a big heavy bag of ssswag at de sssame time! I am an extremely *fantassstic* climber—"

"Good, Iggy," said Measle. "Please do it—*now!*" He pushed the little Wrathmonk firmly toward the wall—because, in the distance, he heard the steady *Clump! Crunch! Clump! Crunch!* as the iron man drew closer and closer.

Iggy did as he was told. He jumped up and grabbed a handhold in the ivy branches and scrambled upward like a monkey, heading fast toward the window. Measle bent down and grabbed Tinker and stuffed him down the front of his leather jacket. Then he seized a rough branch of ivy and began to climb. He wasn't as fast as Iggy, but he managed to haul himself upward at a steady pace and was soon high enough off the ground to worry about falling.

Don't look down! Just keep climbing! Like you did on the Ferris wheel on the Isle of Smiles! Reach up with your hand, then find a new foothold, then pull and push, up and up and up. . . .

But Measle couldn't help himself—he took a quick glance down.

Emerging from the gloom came the huge suit of armor. It paused for a moment at the foot of the wall, its great helmeted head turning this way and that. There was squeak of metal on metal. Then, slowly, the helmet tilted backward and seemed to peer upward, straight at Measle. To Measle's horror, it stepped forward and thrust its gauntleted hands deep into the ivy and began to pull itself off the ground.

Panic gave Measle some much needed strength and energy. Grabbing fistfuls of the dusty branches, he scrambled upward.

Beneath him, the ivy shook.

The branch of ivy to which Measle clung started to

pull away from the ancient stones with the sound of tearing cotton. Measle felt the angle of his body change as the branch ripped off the wall—the ivy shook and bent and, a moment later, his feet slipped away and dangled in midair. The ivy stretched out like a leafy net, away from the wall, the gnarled wood making ominous groaning and creaking sounds. Measle's fingers began to lose their grip.

A moment later he felt a hand on the top of his head. The hand grasped a fistful of his hair and started to pull him skyward.

"I got you, Mumpsss!" hissed Iggy's voice, and he pulled harder, making Measle's scalp feel as if it was being dragged off his head. Measle's eyes began to water from the pain, and he yelled, "It's all right, Iggy—I can manage!" But Iggy took no notice and just went on dragging Measle upward as if he was a sack of potatoes.

More ivy ripped away, then a whole section of it gave a sudden lurch as it was pulled away from the wall—

And then it broke.

But Measle didn't fall.

Instead, the pain from where his hair was joined to his head increased a hundred times as Iggy's iron grip took the entire weight of Measle's—and Tinker's—bodies.

"Oooowwwww!" yelled Measle. He felt himself lifted upward, as if he was on the end of a powerful crane. From beneath him came a ripping, tearing, crackling sound, as the entire curtain of ivy was dragged off the stone wall of the castle. A moment later there was a great crashing, clanging and smashing—like a car running into a concrete wall.

The pain on his scalp was unbearable, and Measle screwed his eyes tightly shut and opened his mouth to let out a really loud yell, but then he was swung sideways and, a second later, his hair was released and he was dropped heavily onto a wooden floor.

When Measle opened his eyes, tears spilled out of them and dripped down his cheeks. Measle never cried, and he wasn't really crying this time, either. The tears in his eyes weren't tears of hurt or misery—they were just a natural reaction to having his hair pulled. Everybody's eyes water when they have their hair pulled.

"Why is you cryin', Mumpsss?" hissed Iggy, close to his ear. "I ressscued you, didn't I?"

Measle glared up at Iggy through blurry eyes.

"Thank you, Iggy," he muttered. "And I'm *not* crying."

Tinker poked his head out from the folds of Measle's jacket and swiped his tongue over Measle's face.

"Stop it, Tink," muttered Measle, wiping his cheeks with the back of his hand. Then he opened the zip of his leather jacket and pushed Tinker gently out on the floor.

Iggy, with Matilda still in his arms, was leaning on the narrow windowsill and staring down toward the distant ground. Measle scrambled to his feet and joined him.

There, far below, lay the iron man. The creature was flat on its back and covered by a great net of ivy, so that all Measle could see of it were its outstretched arms and legs. Measle and Iggy watched as the suit of armor struggled to sit up, but the combined weight of its own iron shell and the leaves and twigs and branches that entwined its huge body like a net was too much for it. All it could do was writhe and squirm and wriggle in a horrible way.

"I did dat, Mumpsss," said Iggy proudly. "I ressscued you—*again*—and den I made all de leaves and ssstuff fall down on top of de fing and now it can't get up and I did dat, too."

"Well done, Iggy," said Measle gratefully. The fact was, Iggy really *had* rescued him this time, even if his scalp did still sting like crazy.

They were in a strange little five-sided room, bare of any furniture and with only the single window and, opposite the window, a single door. A dusty, bare light-bulb hung from a cord in the middle of the ceiling, and it was the light from this that had guided Measle to the window. Measle tiptoed to the door and cracked it open—and, almost immediately, he closed it again, careful not to make a sound as he did so. . . .

He'd heard voices. For a moment Measle felt a sudden surge of relief—*People! Real, live people! They can help us get out of here*—but then his common sense took over. Too many strange and dangerous things had happened here in Caltrop Castle! Who was to say that they wouldn't go *on* happening? Just because he was hearing human voices didn't mean that the speakers would be friendly!

Better safe than sorry. . . .

Measle turned and put his finger to his lips. "We've got to be very quiet, Iggy," he whispered. "There are people out there."

Iggy nodded seriously and took an extra firm grip on Matilda. Measle scooped Tinker up and pushed him down into the front of his jacket.

Oh, here we go again, thought Tinker, wriggling a little to get himself comfortable against Measle's chest. *The smelly kid always thinks his two legs are better than my four.*

Measle flicked the brass light switch by the door and the room was plunged into darkness. Then he carefully turned the doorknob and eased the door open.

As his eyes grew accustomed to the lack of light, he saw they were in one high-up corner of a balcony. A couple of yards over their heads, he could just make out the dim shapes of massive oak rafters that stretched out across the huge space, their extremities lost in the gloom. Well *below* them, its floor probably at ground level, was an enormous room. In the opposite corner, Measle saw a spiral staircase made of iron that circled its way down to the lower level. The voices were coming from down there. Measle shifted Tinker's body and then crawled on hands and knees forward across the dusty wooden boards toward the row of banisters that ringed the balcony.

It was dark up there near the ceiling—the only light came from below, and that was dim, orange, flickering firelight, which still left much of the great room in relative darkness. This made Measle confident that they were unlikely to be seen by any of the speakers. All the same, he was extra careful as he got near the banisters. He pressed his face to the wooden uprights. Now he could see the floor of the room. Below him was a huge stone fireplace, with flames dancing around a great pile of logs. Along the mantelpiece was a whole row of candlesticks, each with a lit candle, their little flames steady in the still air.

Now Measle could see and hear everything quite clearly.

Sitting in a large leather armchair set by the fireside was the long, thin figure of Sir Peregrine Spine. Opposite him, in a matching armchair, hunched Ermintrude Bacon, her pink, piggy face shiny in the light from the fire.

What are these two doing at Caltrop Castle?

Another pair of armchairs came into view. They held Dorian Fescue, his yellow face made even yellower in the candlelight, and Tully Telford, who was polishing his pebble glasses on a handkerchief. Even in this dim light, Measle could see the dark stains on Tully's ear tips.

The Advisory Board! All of them except for that boring looking one—what was his name?

A moment later out from the shadows at one side drifted the dull figure of the government minister—*the one whose face your eyes didn't want to stay on, simply because his face was so incredibly dreary to look at—what was his name?*

The man held two glasses of red wine. As he passed one to Sir Peregrine Spine, the question of the minister's name was resolved, for Sir Peregrine said, "Ah, my dear Underwood, thank you, you're too kind."

Underwood! Quentin Underwood!

Tinker was feeling a little crushed in the confines of the leather jacket and he let out a tiny growl of displeasure. Immediately Measle wrapped his fingers around Tinker's muzzle and whispered, "Shhh!" into a fuzzy ear. Measle felt movement on his other side; Iggy, still holding carefully to the sleeping Matilda, had crawled up next to him. Measle held a finger to his lips, but Iggy only scowled and bent his damp head next to Measle and whispered, "If dere'sss one fing burglarid-ersss know about, Mumpsss, dat'sss being quiet, all right?"

"All right, Iggy," whispered Measle. "Sorry."

"Now den," muttered Iggy, his once-again smelly breath invading Measle's nostrils, "who is dese people and wot is dey doing 'ere, traipsss-passsin' in my cassstle?"

"I don't know, Iggy. Let's just be very, very quiet, so we can listen and find out."

Iggy nodded his agreement and then he, Measle and Tinker settled down to hear the conversation far below.

Sir Peregrine twirled the stem of his wineglass and stared into the dark red liquid. He sniffed delicately, then he lifted his noble head and said, "You asked us here in order to allow us to express our concerns, Prime Magus—"

Mr. Prime Magus! That means that Justin Bucket is down there, too! Well, that makes sense, of course—if the Prime

216

Magus's Advisory Board is here, then the Prime Magus should be as well. . . .

Measle inched forward to get a better angle of view, but most of the floor of the room was still hidden. Justin must be somewhere just out of his line of sight.

Sir Peregrine went on, "—so perhaps we should voice our concerns, one by one—and then you can address them in turn. Would that be agreeable?"

There was no reply, but Sir Peregrine inclined his silver-maned head in what looked to Measle like a grateful way, so perhaps Justin had simply nodded, inviting Sir Peregrine to continue.

"Thank you, Prime Magus," said Sir Peregrine. "Perhaps I shall start? My main concern is this: Just how long are we going to be able to keep the Stubbs family under lock and key before some serious questions will be asked?"

Tully Telford looked up from polishing his glasses. "I agree with Sir Peregrine, Prime Magus," he squeaked. "As a lawyer, I must remind you that—by the rules of the Court of Magistri—charges must be brought sooner or later. If they are not, then the Stubbs family will have to be released. We cannot hold them without accusing them of something, you understand."

Ermintrude Bacon looked toward the middle part of the room. "And then there is the matter of this Mallockee creature, Prime Magus. What exactly are we going to do about her? The dear little poppet!"

Dorian Fescue turned his yellow face away from the fireplace and said, "Personally, Prime Magus, I feel that the Stubbs family was far too powerful even *before* the appearance of this Mallockee. With this all-powerful child joining the family, I don't see how we can possibly allow any of them to go free."

Quentin Underwood had been leaning against the mantelpiece, but the fire was evidently getting a little too hot for him, because he moved away from it, perching himself on the arm of Ermintrude's chair. His flat, dreary, colorless face turned in the same direction in which the rest of his colleagues were all looking, and he said, in a dull and monotonous drone, "And then of course there is the boy, Prime Magus. Our original target. What have you learned about him? Does he in fact possess the powers of which he is suspected?"

There was a pause, while the Advisory Board all stared toward the center of the room, obviously waiting for some sort of response. Measle heard the sound of measured footsteps as the Prime Magus walked slowly toward the fireplace, his back to Measle.

When the Prime Magus reached the fireplace, he turned around.

It wasn't Justin Bucket.

It was Toby Jugg.

12

TOBY JUGG

It felt to Measle as if his blood had turned into ice water. The shock of seeing Toby down there—Toby Jugg, his friend and rescuer; Toby Jugg, a man his mum had said was "very nice"; Toby Jugg, a warm and affable smile on his rugged face, that same smile being directed at each and every member of the Advisory Board, not one of whose members could ever be called a friend of the Stubbs family—well, all that was enough to paralyze Measle. The only thing he could do was stare down at the scene below, his eyes wide and his jaw gaping open.

At his side Iggy took a deep breath and opened his mouth—and somehow Measle knew that Iggy was about to shout a welcome down to his master. . . .

Measle reached over and clamped his hand over Iggy's lips. Iggy, his fishy eyes glaring, huffed and spluttered wetly through Measle's fingers.

"Ssshhhh, Iggy!" Measle whispered as fiercely as he could.

"Mmmmfff?" mumbled Iggy, shaking his head from side to side in an attempt to rid his face of Measle's hand. Measle felt raindrops spatter his cheeks.

"We've got to be quiet, Iggy! We've got to find out what's going on! We can say hello to Mr. Jugg later—all right?"

Iggy's head stopped shaking, and his fishy eyes stopped glaring, and a trace of understanding flitted across them. Iggy nodded slowly, and Measle felt it was safe enough to take his hand off Iggy's mouth. Once he was free, Iggy bent his head close to Measle's and whispered into his ear. "We can sssay hello later, Mumpsss?"

"Yes, Iggy. Later. Right now, we've got to be like little mice, okay?"

Iggy grinned, showing his yellow teeth. Then he turned his head away and concentrated on listening to what was being said down below. Measle, breathing a silent sigh of relief, did the same.

Toby stood casually in front of the fireplace, resting comfortably against the mantelpiece, his legs crossed and his hands thrust deep in his pockets. He looked into the face of each member of the Advisory Board, a small smile on his lips. After a long pause, he took a deep breath and said, "Well, I'm glad you all feel the need to express these concerns of yours, and I shall be happy to address each one in a minute. But first I must ask you all to stop calling me 'Prime Magus.'"

"But—you *are* the Prime Magus, Toby," said Sir Peregrine. "You won the election in a landslide!"

What? thought Measle. *But—surely Justin Bucket won the election?*

Toby laughed. It was a rich, easygoing, friendly sort of laugh—the sort of laugh that would make you like such a person immediately. For a moment Measle felt his suspicions begin to drain away. *Surely, somebody like Toby Jugg couldn't be a bad chap, not with a laugh like that? Or a face like that? Or a smile like that? And Mum said he was very nice—surely Mum couldn't be wrong? Could she?*

Toby stopped laughing, but he kept a broad, amiable

222

smile on his face. He said, "The fact that I won, Peregrine, is neither here nor there. The point is, we agreed that Bucket should believe that he'd won the election and was therefore the new Prime Magus of the Wizards' Guild."

"In name only, Toby," murmured Sir Peregrine Spine.

"Of *course* in name only, Peregrine," said Toby. "The poor idiot certainly couldn't manage the job for real. But you will remember that we also agreed to conceal that I had in fact won, in case my true identity should somehow be discovered."

So—if he's not Toby Jugg, then who is he?

"Therefore, I must insist you stop calling me Prime Magus. If you all continue to do that in *private*," he continued, "then there's the possibility that your tongues might slip and you could—quite by mistake—do the same when we're in *public*. If the secret got out that I was the real Prime Magus of the Wizards' Guild— well, that could be disastrous for us all . . . and for our intended sweeping program of rule changes. Therefore, I must ask you all to call me by my name—and not by my title—at all times. Is that agreed?"

There was a moment of mumbling and murmuring,

during which Measle was unable to catch any of what was being said, and then Sir Peregrine said, "Agreed, Prime Mag—or, rather, *Toby*, I should say."

"Indeed you should, Peregrine," said Toby, smiling so broadly that Measle could see, quite clearly, his flashing white teeth.

There was a little polite laughter and then Toby raised his hand. When the laughter had died away, he said, "Now, to your various concerns. Peregrine, I believe you wanted to know how long we can hold the Stubbs family? My reply? Not long at all. Quite soon questions will indeed begin to be asked, for which we have no adequate answers. Therefore, the problem of the Stubbs family will have to be . . . *disposed* of. You also asked about the boy and whether or not I have learned anything about his possible magic powers. Well—yes, I have."

Measle stiffened. His magical powers—did that mean he might have some after all? And, if he had, what were they? He pressed forward a couple of inches, listening intently.

Toby pushed away from the mantel and began to pace up and down in front of the fireplace.

"I've been watching him carefully for several hours now and I've learned that the boy possesses no magical powers whatsoever," he said quietly. "None at all. The Mallockee, on the other hand, is everything that Octavo said she was. An extraordinary creature. At the moment she tires too easily, but as she grows older, that weakness will disappear, I think. As for young Measle, he has experienced some very dangerous situations down here, and never at any time has he resorted to magic to get out of any of them. What he *has* shown, however, is remarkable courage, an active imagination and some splendid examples of resourcefulness."

Measle felt a pang of disappointment. It was all very fine being called brave and imaginative but not a patch on having magical powers. Well, he'd just have to make the best of what he'd got—and, come to think of it, what he'd got had served him pretty well in the past—

Dorian Fescue's voice interrupted his thoughts. "It rather sounds, Toby," he said, his thin voice dripping with scorn, "that you *admire* the beastly little fellow."

Toby stared at Dorian, and for the first time that night, Measle saw Toby's smile disappear.

"Oh, but I *do* admire him, Dorian," said Toby in a

steely tone. "And for good reason. When your enemy is a dolt, you can sneer at him. But when your enemy is brave and resourceful and clever, then it's stupid *not* to admire him. Even if he is only twelve and a half years old."

"It is a little hard to believe," squeaked Tully, "that a boy so young has managed to overcome so many dangers without the use of magic. Are you quite, *quite* sure, Toby, that he's powerless?"

"I didn't say he was powerless, Tully," said Toby, stopping in his tracks. He grinned amiably. "For a start, he's had the Mallockee with him all this time. But I have thrown a number of obstacles in his way. As you all know, this vast labyrinth of chambers down here is steeped in natural mana—and I'm sure you also know that this free form of magic is programmed to fulfill the wishes of the current Prime Magus. As the actual current Prime Magus, I have been able to direct the power down here to accomplish certain results, all of them extremely unpleasant for young Measle to experience. Several of them were, in fact, downright dangerous. And yet he has survived them all. As I say, quite miraculous, really. And here's another interesting fact about young Measle Stubbs—and, in itself, something of a miracle, as well: the boy and the Mallockee are, at this precise moment, a mere six yards away from us, and while she is mercifully asleep, he has managed to overhear almost everything that we've been saying. And if that isn't an extraordinary feat, I don't know what is."

13

DISCOVERED!

Measle froze.

"*Where?* Where are they?" Dorian Fescue jumped to his feet, his head whipping wildly from side to side as he searched the shadows of the great room.

Toby didn't reply. All he did was grin more broadly—then, slowly, he took his right hand out of his pocket, and extending his forefinger, he pointed up to the exact spot on the dark, shadowy balcony where Measle, Iggy, Matilda and Tinker were lying.

Toby called out, "Officers! Go up to the balcony and bring our eavesdropping guests down here! Quickly now—before they decide to go to another party instead!"

There was a clatter of heavy boots and two black-uniformed men emerged from the shadows. They ran fast up the spiral staircase, and around the balcony and were at Measle's side before he could think of anything to do. With a hard yank, one of the men pulled Measle to his feet and began to drag him purposefully to the iron spiral staircase. The second man put his hand on the scruff of Iggy's neck, lifted him up bodily and then pushed him roughly after them.

Measle's captor clumped down the steps, and Measle half walked, half fell with him until they reached the bottom. The man dragged Measle into the middle of the circle of armchairs and deposited him on the floor at Toby Jugg's feet. A moment later the second man dumped Iggy and Matilda into the circle.

"Thank you, Officers," said Toby. "That will do."

The two men nodded and disappeared back into the gloom.

"Niggle," said Toby firmly, "you will remain perfectly still. You will keep hold of the little girl and you will not—I repeat, you will *not*—allow her to wake up. Is that clearly understood, Niggle?"

Iggy gulped, nodded nervously and muttered, "Yesss, Missster Jugg, sssir."

Toby switched his gaze to Measle and smiled broadly. "Well, Measle old son," he said in his cheerful, friendly voice. "How nice to see you again."

Warily, Measle sat up. He held tight to Tinker, pulling his leather jacket around the little dog's body. He looked around at his audience. Their faces were lit by the candles and the flickering firelight. They didn't look at all friendly.

Sir Peregrine Spine and Ermintrude Bacon were closest, both sunk deep in their armchairs. A little farther out were the two armchairs containing Dorian Fescue and Tully Telford, and beyond them, half obscured by shadows, was the standing figure of Quentin Underwood.

Measle felt the six pairs of eyes boring into him. *It's a bit like being in a forest at night and being watched by a pack of wolves*, he thought. *In this light, their eyes look sort of shiny—and red.*

"May I ask what is going on, Toby?" said Sir Peregrine suddenly. "What are the boy and the Mallockee doing, running free in these quarters?"

"Well, Peregrine," said Toby in a casual voice, "it would appear that they have escaped from *their* section, only to be recaptured in *ours*."

"But—but *how* did they escape?" said Dorian angrily.

"By being brave and resourceful and clever, of course," said Toby.

Measle felt Toby's hand patting his shoulder, as if the man was trying to show his approval. Then Toby's hand stopped patting and settled on his shoulder, and Measle could feel the steely muscles in Toby's firm hand, and he knew that—whatever Toby had in store for him— this time he certainly wasn't going to let Measle out of his grasp.

There was a long silence, then Toby took his hand off Measle's shoulder and walked to a spot directly in front of him. He looked down at Measle, smiling warmly. "Is there anything you want to ask us, Measle old son? I'm sure you're bursting with questions. I know *I'd* be. If so—fire away."

Measle sat there for a moment, his mind buzzing. It was true—there were a lot of questions—but which were the important ones?

"Are you really the Prime Magus?" he blurted, staring up into Toby's friendly eyes.

"Yes, I really am," said Toby.

"Why has it got to be a secret? Why can't you tell anybody?"

"Well, old son—because of who I am, you see."

"You mean—you're not really Toby Jugg?"

Toby laughed—a rich, careless sort of laugh—a laugh that said he hadn't a care in the world.

"Oh, I'm Toby Jugg all right," he boomed. "At least, I was the last time I looked."

There was an appreciative little laugh from the five Warlocks and Ermintrude muttered, "'The last time I *looked*'—so clever."

"But—you said it was because of who 'you *were*," said Measle slowly. "Doesn't that mean you're really somebody else?"

Toby shook his head. "Not so much some*body* else, old son. More like some*thing* else. Here—I'll show you."

Toby squatted down in front of Measle. He raised both his hands and Measle instinctively reared back—but Toby's hands weren't going for Measle. Toby's hands were reaching toward his own head—

Reaching for the long, wavy locks of graying hair that hung on either side of Toby's face, curling the strong brown fingers around the locks of hair, and pulling the locks back from his face.

And revealing—to Measle's astonished eyes—Toby's ears.

14

THE
PLOT

Toby's ears were almost completely black.

The Gloomstains were at their blackest at the tips of Toby's ears, fading down to a dark gray at the lobes. Measle knew exactly what they meant: Toby Jugg wasn't a Wizard at all—he was a Warlock, and a very powerful one at that. Far more powerful than Tully Telford, for example, whose ears were only black at the tips.

"Surprised?" said Toby, grinning cheerfully.

Measle didn't answer. His mind was clicking furiously from gear to gear while he tried to find an explanation for the fact that, a mere twenty-four hours ago,

Toby's ears had been as pink as his own—

And then Measle's agile brain found exactly the right gear.

Click.

"You wear makeup," said Measle quietly. "You wear makeup on your ears."

Toby turned and looked over his shoulder at the rest of the Warlocks. "You see?" he said. "You see what I mean? The boy isn't just brave and resourceful—he's got a quick mind, too."

Toby turned back and looked at Measle thoughtfully. "Indeed I do, Measle—at least, when I want people to think I'm just a simple Wizard. Down here I needn't bother, of course."

"I saw the pot of makeup in your bathroom. I thought it belonged to a woman. I never guessed it might belong to you."

Toby nodded. "I see. Well—now you know what I am, any more questions?"

Measle thought hard. There were lots of questions he wanted to ask, but there was one question that stood head and shoulders above the rest.

"Why?"

"Why what?"

"Why—*everything?*"

Toby laughed. He thought for a moment, shrugged, then pulled himself out of his squat and to his full height.

"You want to know everything, do you?" he said, smiling down at Measle. "Well, why not?

Tully Telford leaned forward again and raised a warning finger. "Ah—Toby—as your legal advisor, I must caution you against saying anything that might incriminate you." Tully glanced around at his fellow Warlocks and added quickly, "And *us*, for that matter."

Toby laughed again. "It won't matter," he said.

"It won't?" said Sir Peregrine Spine, raising both eyebrows as high as they could go.

"No, it won't," said Toby easily. "What we say here in this room, to this boy, won't matter in the least. I hope you all take my meaning?"

There was a long silence. Then, one by one, Measle saw the Warlocks nod. The only Warlock whose head didn't move at all was Sir Peregrine Spine's. Measle saw that Sir Peregrine was biting his lip in a nervous way and twitching his bushy silver eyebrows.

"Toby—my dear fellow," said Sir Peregrine, "do please forgive me—but am I to understand—"

"Yes, Peregrine," said Toby firmly. "You are."

Measle felt himself get cold, and a clammy sweat broke out on his forehead—because he understood what it was that everybody else in the room understood: Toby had no fear that Measle would ever repeat anything to anybody because quite soon after Toby was *finished* telling him everything, there was a strong probability that Mcasle's life was going to come to an abrupt and maybe sticky end.

"Well, what all this is about, Measle old son, is this: there are going to be some changes made. Some big changes, starting with the Wizards' Guild. Now, I'm a Warlock and I'm the Prime Magus of the Wizards' Guild—and that's not allowed, you see. So, first we have to change that rule. The new rule will be that *only* a Warlock can be Prime Magus. Once that's done, the Wizards' Guild is going to have a lot more say in how the world is run, old son. It's always avoided interfering in human affairs—but not anymore. Not with us Warlocks managing things. And there's lots to do. All those silly little countries, with their silly little leaders, all arguing with each other. But not for much longer, old son. Once we get rid of the whole ridiculous lot of them, we Warlocks will be able to make the world so much more—*efficient*.

Measle gasped audibly. He was wondering what horrors the Warlocks had in store for him.

"What's the matter, Measle?" said Toby, all fake concern. "You look a little peaky all of a sudden."

"N-nothing," muttered Measle, staring hard at the floor. *I've got to keep him talking!* "Wh-what other things are you going to change?"

"One of the first things we shall do is begin a worldwide hunt for more Manafounts. There are sure to be a few out there—besides your mother, I mean—that haven't yet been discovered. And when we find them, we'll bring them back here and we'll have a lovely mass wedding."

There was an appreciative little laugh from the other Warlocks and Ermintrude Bacon said, in her coy little baby voice, "I'm *so* looking forward to finding a husband! Now, be sure to find me a really *handsome* Manafount, Toby! I want one at least as attractive as yours, mind!"

Toby bowed in Ermintrude's direction. "I shall do

my best for you, Trudy," he said. Then he turned back to Measle and said, "You see, Measle old son, if we each have a Manafount at our side—well, hand in hand, we can do pretty much as we like, can't we?"

"But—but what if they don't *want* to marry any of you?" said Measle, thinking that nobody in their right mind would ever want to marry Ermintrude Bacon— or Tully Telford, come to that—and frankly, Dorian Fescue and his yellow face was hardly a very attractive proposition, either.

"Oh, that won't be a problem, Measle," said Toby genially. "You'd be amazed at all the pills and potions that we've got in our alchemy labs. Half of them have to do with getting people to fall in love with you, and the other half get people to do exactly what you want. So persuading a few Manafounts to marry us is not going to be all that hard, I promise."

"Besides," cooed Ermintrude, "who *wouldn't* want to marry us? The most powerful group of Warlocks the world has ever seen! I'm sure that silly girl would far rather be married to Toby Jugg than to that ridiculous Wizard!"

"What silly girl?" blurted Measle, though he already

had an idea. "What Wizard?"

Toby cleared his throat loudly and shot an angry look at Ermintrude Bacon. Immediately Ermintrude's piggy face turned pink, and she lowered her eyes to the floor. There was a short, uncomfortable silence. Toby shrugged his shoulders and said, "Well, I suppose it can't hurt to tell him now, can it?"

"Tell me what?" said Measle.

Dorian Fescue got up out of his armchair and poured himself another glass of wine. Then he turned and faced Measle, his yellow face distorted by a broad smirk.

"Toby won't have to search the outside world for *his* Manafount, boy," he said, each word dripping with venom. "Toby already *has* his Manafount, ready and waiting. Her name, boy—her name is Lee Stubbs."

If Measle had felt cold and clammy before, now it seemed as though he was packed in ice. "My mum's got a husband already," he said.

Dorian Fescue let loose a short laugh. He sipped his wine and said, "Not for much longer, boy. Not for much longer."

Sir Peregrine Spine shifted uncomfortably in his

armchair. "This is nothing personal against you, young man," he said smoothly. "I do hope you understand that?"

"No, indeed not," said Toby, shaking his head sadly. "Sir Peregrine's right—we've got nothing against you, Measle old son. It's just that, to achieve our ends, certain unpleasant things are going to have to occur. One of them is the elimination of your dad, I'm afraid."

Measle felt his heart beating very fast. It seemed to be twice as heavy as usual, and a strange little lump was rising in his throat. "And what about my sister?" he said, his voice a little quivery now. "What are you going to do with her?"

"Oh, we're going to keep her, old son," said Toby, in the sort of over-cheerful tone people use when they've just delivered a piece of gloomy news and are then very relieved when they can discuss a happy thing immediately after. "Yes, she's far too interesting to throw away. Her powers will, no doubt, develop splendidly—and, since I'll be her stepfather, I'll be controlling her. Yes, it'll be very interesting having a Mallockee in the family."

Good luck with that, thought Measle—*with controlling*

Matilda—I'm the only one who can do that!

"And—and, what about me?" said Measle.

"*You*, old son?"

"Y-yes. What are you going to do with me?"

"Oh, don't you worry about that," said Toby. "We're just going to keep you safe, while we see what's what. But there'll be no more wandering around the place, I'm afraid. Officers! Come here please!"

Measle watched as the two uniformed men emerged from the shadows and marched into the circle of light.

"Officers, you will escort us all down to the detention center."

Ermintrude coughed a little ladylike cough and said, "And what about this nasty Wrathmonk, Toby? What shall we do with him?"

"A good question, Trudy," said Toby, staring coldly down at Iggy, who was now crouching on the floor and trembling like a whipped dog. Toby sighed irritably. "I've often wondered, what is the *point* of you, Niggle? I've never understood that. As a servant you're a waste of time. In fact, why aren't you in the detention center with all the other Wrathmonks, eh?"

"I was ricky-bended leaningsssea," Iggy muttered,

almost under his breath.

"What?" said Toby, clenching both hands into fists and frowning angrily.

"Ricky-bended leaningsssea," repeated Iggy, a little louder this time.

Tully Telford leaned forward, an amused little smile on his lips. "I think what the creature is trying to say is that he was *recommended leniency*, Toby. It means that the arresting Wizard obviously suggested that, since the crime was not too wicked, the punishment should not be too severe."

Oh, thought Measle, *so that's what "ricky-bended leaningsea" means!*

"I know what it means, Tully!" barked Toby. He pointed a finger at Iggy and said, in a stern and commanding voice, "And who, Niggle, was this Wizard who recommended leniency?"

"It was Misssster Sssam Ssstubbs," said Iggy, smiling nervously up at Measle.

"*Was* it now?" said Toby. "How very interesting." He seemed deep in thought for a moment. Then he said, "You will come with us, Niggle. You will carry the Mallockee. You will carry her very carefully, and you will not wake her up. Understood?"

"Yess, Missster Jugg, sssir," said Iggy, nodding wildly and scattering raindrops in a wide circle.

"Good!" said Toby. "Well, then—shall we go?"

Toby clapped his hand onto Measle's shoulder. To anybody watching, it looked like a friendly gesture, but Measle felt once again the steel in Toby's grip.

The other Warlocks were getting to their feet. Iggy positioned himself next to Measle, and with the two uniformed men leading the way, they all set off—a little procession, with Measle and Iggy in the middle.

15

THE DETENTION CENTER

They walked along a succession of high, paneled corridors, arriving at last at the head of a huge stone staircase. The stairs were brightly lit by a series of modern spotlights set into the ceiling—weirdly, this whole area seemed to Measle to be—well—less like what you might expect to see in a castle and rather more like what might be found in a modern building. As they descended further and further into the bowels of the earth, Measle realized that this was the first set of stairs that he'd seen in Caltrop Castle. Through all his explorations—and, later, during the frantic chases—he'd never come across a single staircase in the entire place! Where were the ones that should, logically, lead to upper floors? What sort of castle had only a ground floor and a deep, deep basement?

After what seemed an age, they arrived at the bottom. There was a single, heavy iron door set into the wall in front of them. Toby tapped Tully Telford on the shoulder and said, "Your department, Tully."

Tully nodded and pressed a small button on a speaker on the wall by the door. A moment later a tinny, gruff voice came out of the speaker. "Officer Offal on duty—kindly state your business."

"Attorney Tully Telford here, Offal. Open up, if you please. We have a—um—a *guest* for the detention center."

"Yes, sir. Right away, sir." A moment later there was a click and the heavy door swung open.

Measle found himself in a brightly lit circular hallway. A stout, uniformed man nodded respectfully at the group of Warlocks and beckoned them toward a door on the far end of the hallway. He took a heavy key ring from a hook on his belt, picked out a key, pushed it into the lock and turned it—and then threw the door wide open and stood aside to let the Warlocks through.

"Thank you, Officer Offal," said Tully. The procession filed into a small, bare office. There was a steel desk in the room, with a swivel chair behind it. On the desk was a big, old-fashioned silver microphone on a short stand and, next to the microphone, what looked like a sort of intercom. Along the walls were several dark green filing cabinets and, in one corner, a door that looked even heavier and more strongly barred than the one through which they had just entered. Next to this door was a panel with a pair of large round buttons on it. One button was black. The other was a dull green and had the number twenty painted on it.

Officer Offal came and stood behind the desk. He was big and heavy looking, with a fat belly that hung over his belt. His face was pink and puffy and his red hair was cut very short, so that his scalp gleamed through the bristles.

"A new tenant for you, Offal," said Tully, and the other Warlocks stepped aside, revealing Measle and Matilda and Iggy and Tinker.

Officer Offal nodded, but it wasn't Measle he was

staring at. His eyes were locked grimly on Iggy.

"I see he's already got his wrathring on, sir," he said, stepping out from behind the desk. "That makes my job a lot easier, I don't mind telling you." Offal marched up to Iggy and said sternly, "Come along then, my lad— and gimme your dolly—you can't take that with you where you're going, you know."

"Wot?" said Iggy, nervously looking about him.

Toby laughed. "That's not a doll, Officer," he said cheerfully. "That's a rather precious little creature who happens to be asleep at the moment. I'd be obliged if you didn't wake her up, so please keep your voice down."

"Ah, right you are, sir," whispered Offal, peering shortsightedly at Matilda. "Er—what do you want me to do with the little thing, sir?"

"Leave her where she is, Officer," said Toby. "You see, it's not Mr. Niggle whom we want you to keep down here. It's this boy here, and his dog. We need to put them somewhere safe for a while—somewhere very, *very* safe, you understand?"

Officer Offal looked doubtful. "Er—right, sir. Yes. The only thing is, sir—well, I understood that the detention center is reserved for Wrathies—I mean Wrathmonks, sir."

Tully Telford nodded impatiently. "Indeed, indeed," he squeaked. "However, this is a matter of some urgency, Officer Offal, and we—the Advisory Board to the Prime Magus—are ordering you to carry out our wishes. Kindly do so without further delay."

Officer Offal's face went even redder than it was before. He stood up very straight and saluted smartly. "Yessir!" he whispered. "Right away, sir!"

Offal stepped toward Measle, and Toby said, "And gently, Officer, if you please. Young Measle Stubbs is our guest, not our prisoner."

"Right, sir."

Officer Offal stared at Measle for a moment, as if unsure how to treat a guest. Then he turned on his heel and went to the heavy door on the far side of the room. He pulled it open and stepped through, calling back, "This way, young feller."

Measle felt the pressure of Toby's hand on his shoulder as he went through the door and into a broad corridor. There was a series of cells on either side of the corridor. While the doors to the cells were made of very solid-looking studded iron, the outer walls of the cells were of thick heavy glass, with wire embedded in it, so that it was practically unbreakable. These glass walls allowed you to see into the cells, which meant that the occupants had no privacy whatsoever.

Iggy Niggle nudged Measle. The little Wrathmonk looked frightened.

"What's the matter, Iggy?" whispered Measle.

Iggy bent his head close to Measle's ear and muttered, "Disss is de *uvver place*, Mumpsss! Where all de really *bad* Wraffmonks go!"

As they all walked down the wide corridor, following the massive figure of Officer Offal, Measle peered into each cell as he passed. Most were occupied by Wrathmonks, of all shapes and sizes. They were dressed in white, one-piece jumpsuits—which was, Measle realized, in sharp contrast to the black clothes that Wrathmonks always wore in the outside world. Each had a dull gray steel wrathring around his neck.

Measle didn't recognize any of them.

No—wait! There, in that cell—a huge, hulking figure, sitting on the edge of his bunk and staring curiously out at the passing procession! It's Mr. Cudgel! Buford Cudgel!

Buford Cudgel's face changed the moment the giant Wrathmonk caught sight of his old enemy Measle Stubbs. His eyes narrowed, a frown appeared in the middle of his narrow forehead, his nostrils flared like a racehorse—and then Cudgel jumped up from his bunk and began to beat both huge hands against the glass. He opened his mouth and roared with rage.

"Somebody you know, old son?" said Toby.

"That's Mr. Cudgel," said Measle.

"Ah, yes. From your adventure with the Dragodon. He looks quite pleased to see you. Perhaps you'll find a few other old friends down here."

And Measle did.

Right next to Cudgel, in the neighboring cell, Frognell Flabbit was sitting moodily on his bunk, scratching at his red and lumpy face. Next to him, Judge Cedric Hardscrabble, one hand pressed to his long jaw, was pretending to read a book (Measle noticed that the book was *upside down*); next to him, in a cell that seemed a little cleaner and tidier than all the others, stood the small, round figure of Griswold Gristle, the bank manager.

As the procession passed, each of the remaining

three Wrathmonks caught sight of Measle and each had a different reaction. Where Buford Cudgel had become enraged, Frognell Flabbit simply stared for a moment, an angry look in his little red eyes. Then he shrugged his shoulders and went back to scratching his face. Judge Cedric Hardscrabble looked up from his book, saw Measle, and waved, a vague smile of recognition hovering on his thin lips.

Griswold Gristle's reaction was the most disturbing: he simply stood and stared, his snub nose pressed flat against the glass wall in front of him. His round, white face was completely expressionless, and the only movement was in the pair of tiny black eyes that followed Measle fixedly as he walked by.

"Seems like a friendly crowd," said Toby.

"Can—can they get out?" asked Measle nervously.

"*Can* they get out, Officer Offal?" called Toby.

Offal stopped in his tracks and turned around. "Not unless I let 'em out, sir," he said. "That happens once a day. They get an hour of mixing together, out here in the corridor. Then I give them their marching orders over the microphone in the office and they all 'ave to go back to their cells. And they do it pretty smartish, too, I don't mind telling you. The Wrathies do as I tell 'em, 'cause they know what'll 'appen if they don't, see?"

"What will happen?" said Measle, using his most innocent voice. (Measle had discovered that, if you wanted the answer to a difficult question, putting on an innocent-sounding voice often got it for you.)

Officer Offal looked down at him and winked. "Let's just say that the Wrathies don't like me, and I don't like them—but they know who's the boss, see?"

"Why are the walls made of glass?" said Measle, who wanted to find out as much as he could before anybody thought to tell him to be quiet.

"Because we like to see what they're doing, young feller," said Officer Offal. "They got the wrathrings on, see? Well, those are fine for stopping their major spells, but they don't do nothing for their breath. Nothing stops that. Disgusting, that's what it is. 'Ave you ever smelled a Wrathmonk's breath, young feller?"

"Yes," said Measle, remembering the terrible stink of Basil Tramplebone's breath.

"Well then, you'll understand why we 'ave the glass walls. We want to see them, but we certainly don't want to smell 'em, do we? And some of their breathing magic is very nasty indeed."

"Mine is *'orrible!*" announced Iggy, proudly.

Officer Offal took a step away from Iggy and frowned. "Well, you'd better not use it down 'ere, chummy. Not if you know what's good for you."

They had reached the end of the broad corridor. The last cell on the left was empty and open, its door pushed back against the wall. There was a number painted on the cell door—the number twenty.

"There you go, young feller," said Offal. "You'll be all right in there."

Measle felt the pressure of Toby's hand on his shoulder, pushing him gently but firmly toward the open door. There was nothing he could do—so he said, "Come on, Tink," and, together, he and Tinker entered the cell.

"He'll be quite safe here, will he, Officer Offal?" asked Toby, leaning carelessly against the door frame and smiling in at Measle.

"Oh, yes, sir," said Officer Offal. "See, what 'appens is this: when it's time to let the Wrathies out—that'll be in a couple of hours now—I push the big black button in the office and that unlocks all the cell doors, see? We're all very up-to-date down here, sir. All electronic, see? I can talk to them, too, and hear 'em as well—every cell has got a two-way communication system in it. Mind you, I keep that turned off most of the time—Wrathies' conversations aren't my cup of tea at all. Oh, yes, we're all very high-tech, sir. Now, as to the young feller being safe. I can isolate *this* cell, see, so that it don't get unlocked when I push the black button. This number twenty cell is operated independently—that's what the *green* button is for. It's a special cell, where we put the ones we 'ave to keep separated from the rest—'cause you see, sir, some Wrathies really hate each other—and, when that 'appens, well, we 'ave to keep 'em apart."

"I understand," said Toby thoughtfully. He seemed to think for a moment—then his face cleared and a smile twitched at the corners of his mouth. "Excellent!" he boomed. The he turned to Iggy and said, quite casually, "Let me have the Mallockee, Niggle."

Iggy thought about this. It was a request he quite obviously was reluctant to grant, because his face muscles started to twitch and writhe, so that it looked as if he had a whole mass of wriggling worms just under his skin. Toby Jugg waited for Iggy to make a decision, but when it didn't seem likely that Iggy was going to come to one any time soon, he barked, "The Mallockee, Niggle! *Give her to me!*"

Iggy shuddered and then, mutely, he disentangled Matilda's arms from around his neck and held out her sleeping form—and Toby scooped the little girl gently into his own arms.

Measle wanted to shout out that Toby must give her back! That he couldn't take her away! That he wanted Matilda here with him!

But before he could do so, Toby shot out his free hand and grabbed Iggy by his collar. Without a word, Toby dragged Iggy to the door and pushed him into the cell, making Iggy totter out of control across the floor and crash against the far wall.

"Oooowwww!" wailed Iggy, slumping into a heap on the floor.

Toby hissed, "Once a Wrathmonk, always a Wrathmonk! We are withdrawing the recommended leniency! Welcome to your new home, Niggle!"

Then, before Measle could react, the door swung

shut with a *clang!* and there was the sound of a heavy bolt slamming home.

"Oooh!" cried Iggy, bursting into a flood of tears. "Wot did he do dat for? Why did he take my little fing away? Oooh!"

Measle watched through the glass wall of the cell as Toby beckoned to Officer Offal. He spoke to him, and Officer Offal's eyes widened in shock, then Officer Offal looked in the direction of Measle's cell. Toby did some more talking. Officer Offal shook his head firmly. Then Measle saw Toby reach into his pocket and pull out a great wad of money. Measle had never seen so much money in his life. The money was pushed into Officer Offal's beefy hand—more talk—and soon Officer Offal was nodding slowly. One by one he and the Warlocks each glanced back at Measle's cell, and each one had a small, satisfied smile on their lips. Toby patted Officer Offal on his shoulder in a friendly manner, and then the whole group walked away down the broad corridor. Measle watched them, his mind awhirl, until they all disappeared through the door at the far end.

Iggy was whimpering piteously, so Measle went and

sat down next to him, leaning his back against the cold glass wall. Tinker, guessing that the smelly kid wasn't going to want him to go anywhere in a hurry, lay down, closed his eyes and was soon asleep.

Measle's main concern was for his sister. *Where were they taking her? What would they do to her?* But then he thought about what he'd just seen. *And why did Toby give Officer Offal all that money? What are they going to do with me?*

It was that last question that stuck in Measle's mind—*What are they going to do with me? Toby said they're going to keep Mum and Matilda alive—they're going to get rid of Dad—and what about me?*

Slowly a sick realization began to seep into Measle's mind, and then he knew exactly what was going to happen to him. It was all linked to that wad of money—and the wad of money was linked to Officer Offal—and Officer Offal was linked to the opening of all the Wrathmonks' cell doors—all except this one, if Officer Offal so decided—and Officer Offal had shaken his head at something Toby had said, but when Toby had given him the money, Officer Offal had nodded—and all the Warlocks had looked back at him and grinned their horrible grins—

Officer Offal wasn't going to keep Measle's cell door locked!

Officer Offal was going to open the door to Measle's cell, so when it was time for the Wrathmonks to mingle in the corridor, there was going to be nothing to stop Griswold Gristle, Buford Cudgel, Frognell Flabbit and Judge Cedric Hardscrabble from marching up to Measle's cell and walking in and—

And breathing on him.

Measle remembered what those four Wrathmonk exhalation enchantments did to a person. The first two were nasty and very painful. Judge Cedric's breath gave you horrible, painful red boils all over your face and body. Frognell Flabbit's caused the most terrible, agonizing toothache. But the breaths of the other two Wrathmonks were deadly. Buford Cudgel's made all the microscopic organisms on your body grow to the size of beetles, and Griswold Gristle's dried up all the moisture in your body—all the sweat and the tears and, most importantly, all the *blood*—until you were nothing more than a little, dried-out, shriveled corpse.

A very *dead* little shriveled corpse.

And this time there was no Dad or Mum or Nanny Flannel to help him out. This time there was no Matilda to do a helpful spell. This time there was only Tinker—and Mr. Ignatius Niggle. And Mr. Ignatius Niggle was a Wrathmonk himself! Measle looked at Iggy, who was still sniveling. *He won't be any use,* thought Measle, *not against those Wrathmonks. And why should Iggy even try—he's one of them!*

Measle got up abruptly and went to the cell door and pushed against it. It was a pointless thing to do, but it's something everybody does if they've been locked in somewhere.

The door didn't budge.

Two hours! thought Measle. *That's what Officer Offal said—he'd be opening the cell doors in two hours! So I've got two hours to get me and Tinker and Iggy out of here!*

But how? How to open a massive, electronically operated cell door?

16

IGGY GOES TO WORK

Measle had discovered that, if he sat down and thought about a problem—*really* thought about a problem—then more often than not, the solution would simply pop into his brain like a shaft of sunlight. In the past some of these solutions had come to him very quickly, simply because they *had* to come to him quickly, or else he would certainly have died—but this time Measle had a little longer to come up with one of his brilliant ideas, so he went and sat down on the bunk and started to think.

How to open a door?

Iggy. Iggy said he could open things with his one and only spell—so perhaps Iggy could open this massive door and let them out?

But Iggy was wearing a wrathring—and a wrathring stopped all magic, except for a Wrathmonk's exhalation enchantment, and Iggy's exhalation enchantment did nothing more spectacular than kill a few insects.

But—without the wrathring . . .

Click—Click—Click—went Measle's brain—and here was a shaft of sunlight!

Measle crossed the cell and sat down again at the little Wrathmonk's side. Iggy raised his tear-stained face and stared mournfully at Measle through his fishy eyes.

Measle said gently, "Iggy, you know when you were a burglar—I mean, a *burglarider*—did you ever want to open something *without* using your magic spell?"

Iggy thought for a moment, his face twisting with the effort. Then he nodded, cautiously.

"What did you open, Iggy?"

"Locksss."

Measle frowned. "But—but I thought you used your spell for locks?"

"I *did*, Mumpsss," said Iggy, in that patient sort of voice that people use when they're trying to explain something to somebody who's not all that bright. "I *did* use my ssspell to open locksss—but only de *'ard* ones. Sssee, you can only do a big ssspell like dat once a day."

"I know that, Iggy."

"Well, den, I didn't do my big ssspell on de *easy-peasy* ones."

"So how did you open the easy-peasy ones, Iggy?"

Iggy's eyes narrowed suspiciously. "Why do you want to know dat, Mumpsss?" he said. "Dat's a sssecret. Only burglariders know dat—and you're not a burglarider."

Measle thought furiously. How could he get Iggy to tell him? Wrathmonks weren't too bright, and Iggy Niggle was one of the dimmest. . . .

Flattery. I could try flattery.

"Well, the thing is, Iggy—I really, really, *really* want to *be* a burglarider! I want to be the best burglarider in the whole wide world—just like you! You're so clever and brave—look at all the times you've rescued me! You're wonderful, Iggy! And, if that's what being a bur-glarider means—then I want to be one, too! I want to learn how to be one, Iggy—will you teach me?"

Iggy's face transformed. It went from sad and hurt and suspicious to pleased, confident and even a little boastful.

"Ho, Mumpsss—I will be *'appy* to teach you how to be a burglarider. And you will be learning from de bessst, too! 'Coz I was de bessst burglarider in de whole wide world! I was de bessst roof climber, I was de bessst window breaker, I was de bessst night creeper, I was de bessst picklepocket, I was de bessst—"

"I know you were, Iggy! And you know what I want to learn first?"

"What, Mumpsss?"

"I want to learn how to open *little* locks. Can you teach me how to do that?"

"'Courssse I can, Mumps. Dat's not difficult at all! What you do is—you get a little bit of metal—'bout ssso long"—Iggy held up his hand and measured a distance of about half an inch between his thumb and his forefinger—"and den you put de little bit of metal into de lock and you go twisssty-twisssty one way, den you go twisssty-twisssty de *uvver* way, den you go wiggle-wiggle-wiggle *very* fassst and den, if you're good at it like me, de lock opens!"

"Have you got a bit of metal like that, Iggy?" said Measle.

Iggy's face fell. "Not anymore, Mumps. Dey took mine from me when your dad ricky-bended lean-ingsssea."

Measle's heart sank—then, a moment later, he pushed his hands, one by one, into each pocket in his clothes, searching for something—anything—which might fit the description of "a little bit of metal." All Measle found was the small plastic bag of jelly beans.

The jelly beans! He'd forgotten all about them. Everything that had happened at Caltrop Castle had been so weird and unexpected, he'd never thought to use the jelly beans—and now, with the knowledge of just how useful they could be, finding a little bit of metal for Iggy seemed even more urgent.

Iggy had been watching Measle rummaging about in all his pockets. It looked rather an important and urgent thing to do, so Iggy—without any idea what he might be looking for—started rummaging in his own pockets. They were all empty, apart from one. Iggy reached in and pulled out . . . Measle's toothbrush.

Measle glanced over and saw Iggy examining the

toothbrush. He noticed that the bristles had already picked up a lot of dirty fluff from the bottom of Iggy's pocket. *I'll have to clean that before I use it,* he thought glumly. *I'll have to give it a really good scrub—I'll probably have to take the top off and put it in boiling water. . . .*

And the image of what the toothbrush looked like when the brush section was removed from the handle came popping into his mind.

An idea . . .

"Can I borrow that for a moment, Iggy?"

Reluctantly Iggy handed Measle the toothbrush—and Measle, without hesitation, instantly pulled the brush section away from the handle.

"Aaaaah!" screamed Iggy. "You've *broked* it!"

"I haven't broken it, Iggy!" said Measle quickly. "Look—see? It goes back together again! See?"

Iggy watched dubiously as Measle slipped the brush section back onto the handle, his face relaxing as Measle pulled it off again and then slipped it back on, each time fitting it precisely over the slender spike of metal, a slender spike of metal that was about half an inch long—

Once again Measle pulled the brush section off and,

this time, he kept it off. He held up the handle of the toothbrush, right in front of Iggy's staring eyes, forcing Iggy to look at the metal spike that protruded from the handle.

"Is this like the bit of metal that you used, Iggy?"

Iggy shook his head. "No, dat's not like it at all, Mumpsss," he said dismissively. "Dat's got a 'andle on it. My little bit of metal didn't 'ave no 'andle on it."

"Yes, but would this one *work*, Iggy?"

"I sss'pose ssso," said Iggy.

"Good," said Measle. "Now, will you show me how to open a lock, Iggy?"

"What lock, Mumpsss?"

Measle extended his left hand and touched Iggy's wrathring with his forefinger. "That one, Iggy," he said softly.

Iggy pulled away from Measle's finger, a look of shock on his face. "Open my wraffring? Dat would be wrong, Mumpsss!" he hissed. "Missster Jugg wouldn't like dat at all!"

"But Mr. Jugg doesn't *like* you, Iggy!" said Measle urgently. "He threw you into this cell with me and Tink! He took Tilly away from you! So you don't have

266

to do what Mr. Jugg says anymore!"

"Don't I, Mumpsss?" said Iggy, looking unconvinced.

"No, Iggy! And just think how nice it will be, not having a nasty great thing around your neck! So please—show me how to open the lock!"

Measle pushed the toothbrush handle at Iggy—but Iggy shook his head and said, "I can't do it, Mumpsss."

"Why not? Is it a difficult lock?"

Iggy snorted contemptuously. "Nah, it'sss a easy-peasy one. But I can't open it 'coz I can't *sssee* it, Mumpsss. I got to be able to sssee it."

Iggy demonstrated by tilting his head so that it was bent over as far as it would go. He squinted his fishy eyes downward and Measle could see that it was true—there was no way that Iggy could look directly at the wrathring that was around his scrawny neck.

"Well, maybe I could do it, Iggy—if you just tell me what to do?"

"I already *told* you, Mumpsss. You twisssty-twisssty one way, den you twisssty-twisssty de uvver way, den you wiggle-wiggle-wiggle it very fassst and den, if you is lucky, de lock opens. Dey always opened when *I* did it."

"Can I try, Iggy?"

"You can *try*, Mumpsss," said Iggy smugly. "But you won't be able to *do* it. 'Coz you isn't a burglarider, sssee?"

Iggy lifted his chin, exposing the dull gray wrathring. Measle saw that there was what looked like a simple lock, in the front, that fastened the two halves together. Very carefully, he pushed the metal spike into the small keyhole. He twisted the handle one way. Then he twisted the handle the other way. Then he wiggled the handle backward and forward.

Nothing happened.

"You have to do de wiggly-wiggly fassster dan dat," said Iggy scornfully, staring up at the ceiling.

Measle was concentrating so hard—and clutching the toothbrush handle so tightly—that he let one finger slip over the toothbrush switch. Instantly he felt a buzzing sensation in his hand as the little metal spike started to vibrate back and forth.

"Oooh," said Iggy, a trace of admiration in his voice. "Dat is *very* fassst wiggly-wiggly. Dat is nearly as fassst as *my* wiggly-wiggly. You is quite a good learner, Mumpsss—but you have to do it jussst a little bit fassster dan dat if you want de lock to open."

And then, without Measle doing anything more, the wrathring made a sort of *doingggg!* sound and the two halves suddenly sprang apart.

Iggy lowered his chin, a look of astonishment on his face. He reached up and took hold of the wrathring and slipped it off his neck. Then he grinned, showing his pointed yellow teeth.

"Dere! Sssee, Mumpsss? Dat's 'ow to do it! Oooh—how clever I am!"

Measle took the wrathring from Iggy's hands and threw it into a corner of the cell. Iggy went on prattling how incredibly clever he was when it came to opening locks, until Measle took hold of his damp shoulders and gave Iggy a little shake.

"Iggy! Listen! Now you haven't got your wrathring on—do you think you could use your spell and open the door?"

Iggy turned and stared at Measle, his eyebrows raised as high as they would go. "Open de *door*, Mumpsss? Disss door 'ere? *Disss* door—wot is a door in de *Uvver Place*? But—dat would make Missster Jugg really, *really* crosss, dat would! Missster Jugg would *kill* me if I did dat! No—no, I couldn't do dat! Not *never*! Not *nohow*! Not *noden*, neither!"

Iggy turned away, crossed both his arms across his skinny chest and stuck his nose in the air, and Measle realized that Iggy was drawing the line. He simply wasn't going to cooperate with this idea at all.

Measle thought desperately. Flattery wouldn't work, not a second time. There was no point threatening Iggy, because Iggy wasn't as frightened of him as he was of Toby Jugg. So, how to get him to do what he wanted? *There must be a way. . . .*

Another idea! It might work—it did with breakfast!

Measle turned away and folded his arms and put his nose in the air, just like Iggy had done. Then he sniffed loudly, in a contemptuous sort of way and said, "No, I don't suppose you could."

Iggy glanced over his shoulder and said, "Don't sssuppose I could wot?"

"Open the door, Iggy. I don't think you can do it at all."

"You wot?"

"I don't think you've even *got* a spell, Iggy. I think you were telling a big fibby-dib about that. In fact, I don't think you've got any magic at all."

"I 'ave too!"

"No, you haven't."

"I *'ave!* I *'ave!*"

"Don't believe you, Iggy."

"I 'ave, I 'ave, I *'ave!*"

"No, sorry, Iggy. I mean, just look at your silly little rain cloud. It's not even a proper one, is it? And that means you're not really a proper Wrathmonk, are you?"

"I am, I am, I *am!*"

"Not, not, *not,*" said Measle, in a singsong voice.

"Am, am, AM!" screamed Iggy, his white face going a little pink.

"Then prove it," said Measle, leaning back against the cell wall and closing his eyes in pretend boredom.

There was a pause and all Measle could hear was Iggy's heavy breathing. Then Iggy said, "Right! You watch disss, Mumpsss! Come on—open your eyes and watch *disss!*"

Lazily Measle opened one eye. Iggy was standing up, facing the heavy door. When he saw that Measle was watching him, he took a deep breath and yelled,

"*Unkasssshhhriek gorgogasssshhh plurgholipsss!*"—and, at the same moment, a pair of bright, lavender-colored beams shot from his eyes and sizzled their way across the cell. The beams struck the lock with the sound of bacon frying—and then, a second later, Measle heard quite clearly a heavy, metallic *thonk!*

The twin beams disappeared and Iggy stood there, looking pleased with himself.

"Did—did you do it, Iggy?" said Measle, staring at the door, which hadn't moved at all.

"'*Coursssse* I did, Mumpsss," said Iggy. He strode across the cell, put his hands flat against the heavy iron door and pushed—and, silently, the door swung open on its oiled hinges. "Sssee? Now—'ave I got magic or 'aven't I? Eh? An' am I a proper Wraffmonk, or am I not? Huh? *Huh?*"

"Oh, you certainly *have* got magic, Iggy!" whispered Measle, with delight. "And you most certainly *are* a proper Wrathmonk, too!"

He carefully stuck his head out into the corridor. He looked down its length, toward the far end—and then his heart sank. He'd forgotten about the *other* iron door—the one that led to Officer Offal's office. That

272

door was sure to be locked as well—and, almost certainly, could be opened only from the other side.

For a moment it seemed to Measle that using Iggy's spell had accomplished nothing useful at all—they were still locked down tight in the detention center, with a heavy iron door and a heavy fat guard between them and freedom.

Measle started to use his brain to its fullest capacity. And then an idea came. It was, like so many of Measle's ideas in the past, a terribly risky idea—but it was the only thing he could come up with at the moment, and time was running out.

Measle hurried to Iggy's side and began to explain the idea. It took six explanations before he thought that Iggy might perhaps just about understand what they were going to do. So, just to be on the safe side, Measle explained the idea another three times and, at the end of it, Iggy nodded solemnly and said, "Right, Mumpsss. I got it."

I hope you do, Iggy, thought Measle. He turned to Tinker who, ever since he'd been woken by the sound of the wrathring clanging into the corner of the cell, had been watching the proceedings with some interest.

Tinker was doing his best to like the nasty little damp thingy, if only because the smelly kid seemed to get on with it all right. In fact, the smelly kid had been doing an awful lot of the talky-talky business, right in the nasty little damp thingy's ear—and the smelly kid didn't do that unless he *liked* doing it—so Tinker was doing his best not to show his teeth every time the nasty little damp thingy came near him.

"Tink! Sit! Sit and stay, Tink! *Stay!*"

Tinker knew what *sit and stay* meant. It meant, *don't move from this spot until the smelly kid says you can—but not for too long, mind, 'cause a little dog's only got so much patience. . . .*

Tinker sat down on the cell floor, his stubby tail flipping to and fro. He watched as Measle and Iggy backed slowly away, toward the open door. Then they were gone.

Measle and Iggy hurried down the corridor. Measle sensed movement in the cells as they passed. Out of the corner of his eye, he saw several Wrathmonks approach the glass walls of their cells and stare at them with wonder as they hurried by—Buford Cudgel's face twisted with fury and Judge Cedric's face screwed up into a look of deep bewilderment—but there was no time to linger, so Measle averted his eyes and hurried Iggy along, until they reached the heavy iron door that led to Officer Offal's office.

Very gently Measle tested the door. It was locked fast, as he guessed it would be. Standing close to the wall, Measle turned to Iggy and put one arm tight around the little Wrathmonk's skinny waist.

"Ready?" he whispered.

"Ready, Mumpsss."

"And you know what's going to happen, Iggy?"

"*Yesss*, Mumpsss! You told me a *sssquillion* times!"

"All right. Here we go."

Measle reached into his pocket and took out the bag of jelly beans. He poked around until he found one of the two remaining yellow ones. He took the yellow jelly bean between his finger and thumb and held it close to his mouth—

And then he waited.

It wasn't long before Tinker got bored of staying. He never could do it for very long before deciding that enough was enough.

It's a bit much, expecting a little dog just to sit here, for-ever and ever—and perhaps the smelly kid's gone and forgot-ten all about me, forgotten all about a poor little doggie, that's been sitting here for a hundred years at least—perhaps it's time to remind the smelly kid that I'm here. . . .

And Tinker—as Measle knew he eventually would—raised his nose in the air and started to howl at the top of his voice.

Measle clutched Iggy and waited. This was the one part of the plan that had a big element of doubt about it. What if the door was so thick that not even the loud-est sounds could get through it? What if Tinker decided to stop howling and simply left his post and came after them instead? What if . . .

A moment later his doubts vanished. There was a *clunk!* and the door beside him began to swing open—and, as it did so, Measle popped the jelly bean into his mouth and bit down hard on it.

He and Iggy vanished.

Iggy gasped and Measle could hear the sudden terror in the sound. Measle had explained to Iggy—nine times, in fact—exactly what would happen when he bit down on the jelly bean, but Iggy was easily frightened. Measle knew that terror like Iggy's could easily lead next to a loud, Iggy-type shriek—so Measle reached up and clamped an invisible hand over Iggy's invisible mouth.

The door swung wide and Officer Offal's heavy body stepped into view. Measle watched as Offal took in the long corridor, the open cell door at the far end, the howls coming from the open cell. . . .

"What the——?" muttered Offal. The big man set off at a shambling run toward the end of the corridor. Measle let him get about halfway down the passage— then he let go of Iggy and, pushing him toward the open door of the office, hissed, "Go, Iggy! *Go!*"

The moment Measle released Iggy, he reappeared. Iggy reacted with delight to the sight of his own hands materializing in front of his face—and then Measle's heart almost stopped beating, because Iggy wasn't going through the open door! Iggy was just standing there, staring down at himself.

"*Iggy!*" hissed Measle. "Don't just stand there! Go *on!*"

Iggy's skinny body jerked at the sound, and he seemed to remember what he was supposed to be doing, because he suddenly scuttled like a black spider through the open door and into Offal's office. The moment he had disappeared around the corner of the door, Measle began to sprint after Officer Offal. He ran as silently as he could, hoping that Tinker's howls would cover any sound he made. Officer Offal reached the open door of the cell and peered inside . . . Offal walked into the cell. . . .

Only a few more yards to go! Measle put on an extra burst of speed and reached the open door.

He threw himself against it as hard as he could and, immediately, the massive door began to swing on its oiled hinges. . . .

"Tink!" screamed Measle. "Tink! Come on, boy! Come on, Tink!"

The moment Tinker heard the urgent sounds coming from the smelly kid outside, he stopped howling. He jumped to his feet and darted—like a fuzzy white bullet—through the legs of the big man with the red face and fat belly, who had been staring at him with a look of utter bewilderment on his face. *Almost like he'd never seen a little howling doggie before. Well, excuse me, no time to explain, gotta dash—*

Tinker burst out of the cell just as Measle was closing the last few inches of the gap.

The door thudded against the frame and Measle turned his head and yelled, at the top of his voice, "Now, Iggy! *Now!*"

It should have worked. Iggy's job in this operation was such a simple one. All Iggy had to do was stand by the panel with the two big buttons and—when Measle shouted "Now, Iggy!"—push the green button with the number twenty painted on it.

But, in the short time between Iggy getting his orders and actually carrying them out, Iggy had forgotten what it was he was supposed to do. *Sssumfing about pushing buttons, wasn't it? Dere'sss two of dem 'ere—a black one and a green one.*

From down the corridor came Measle's panicking voice. "Iggy! Push the button! Push the *button!*"

All right, Mumpsss! I'll push it! De only fing is—which one?

And then Iggy, doing what only a small, confused and very silly little Wrathmonk would do, extended an index finger on each hand and pushed both the black and the green button at exactly the same moment.

17

SURROUNDED!

When Iggy pushed both buttons, the first thing that Measle heard was a wonderful sound—a heavy *thunk!*—as the electronically driven bolt in the door of cell number twenty slammed home into its slot.

Measle heaved a sigh of relief. It had worked! Officer Offal was securely locked into cell number twenty— and, in fact, Measle could see the big man staring toward the door with a puzzled look on his pink face. Measle watched through the glass wall as Offal marched to the door and gave it a great shove—but the door was locked fast and nothing short of another press on the green button back in the office was going to budge it.

Officer Offal stared furiously out through the glass wall, his pink eyes swiveling in every direction. At first all he could see was the little white dog—but then, like swirling gray smoke, the boy suddenly materialized on the other side of the wall. For a moment Offal could only gape—but then his fury overcame his wonder. He shook his fist, opened his mouth and—his voice muffled from behind the thick glass—he yelled, "Let me out, boy! You let me out this instant!"

And then Measle heard someone else.

"Well, well, well," said an oily voice from close behind Measle—an oily voice that wasn't muffled at all. "Ssso, we meet again, Massster Ssstubbs."

Measle whirled around.

There, only a few feet away, stood little, round, bald-as-a-billiard-ball Griswold Gristle. Griswold was smiling unpleasantly, showing his two sets of pointed yellow teeth. Measle saw that the door to Griswold's cell was wide open—

And beyond Griswold's cell, other doors were slowly swinging open and Wrathmonks—*lots* of

Wrathmonks—were cautiously stepping out into the corridor.

Measle felt himself rooted to the spot, unable to move and almost unable to breathe. *What's happened? How are they all getting out?*

Iggy! Iggy must have pressed both buttons!

"Cedric! Missster Cudgel! Missster Flabbit! *Do* come and sssee who's here!" Griswold's smile was even broader than before. He rubbed his podgy little hands together in glee.

The enormous figure of Buford Cudgel emerged from his cell. The huge Wrathmonk looked strange without his motorcycle helmet and his black leather jacket—and somehow, in his white prison clothes, appeared larger and even scarier than he had back at the Isle of Smiles.

Frognell Flabbit stuck his head out of his cell. He had lost a little more of his precious hair, and now his greasy comb-over looked even more ridiculous than before. Flabbit's face was still red and lumpy from Judge Cedric's old boil spell, and the redness was even worse because Flabbit had been scratching at the sore patches for a very long time—ever since he and his fellow Wrathmonks had been locked up in the detention center, in fact. Flabbit came out of the cell and strolled to Griswold's side.

"Well, well—look who it is," said Flabbit, smoothing his greasy hank of hair over his shiny head. "I've been hoping for thisss day, I don't mind telling you."

Buford Cudgel stood behind Flabbit and Griswold, towering over them both. His great fists were clenching and unclenching and a dark frown creased his narrow forehead.

"I should have sssquashed you before, boy—like a beetle," he rumbled, his voice like distant thunder. "Well, I shan't misss the opportunity again."

Griswold turned his round head and looked back over his shoulder.

"Cedric!" he called. "Cedric—come and sssee!"

The frizzy, white-haired head of Judge Cedric Hardscrabble poked nervously out of his cell. One hand was pressed against his jaw. He was obviously still in some pain from Flabbit's old toothache spell.

"What is it, Griswold?" he asked, his vacant eyes staring vaguely around the corridor. "Surely it'sss not yet time for our exercise?"

"Oh, but it is, Cedric!" said Griswold excitedly. "And sssuch exercise we shall have! Sssee—young Measle Ssstubbs is here, at our mercy—and oh what fun we shall have with him!"

Judge Cedric tottered up the corridor on his ancient legs, and when he got near enough, he stopped and peered shortsightedly at Measle.

"Goodnesss graciousss me!" he exclaimed. "It'sss that boy—but surely he was eaten by a dragon, wasn't he?"

"No, Cedric," said Griswold patiently. "He essscaped the dragon—more's the pity. However, thisss time, he won't essscape *usss*!" Griswold turned to Measle and said, quite loud enough for Judge Cedric to hear, "Poor Cedric! Ever sssince he's been in here, his memory has been getting worssse and worssse. And you are to blame for that, boy! You are to blame for all our misssfortunes! And now, we have you at our mercy! And thisss time, there is no father to protect you! And no mother to help your father! And no Nanny to ssstand between usss! Jussst *you*, Measle Ssstubbs—on whom to wreak our revenge! Jussst you—you and your beassstly little dog, I sssee!"

Griswold was staring down at a spot on the floor by Measle's feet. Measle looked down and saw Tinker standing at his side, all the wiry hair on his back sticking up in a line of bristles. Tinker's lips were curled back and he was showing all his teeth at the Wrathmonks, and the beginnings of a growl were starting deep down in his throat.

Measle instinctively bent down and scooped up Tinker into his protective arms. As he did so, Measle felt a small pressure in one of his pockets—the action of bending and lifting pressed a lumpy object against his thigh. . . .

The jelly beans!

"Ssso, young Measle Ssstubbs!" Griswold Gristle exclaimed cheerfully. "How shall we ssstart to wreak our revenge, eh? Both Missster Cudgel's and my exhalation enchantmentsss end in ghassstly death, ssso we shall sssave them for later—but to whom of my other colleagues shall go the honor of ssstarting, eh? Shall we let Judge Cedric give you sssome horrible, painful boils? Or shall we have Missster Flabbit breathe his agonizing toothache onto you? Either way, it will be mossst entertaining for all the ressst of usss!"

Griswold made a sweeping gesture and Measle saw that a small crowd of curious Wrathmonks had now gathered behind his four arch enemies. They were all peering over the shoulders of Griswold Gristle, Frognell Flabbit and Judge Cedric Hardscrabble—but they were all peering around the *sides* of Buford Cudgel, whose shoulders were far too high to peer over.

"Fellow Wrathmonks!" shouted Griswold in his squeaky, oily little voice. "Thisss horrid boy is the ssson of the notoriousss Wrathmonk hunter, Sssam Ssstubbs! Sssam Ssstubbs, of the infamousss Ssstubbs family!"

There was a sudden hissing from the collected Wrathmonks as they all spoke the name of Sam Stubbs. Measle could hear the hatred in their voices.

Griswold Gristle held up his fat little hands. "And that's not all, fellow Wrathmonks! Thisss Ssstubbs child was the one resssponsssible for capturing mysssself and my friends! It was through his actions that we were brought to thisss terrible place! It was he who . . ."

Griswold trailed off, because he became aware that this latest piece of news was being greeted by some among the crowd of Wrathmonks as something of a joke.

"Aaah, poor old Grissstle!" called out a young, skinny Wrathmonk at the front of the crowd. He had bright ginger hair and pointed ears that stuck out of his head like jug handles. "Did 'e get 'imssself caught by an itty-bitty kiddy-wink, then?"

Buford Cudgel turned his massive head and glowered down at the young Wrathmonk. "Shut your ssstupid mouth," he growled, and instantly the young Wrathmonk shrank away from him, a look of pure terror on his face. Every Wrathmonk eye turned toward the two, eager to see a fight.

It was in that moment that Measle saw his opportunity. He dived his free hand into his pocket and into the plastic bag, closing his fingers around as many jelly beans as he could hold. Quickly he pulled his fist back out of his pocket and darted a glance down at it. There were about twenty jelly beans in the palm of his hand—

And not a single yellow one among them.

"What'sss that you have there, dear boy?" said Griswold, who had turned back just in time to see a look of despair cross Measle's face.

"Nothing," muttered Measle, closing his fist around

the useless jelly beans.

"Oh, I don't think it'sss nothing, dear boy," said Griswold. "And we've had thisss sssort of trouble with you before, haven't we? Hiding little magical things on your perssson? Oh yesss—Missster Cudgel, kindly show usss what is in the boy's hand!"

Buford Cudgel turned away from the frightened young Wrathmonk and lurched like a small mountain toward Measle.

"Open your hand, boy," he rumbled.

Measle thought fast. There was only one thing he could think of and he wasn't at all sure that it would work, but it was the only chance he had.

"Anybody like a jelly bean?" he said loudly and cheerfully, as if they were all at a party and he was the host, offering his guests a slice of cake. At the same time, he brought his hand up and threw the handful of jelly beans as hard as he could, over the heads of the crowd of Wrathmonks. He even managed to get the jelly beans to sail over Buford Cudgel's head—and Buford Cudgel's head almost scraped the ceiling.

The effect was immediate.

Measle knew quite a lot about Wrathmonks—after

288

all, he'd lived with his horrible old Wrathmonk guardian, Basil Tramplebone, for several years. One of the things he knew about Wrathmonks was that they liked sweet things; when Basil played with his train set up in the attic of the horrible house, he always used to eat a plateful of glazed doughnuts and drink a whole jug of pink lemonade while he was doing it. And Iggy had almost eaten his way through the whole bag of jelly beans.

The other thing Measle knew about Wrathmonks was that, on the whole, they weren't very bright.

The head of every Wrathmonk—including those of Gristle, Flabbit, Judge Cedric, and Cudgel—turned to watch the little brightly colored ovals as they landed— and then scattered—across the stone floor behind them.

"Oooh! Sssweeties! Lovely sssweeeeties!" screamed the Wrathmonks—and even Griswold Gristle took a couple of steps toward the mob, who were now scrabbling about on the floor and grabbing every jelly bean they could find and stuffing them into their mouths.

Measle reached back into his pocket and pulled out the plastic bag. There weren't many jelly beans left now, but there—nestled among them—was the single remaining yellow one! Measle poured all the jelly beans into his open palm and then plucked out the yellow one. He threw the rest into the scrambling mob.

Griswold Gristle—whose brain was a little sharper than others of his kind—turned back toward Measle just in time to have his suspicions confirmed. *Why is he throwing sssweets all over the place? The boy is up to sssomething!*

Measle popped the yellow bean into his mouth. He bit down on it, tasting the familiar sugary lemon taste—

"Aaaaarrrgh!" screamed Griswold, his piggy little eyes swiveling around madly. "He has gone! The boy has gone! But he is ssstill here! Quickly, all of you—feel for him! *Feel* for him!"

Griswold, Cudgel and Flabbit immediately stretched out their arms and started to feel the air with their fingers. Judge Cedric, with a look of extreme puzzlement on his face, started patting his own body, as if Measle might perhaps be in one of his pockets. But the rest of the Wrathmonks were still too busy gathering up the scattered jelly beans to take any notice of a fat little Wrathmonk who was screaming about a boy disappearing into thin air—*as if a human boy could do that!*

It wasn't just Measle's brain that was quick. His legs could go pretty fast, too. He tucked his head down and, clutching tightly to an invisible Tinker, started to scurry down the corridor, toward the open door that led to Offal's office. He darted around Flabbit, ducked under Cudgel's waving, searching fingers—each one was the size of a banana!—and slipped past Judge Cedric as if he was made of smoke.

The corridor ahead was clear, apart from a couple of Wrathmonks still grubbing about on their knees. Measle jumped over them, like a hurdler in a race. Behind him, he could hear Griswold's impassioned screams.

"You fools! Don't let him get away again! *Don't let him get away again!*"

And then Measle was through the doorway—and there was Iggy, still staring at the two buttons on the panel and looking a little bewildered. Measle had never been so glad to see a Wrathmonk in his entire life.

But there was no time for reunions. Any second now Griswold and the others would guess that Measle was now safely past their searching hands and inside Offal's office. . . .

Measle looked back over his shoulder and saw, to his horror, that Buford Cudgel was charging, head down like a rhinoceros, at full speed toward him. Measle threw a quick glance at his hands—or where his hands would have been, if they hadn't been invisible. *No, he still can't see me—but he can see this open door! I've got to get it shut!*

Measle put his shoulder against the massive door and shoved as hard as he could, and the great iron door swung smoothly on its oiled hinges and slammed shut. There was an audible click as the latch fell into place— then, a moment later, a thunderous *thump*! against the outer surface of the door as the full weight of Buford Cudgel slammed against it. Measle felt the door shudder under the impact, but even Buford Cudgel's great mass could never break through a door like this.

"Dat door jussst closed all by itssself," muttered Iggy to himself. "And den dere was a big bump! And where is Mumpsss? And de little dog? Where is dey, I wonder?"

"Here I am, Iggy," said Measle, watching his fingers change from wispy gray smoke to their usual, solid pinkness (although, by now—what with all his adventures in the last few hours, his hands were pretty dirty). "We're both here."

Iggy blinked a couple of times and then stared in fascination as Measle and Tinker solidified in front of him. Then Iggy seemed to forget all about the wonder of the magic, because he said, "I pushed de buttons, Mumpsss! I pushed dem like you told me—and I sssaved you! I sssaved you—again!"

"Yes, Iggy, you did," said Measle. He put Tinker down on the floor. "And thank you very much—again."

"Dat'sss all right, Mumpsss," said Iggy grandly. "Any time."

What to do now? thought Measle, listening with half an ear to the steady thumping sounds against the door. Obviously Buford Cudgel wasn't going to give up that easily. *Meanwhile, where to go? How to get Matilda back from the Warlocks? How to get out of this castle? How to get back to the city and find Mum and Dad—*

And then something occurred to Measle that he hadn't thought of before. If all the Wrathmonks who'd

been caught were imprisoned here in Caltrop Castle—
was it possible that his mum and dad were imprisoned
here, too?

There was only one way to find out.

Measle went to the desk and sat down in the swivel
chair. He reached forward and pulled the big silver
microphone toward him. He looked down at the intercom panel next to it—there was a row of switches,
numbered one to twenty. Measle flipped the switch
with the number twenty.

He listened.

There was the sound of heavy breathing.

"Officer Offal?" said Measle into the microphone.

"What? Who's that?" Officer Offal's voice sounded
tinny and distant, coming out of the intercom loud
speaker.

"It's me, Officer Offal. Measle Stubbs."

There was a long pause. All Measle could hear was
the sound of Offal's lungs, going like a pair of wheezy
old bellows.

"You're in a lot of trouble, young feller. A *lot* of trouble! Best thing you can do is go and tell the gentle-
men—and the lady—who brought you down here

what you've gone and done. It's very *bad*, what you've gone and done, see? But, if you make a clean breast of it, young feller—maybe they won't be too angry, eh? What do you say, eh?"

Measle felt a little strange. He'd never had a grown-up in his power before—not *completely* in his power, like Officer Offal was right now. Half the feeling was exciting; the other half was frightening. But this wasn't the moment to be frightened.

"Do you know where my mum and dad are, Officer Offal?"

There was another pause, filled with Offal's breathing. Then the gruff voice came again. "Never you mind about that, boy. You just go and—"

"No. Not until you tell me if you know where they are."

"Now look 'ere, boy—"

"Do you know where my mum and dad and sister are?"

"Yes, I do, boy—but I'm not going to tell you! Now don't make things worse for yourself, eh? Just go and get—"

Measle leaned close to the microphone and spoke into it. He spoke very slowly, carefully picking out each syllable, so that there would be no doubt at all in Officer Offal's mind that he meant every word.

"Officer Offal, if you don't tell me where my mum and dad are, I'm going to push the green button."

This time the pause went on for a very long time—and Officer Offal's breathing was twice as heavy as before. To Measle's ears, it sounded a little—well, a little *nervous*.

Then—

"Now—you don't want to go and do a thing like that, young feller," said Officer Offal's tinny voice. There was a tone of great friendliness in his voice, of great reasonableness—but also a faint trace of trembling. . . .

Officer Offal was *scared*.

Measle leaned into the microphone again and whispered, "Officer Offal—when I've finished talking to you, I'm going to get up and go over to the door and I'm going to push the green button. And then the door to cell number twenty is going to open. That's *your* cell, Officer Offal. The only trouble is, all the Wrathmonks are out of *their* cells—you can probably see them, can't you? And they don't like you, do they, Officer Offal?

And you won't be able to stop them getting at you, will you? Now, I'm going to ask you again—where's my dad and my mum?"

The breathing was now very heavy—but Officer Offal said nothing.

"All right, then," said Measle. "I'm getting up now—"

Measle pushed with his legs, making the feet of the swivel chair scrape loudly against the stone floor of the office—and instantly, the intercom burst out with sound. A very panicky, pleading sound.

"All right, all right! No need for that, young feller! I'll tell you! *I'll tell you!* Just don't you go near that green button, all right?"

Wow! thought Measle. *The Wrathmonks must really hate Officer Offal!*

"They're in the next section but one, young feller, second door on the left. They're in high security."

Measle's heart jumped into his throat. *They're just around the corner!*

"Is there another guard there, Officer Offal?"

"No—I'm in charge of everything down 'ere, young feller. Now then, seeing as how I've told you what you wanted to know—how about getting me out of here, eh?

I mean—without touching that green button, of course!"

But Measle never heard those last words from Officer Offal, because the moment Offal had said the word "No," Measle had whistled once at Tinker, grabbed Iggy by the arm and had run out of the office.

Measle heaved open the second door off the circular hall and ran into an office that seemed almost identical to the one they had just left. Another steel desk, another row of filing cabinets, another silver microphone with an intercom next to it. The only difference in this office was the panel by the inner door. There were only four numbered buttons on this panel—and all were colored a bright, fire-alarm red.

Measle's first instinct was to run to the inner door, yank it open and then press all those four red buttons, releasing—

Releasing what? Perhaps his mum and dad and sister weren't here at all. Perhaps it had been a trick on Officer Offal's part? Well, there was one way to find out.

Measle hurried to the desk, leaned toward the microphone and flipped the first switch.

"Mum? Dad? Are you there?"

There was nothing but a faint electronic hiss of static from the intercom. Measle was about to try another switch, when he heard a faint and horrible throaty, choking, gurgling sound—as if somebody was being sick, a long way away.

Measle didn't like the sound at all. There was something very *different* about it, as if it was coming from something not at all human—in fact, something terribly, terribly alien.

Measle hurriedly let go of the switch and tried the second one.

"Mum? Dad?"

This time, there was no silence, no pause. . . .

"Measle?" came the voice of his mother from the intercom. "Measle—is that you?"

"Yes, Mum—it's me!"

"But—but where are you, darling?"

"I'm right here, Mum! I'm in the office! I'm going to let you out!"

"Oh, Measle—we've been so worried about you! And now you're safe! Oh, thank goodness!"

"Where's Dad, Mum?"

"Dad's in the third cell. Now, darling—can you get us out?"

"All right, Mum—I'm going to open all the doors now—"

Lee's voice changed suddenly. It changed from a sort of joyful astonishment at hearing that Measle was safe and coming to the rescue, to a sudden, panic-stricken scream.

"No, Measle! Don't open all the doors! NO!"

18

MEASLE
AT LARGE

But—"

Lee took charge of her terror and managed to bring her voice back under control, because the next thing Measle heard was his mother, saying calmly but very firmly, "Measle, my darling, be very, *very* careful. Whatever you do, don't open the door of the first cell. Understand? Not cell number one, whatever you do. If you open the door to cell number one, *you might kill us all*. Only open number two and number three, and please, *please*—don't touch the button that opens number one. Understand, darling?"

Measle said, "Right, Mum—I've got it. Not number one. Okay—hang on a sec."

Measle left the desk and crossed over to the panel by the inner door. Very carefully avoiding the button marked one, he pressed the buttons marked two and three. Then he grasped the big iron lever on the door and twisted it, and the door clicked open. Measle heaved and it swung wide. He stepped into a short, dark corridor. There were no glass walls here, just solid stonework, with four massive ironwood doors set into its surface. Two of the doors were open wide—

A pair of arms suddenly threw themselves around his neck and he felt himself being pressed against something warm and soft and very familiar. Measle looked up at his mother's face and saw tears streaming down her cheeks, but she was smiling and laughing at the same time—despite the dull silver ring around her neck.

A moment later another pair of arms was around him as well, and *these* arms were hard and strong and were hugging him with enormous power. Measle looked sideways and saw his father, his face a little pale and a little drawn, beaming down at him—and Sam too had a dull silver ring around his neck.

Then a very small pair of arms went around Measle's right leg and clutched him fiercely and Measle looked down—and there was Matilda sitting at his feet and grinning up at him and showing off all her six teeth—and around her chubby little neck was yet another silver ring.

"Are all dese people 'urtin' you, Mumpsss?" said Iggy, peering anxiously around the doorframe. "And, if dey are—do you want me to ressscue you—*again?*"

Measle's reply was a little muffled, because both his parents had their arms wrapped so tightly around him that he was having a slight difficulty in breathing—but he managed to gasp out, "No, Iggy—look, it's my mum and dad! And Tilly, too!"

Iggy came slowly into the corridor. When he saw Matilda sitting on the floor, a great beaming smile split his face in two. And when Matilda caught sight of Iggy, she stopped hugging Measle's leg and held out her arms in Iggy's direction and started to kick her legs furiously against the stone floor.

"Cubba doogy *wump!*" she yelled, and Iggy darted

forward and scooped Matilda off the floor and into his arms.

"Where you bin, den, you naughty fing, you?" he crooned into Matilda's face.

Matilda wrinkled her nose at the smell of Iggy's breath and waved her hands to make it go away—but this time, the nasty smell didn't to go away at all. Then Matilda tried to change Iggy's teeth—but they stayed as yellow as ever. So Matilda gave up trying to do her special things—because obviously they weren't going to work this time—and played with Iggy's wet hair instead.

Measle felt his father's arms drop away from him. Then Sam said, "I don't believe it! Mr. Niggle? Is that you?"

When Iggy recognized Sam, he became so excited that he could hardly speak. All he could do was cling tightly to Matilda and dance about on the spot and grin so widely that all of his pointed yellow teeth were exposed.

"Ricky-b-b-bended leaningsssea!" he stuttered. "You ricky-b-b-bended leaningsssea!"

"I did, didn't I?" said Sam, smiling a little uncertainly

at the Wrathmonk. "And I just hope I was right to do so."

Lee stepped forward, a worried look on her face. She said, "But I'm afraid I don't trust you with my daughter, Mr. Niggle. Please give her back immediately."

Measle grabbed his mother's hand. "It's all right, Mum," he said. "Iggy's been carrying her everywhere. They're friends. Tilly really likes him—see what she's doing to his hair? And Iggy's rescued us lots of times, Dad—really he has!"

Sam looked a little dubious at this. He leaned down and whispered into Measle's ear. "I didn't think he was all that bright, son. Are you sure it wasn't the other way around?"

"Well—mostly yes, Dad," whispered Measle back into his father's ear. "But once he really did rescue me. He pulled my hair and it hurt really bad but that didn't matter because the suit of armor was about to grab me and he pulled me up so it couldn't reach me anymore—"

"Don't you know it's rude to *whipssser?*" said Iggy, who had got over his initial excitement and was now looking at them all with a slightly hurt expression on his thin little face.

"I'm so sorry, Mr. Niggle," said Sam, straightening up. "Measle was telling me all about how very helpful you've been to him and to Matilda and I'd like to say a very big thank you."

"Oh," said Iggy, his face brightening. "All right. Go on den."

"Go on?" said Sam. "Go on—what?"

"Sssay a very big fank you."

"Thank you, Mr. Niggle," said Sam. He stepped forward and shook Iggy's hand. "Thank you very much indeed. Now—perhaps you'd like to give Matilda back to us?"

Reluctantly Iggy held Matilda out to Sam, but Matilda, sensing what was about to happen—and determined not to be wrenched away from her wet friend again—screamed "Cubba doogy *wump!*" and wrapped her arms tightly around Iggy's scrawny neck.

Sam smiled a little ruefully and said, "Or—er—or you can hang onto her if you like, Mr. Niggle."

Iggy nodded seriously and tightened his grip on Matilda—and Sam and Lee glanced at each other and, smiling, shrugged their shoulders.

Measle pointed at Matilda's wrathring and said, "When did Tilly get that ring put on her?"

"I don't know, darling," said Lee. "Wasn't it on her all the time?"

"No, Mum. It's new."

"Oh. Well, all I know is that my cell door opened a few minutes ago and Toby Jugg was there. I couldn't believe it! He had Tilly in his arms. He handed her to me and she had the wrathring on then."

"Did he say anything, Mum?"

"Well, it was rather odd, darling. He smiled in a really weird and nasty sort of way and then he said, 'A little present for you, Lee. The first of many, I hope.' Then, before I could say anything, he slammed the door and went away. I didn't care—I was just so happy to see Tilly. And then, a few minutes later, here you are, too! It's like a sort of miracle."

Lee broke off because, suddenly, something thudded against the closed door of cell number one. It was a soft, squelchy sort of thud, as if somebody had thrown a sack full of jelly against the door. A very large sack of jelly—

At the same moment, a wisp of what looked like yellow smoke drifted out from under the door—and a dreadful, disgusting, revolting stink seeped out into the corridor. It was so strong that it made them all choke—even Iggy, who Measle thought should be quite used to that sort of thing.

"Let's get out of here," muttered Sam, holding his hand against his nose.

They hurried back into the outer office and Sam closed the heavy door with a clang.

"Wh-what is that thing?" asked Measle nervously.

"Some sort of manifestation," said Sam. "They say it was conjured up by a crazy Warlock many, many years ago. Apart from that, all we know about it is that it's horribly dangerous. That's why it can never be let out of here. Speaking of which, how did you get in here?"

For the next ten minutes, Measle told them everything that had happened to him and Matilda and Tinker ever since Toby Jugg had brought them to Caltrop Castle. Because Iggy was right next to him, Measle exaggerated just a little when he described Iggy's part in the adventure, making out the little Wrathmonk to be more of a hero than he really was—and Iggy listened to the story with rapt attention, as if he was hearing about the events for the very first time. When Measle finished, there was a long silence. Then Sam said, "Right," and Measle saw that his father's face was dark with anger.

"First things first," said Sam. "Mr. Niggle, do you think you could let go of my daughter for a moment and get us out of these wrathrings?"

Iggy was so eager to do something—anything!—for Sam that he happily handed Matilda over to Lee and rushed to Sam's side, pulling the brush section away from the toothbrush handle as he did so. Sam shook his head.

"My wife first please, Mr. Niggle."

Iggy dealt quickly with Lee's wrathring. It took only a few seconds before the two halves clicked apart. Lee ripped it off her neck and threw it into a corner of the office.

"That's wonderful, Mr. Niggle!" cried Lee, and Sam said, "What a talent!"

A few more quick twists of the toothbrush handle, and Matilda's wrathring fell away from around her neck and clattered to the floor.

Measle picked it up and stared at the thing.

"Why are they so easy to open, Dad?" said Measle, wondering (not for the first time) why such an effective magical device seemed to be so easy to break open.

"I guess it's because they're anti-magic, Measle," said Sam. "They neutralize any magic their wearers try to conjure. So the locks *themselves* can't be magical—they wouldn't work, you see. The lock part *has* to be mechanical. And we Wizards aren't all that good at making mechanical objects. So, for somebody as good at picking locks as Mr. Niggle, they don't present much of a problem."

Iggy came shyly up to Sam, who tilted his head back to let Iggy work. Iggy carefully pushed the spike into the keyhole, turned the toothbrush handle this way, then that—he wiggled it—turned it again backward and forward—

"Sssumfing's wrong," he muttered.

"Try pressing the button, Iggy," said Measle. "That worked for me."

Iggy pressed the button on the handle and the toothbrush began to buzz in his hand. Iggy gritted his teeth and went back to work—twisting, wiggling, twisting again—

Nothing happened.

"Dere's sssumfing wrong wiv de lock," announced Iggy, pulling the spike out of the keyhole and turning off the toothbrush's vibrations. "Sssomebody's been messsin' about wiv it. It'sss all jammed up inssside."

"That was probably me, Mr. Niggle," said Sam. "I've been pulling on it with all my strength—maybe I've damaged it."

Iggy put a look on his face that reminded Measle of the expression that one of his teachers at school had used when she'd caught him passing a note to a friend.

"Dat wasn't very clever, Missster Ssstubbs, sssir," he said disapprovingly. "You've broked it—and dat means I can't open it!"

"Hmm," said Sam thoughtfully. "That gives us a bit of a problem, doesn't it? If I can't use my magic—"

"We won't be able to get out of here!" blurted Measle. "How are we going to get past the guards—or the Warlocks?"

"A hacksaw, that's what we need," said Sam. "I've got a terrific one back at home."

"But how are we going to *get* home, Dad?" said Measle. "It's miles away! And how are we going to get out of *here* in the first place?"

Measle's voice trailed away. He felt very small and

very useless. The last time he'd felt as small and as useless as this was back on the tabletop of the great train set in Basil Tramplebone's attic, when Basil had shrunk him down to the size of a paper clip.

But even now that he was his full size, he was still too small to do much about protecting them all. If only he was as big and powerful as his dad, then he could really do something! But Sam himself couldn't do much at the moment, not with that wrathring stuck around his neck.

What they needed right now—to get them out of this place—was something so big and powerful, that even guards and Warlocks might think twice about interfering with it.

Then, with a sort of thud, a new idea popped into Measle's mind. Like so many of Measle's ideas, it was pretty wild and crazy—but it was the only one he could think of.

Measle went to Matilda and put his face close to his sister's.

"Tilly!" he whispered, putting a sort of fun and excited tone into his voice. "Tilly—make me big, Tilly! Make me really, *really* big, Tilly!"

Matilda listened with interest. She'd always wanted a big brother. Measle was wonderful and fantastic and brilliant and funny and handsome—Matilda especially loved his sticky-up hair—but there was no way he could be described as big. Measle was small and rather skinny and not particularly strong. . . .

And now he was saying he wanted to be big.

Well, that was easy.

Matilda waved her hands.

And for Measle, quite suddenly, everything around him got smaller.

Sam and Lee and Iggy and Matilda and Tinker all seemed to be moving away from him, moving *downward*, in fact—as if Measle was in an elevator and the elevator was going swiftly *upward*—

Measle looked around him. The office was shrinking, the floor was getting farther away, the walls diminishing, the desk becoming the size of a matchbox. . . .

Measle felt his head brush against the ceiling.

"All right, Tilly," said Measle. "That's enough now."

"Grubble?" said Matilda, smiling up at the giant in front of her.

"Yes, Tilly! Grubble!"

Matilda stared up at Measle, admiring her handiwork. She wasn't at all sure that she was going to "grubble." Perhaps he ought to be just a bit bigger. . . .

Measle's head was now being bent sideways by the ceiling and he could feel his shoulders pressing against one of the fluorescent lamps.

"Ow, Tilly! That hurts!"

Matilda saw that her really, *really* big brother was getting squashed—and it was all because the room wasn't big enough. Well, that was easy to change—

Matilda waved her arms and the room got bigger. Much, much bigger. And Measle got bigger with it. Up and up and up he grew, his head getting farther and farther away from the floor, but no closer to the ceiling because the ceiling grew taller with him. Now Measle was four yards tall, then five yards, then six yards, seven, eight . . .

"All right, Tilly! Stop it! Stop it right now!"

Measle's voice was just a little bit fierce, so Matilda decided that she'd done enough. She waved her chubby fists and, instantly, Measle felt the upward movement of his head come to a halt. He looked down at his tiny family, clustered around his feet. They looked no bigger than plastic action figures.

"Good girl, Tilly," he said, his enormous voice booming around the office. Matilda hardly heard him. She was already dropping into a deep sleep, her head sinking down onto Lee's shoulder.

"Interesting," said Sam, edging carefully away from Measle's enormous sneakered foot. "But what was the point of it, son?"

"I thought—well, in case we meet some guards, Dad," said Measle lamely.

"Yes, fine," said Sam. "But what if we meet some *Warlocks*, eh? You could be the size of Mount Everest and it wouldn't do you any good. Not against them— and I can't help you at the moment."

Measle looked down at his tiny father. Sam's head now came to just above Measle's ankle. Sam was doing what he always did when he was thinking hard about something—he was frowning and tapping the front of his teeth with the nail of his index finger. Lee was staring up at her giant son with wonder, and Tinker was busy sniffing curiously at Measle's left foot and making up his mind that, since this mountain in front of him *smelled* like the smelly kid, then that's what this mountain *was*: just the smelly kid and therefore nothing to worry about.

Sam seemed to come to some sort of decision because suddenly he stopped tapping his teeth. He looked up at Measle and said, "Well, under the circumstances, Measle, I think it's probably the best idea any of us could have had. Well done. At least it'll give them something to think about, won't it?"

"I hope so, Dad," said Measle. Then a thought occurred to him. "One other thing, Dad—Tilly's spells don't last very long. I'm only going to be this size for a few minutes, so we ought to get going. The only trouble is, I don't know the way."

"I do," said Sam firmly. He pointed to the office door and said, "Do you think you can squeeze through the door to the hall out there?"

"I think so," said Measle, wondering how, exactly, Sam could be so sure about knowing the way out of the labyrinth that was Caltrop Castle.

Measle shuffled his enormous body around, lay down flat on the floor and started to edge through the doorway. He had to turn his shoulders sideways to wriggle through the opening, and when he got as far as his hips it suddenly became a very tight squeeze indeed—but he worked the rest of his body through the opening inch by inch until—with a *pop!*—all of him was at last in the outer hall.

He felt something in his hand—a little circle of metal. He looked down and saw Matilda's wrathring nestled in his palm. It was big enough to have been fastened around Matilda's neck, but now it looked tiny.

Small enough to fit around his little finger.

Measle sat up. A moment later Sam, Lee, Iggy, Matilda and Tinker came out of the office and joined him in the circular hallway.

"Well done, son," said Sam. "Now then—let's get out of here, shall we? Squeeze yourself through that next door and I think you'll be fine after that. Once we're clear of the detention center, the rest of this section has fairly high ceilings and it shouldn't be too much of a squash for you."

Measle lay down and wriggled his body through the outer door. Once on the other side, he found he was able to stand up. His head brushed the high ceiling and the walls of the corridor came uncomfortably close to his sides—but there was just enough room to move if he was careful.

"Right, let's be off," said Sam. Then he appeared to

get an idea, because his face brightened and he grinned widely.

"Put us in your pockets, Measle," he said. "You can move a lot faster than we can and it'll save time. Mum and I up front, so I can tell you which way to go. Perhaps Mr. Niggle won't mind being in one of the side pockets—and Tilly and Tinker can go in the other. Quickly now!"

Very carefully Measle picked up the members of his family and distributed them in his jacket pockets. He put Sam and Lee in his top pocket, which was shallow enough to allow their heads to poke out of the top. He slipped Matilda and Tinker into one side pocket. Matilda was fast asleep now and Measle knew that nothing short of an earthquake would wake her for a long while. Once Tinker found himself in the warm darkness of the pocket, he curled up next to Matilda and went to sleep himself.

Iggy, alone in the other pocket, initially felt a bit resentful that the little doggie had got Matilda for company and not him. But he soon forgot all about that because, for a start, there was no room for his rain cloud in there, so Iggy was warm and dry for the first time in ages—but even better was the thing that Iggy found in there—a red jelly bean. It had slipped out of the plastic bag during one of Measle's fumblings. The jelly bean was now the size of Iggy's head and Iggy forgot all about everything that might be happening outside the pocket and settled down in the warm darkness of the pocket to eat his way through the enormous thing.

"Perfect!" said Sam, leaning forward against the front of Measle's top pocket, like the captain of a destroyer leaning on the bridge of his ship. "Thattaway."

19

FREEDOM!

This, thought Measle, *is fun!*

The long staircase, which had taken him and the Warlocks a good two minutes to walk down, he climbed in a mere five giant steps. Next came the series of paneled corridors—they were tall and wide and Measle only had to duck his head a little bit to avoid bumping against the ceiling. Each corridor took only four or five of Measle's huge paces before he was at the end of it. Sam called out directions as they went along—"Left! Now right! Left again!"—and quite soon

Measle realized that they were approaching the double doors to the great room where he'd been caught by the Warlocks. Instinctively he slowed down.

"What's up, son?" said Sam, staring up at Measle from the top of the pocket.

"That's where the Warlocks found me," said Measle quietly. "They might be in there now."

"So—they're using the grand salon, are they?" said Sam, equally quietly.

This took Measle by surprise. *How does Dad know so much about Caltrop Castle? How does he know his way around the place?*

"How do you know about that room, Dad?" whispered Measle.

"I know a lot about this place, Measle," muttered Sam. "You'd be surprised. Come on, let's get past those doors. Quiet as we can, everybody—we don't want to meet any Warlocks right now, not while I'm helpless."

Measle moved forward as cautiously and as quietly as his enormous bulk would allow. *It's lucky,* he thought, *that the floor here is stone. If it had been wooden floorboards, they'd have been sure to creak under my tremendous weight.*

Then, quite without warning, Iggy stuck his head

out of Measle's pocket. His lips were smeared with red sugar. He cupped both hands around his mouth and yelled up at Measle at the top of his voice.

"OY! MUMPSSS! I CHANGED MY MIND, MUMPSSS! I DON'T LIKE DE YELLOW ONES BESSST NO MORE! I LIKE DE *RED* ONES BESSST NOW! GOT ANY MORE RED SSSWEETIES, MUMPSSS?"

For a small and skinny Wrathmonk, Iggy's voice was extraordinarily loud. It echoed around the stone corridor, bouncing off the walls and the floor and the ceiling, with the effect that, to Measle's ears, it sounded louder than it really was.

"Shhh, Iggy!" hissed Measle. He put his finger on top of Iggy's tiny head and tried gently to push him back down into his pocket, but Iggy was having none of it.

"OY! DON'T PUSH, MUMPSSS! I'VE 'AD ENOUGH PUSHIN' TODAY, FANKSSS VERY MUCH! NOW DEN, 'AVE YOU OR 'AVE YOU NOT GOT ANY MORE OF DOSE RED SSSWEETIES?"

Any hope that Iggy's voice *hadn't* penetrated into the grand salon suddenly disappeared, because the two great double doors were flung wide, revealing, to

322

Measle's horrified eyes, the figures of Toby Jugg, Tully Telford, Ermintrude Bacon, Dorian Fescue, Quentin Underwood and Sir Peregrine Spine.

The six Warlocks stood in the open doorway, their jaws gaping with astonishment—and a certain amount of fear as well. For several seconds nothing happened and nothing was said. Then Toby Jugg recovered himself. He stepped forward and stared up at Measle with a puzzled smile on his rugged face.

"Well, well, Measle old son," he said. "Look at you! Now, how on earth did you manage that, eh?"

Measle didn't reply. He simply stared down at Toby, with what he hoped was a fierce, grim look on his face. He didn't know how successful he was—when you're twelve years old, it's pretty hard to look really grim and really fierce when faced with a brawny grown-up who also happens to be a very powerful Warlock—and, somehow, the fact that Measle was about eight yards tall and was towering over Toby and the other Warlocks like a tidal wave didn't seem to make all that much of a difference right now.

"See what I mean?" said Toby, turning his head and looking back at the rest of the Warlocks who were clustered behind him in the doorway. "See what I mean about this boy? Brave and resourceful and imaginative! And now, somehow, he's grown to the height of a decent-sized tree! A worthy enemy indeed!"

Toby turned back to Measle and stared up at him, and Measle thought he detected a slight look of admiration in Toby's expression.

"I'm not going to ask you how you did this, old son," said Toby. "There'll be plenty of time for that later. I'm also not going to ask how you got out of the detention center, when nobody and nothing has ever managed to do that before. But you obviously did and I congratulate you. However, right now we must stop all this nonsense, you know. We need to cut you back down to size and put you somewhere secure—somewhere obviously a bit more secure than the detention center, I think. So, I'm going to use a spell on you—a simple diminishing spell, which will reduce you to a more manageable size. Now don't worry, this won't hurt—"

Toby broke off, because he suddenly caught sight of Sam's and Lee's heads, sticking out of Measle's top pocket. A look of fear flooded Toby's face and he took a hurried step backward.

"Oh—hello Sam, old chap," he said, smiling warily up at them. "And there's the lovely Lee, too! What a pleasure to see you both!"

"Hello, Toby," said Sam quietly. "I won't say it's a pleasure to see *you*." There was an edge of steel in Sam's voice. To Measle, his dad sounded very, very dangerous.

Toby's eyes narrowed and he squinted up at Sam.

"Ah—I see you still have your wrathring on, old man," he said, his voice relaxing and a cunning grin appearing on his face. "Now that's interesting. Sam Stubbs, with no magic. You know, old man—with all due respect, you're not much of a Wizard at the best of times. In fact, without your lovely Lee, you're a bit of a nothing, aren't you? A few minor defensive spells is pretty much all you're good for—and, with a wrathring around your neck, you're not even good for *them*, are you? Poor old Sam—now I come to think of it, you really are the least admirable of the Stubbs family. The lovely Lee is magnificent and I have some very interesting plans for her. The baby Mallockee is a fascinating creature. And, as for young Measle, well I think he's probably the best of the sorry bunch. But making him this ridiculous size! It won't help you, I'm afraid. Not without your magic to protect you, Sam. Now then, let's put a stop to this nonsense, shall we?"

Toby pointed his finger straight up at Measle and shouted, *"Reductiornus bekswakwee sagaftra!"* Instantly, twin beams of light—beams of light that appeared, to Measle's horrified eyes, to be *black (But how can light be black?)*—sizzled out from Toby's eyes and up toward Measle's head.

Instinctively Measle threw up his hand to ward off the spell—and, even as he did so, he was thinking, *This won't do any good, you can't stop a spell just by putting your hand in front of it.*

And yet—

And yet—

That was *exactly* what happened.

The twin beams of dark light splashed against Measle's hand like two jets of black water. Where they hit, they exploded outward in two rippling circles of darkness; then the ripples became a small, fast-running stream of shiny blackness that trickled directly across Measle's palm and into—*into something that hadn't been there before.*

Measle slowly turned his hand and stared at his palm

in amazement. Apart from its hugeness, it looked the same as always—a bit grubby, with all the familiar lines and creases in all the right places. The only small difference was the dull silver ring around his little finger—

Matilda's wrathring.

Matilda's wrathring, which had been around his sister's neck but which now sat snugly around Measle's little finger. He'd slipped it on back in the circular hallway, without giving the action a second thought.

Matilda's wrathring, which stopped her magic dead in its tracks—and which seemed to be stopping somebody *else's* magic dead in its tracks as well.

Sam stared up at Measle's hand. "Well, that's very interesting," he muttered. "I don't suppose a wrathring has ever been put on a nonmagical person before. I mean, what would be the point? And, since the ring had no magic to absorb from *you*, the only thing it could do was absorb magic from somewhere *else*."

Toby whirled around on his companions. His face was dark with fury and bewilderment. "What are you all *waiting* for?" he bellowed. "*Do* something!"

Dorian Fescue stepped forward, raised his yellow

face and screamed, "*Reductiornus bekswakwee sagaftra!*" The twin beams that shot from his eyes were yellow, too, just like his face.

Measle moved his hand. The yellow beams splashed against his palms and Measle noticed that, as with Toby's dark beams a moment before, he felt nothing other than a slight tickling sensation against his skin.

"*Fascinating,*" muttered Sam from Measle's top pocket.

"All of you!" shrieked Toby. "All the rest of you—*together!*"

Ermintrude Bacon, Quentin Underwood, Tully Telford and Sir Peregrine Spine all stepped forward and screamed the spell in unison. "*REDUCTIORNUS BEKSWAKWEE SAGAFTRA!*" The twin beams of light that shot from Ermintrude's eyes were a sickly pink; Sir Peregrine's were silver; Tully's were gray; and Quentin Underwood's were a dusty beige. All four beams merged as they neared Measle, their colors twisting together like a braided length of hair. Once again Measle intercepted the beams with the palm of his enormous hand. There was a brief, tickling sensation as the spells splashed against his skin.

"Oh dear," said Sam, leaning comfortably out of Measle's top pocket and grinning down at the group of Warlocks. "It looks like you've used up all your mana. So . . . what are you going to do now?"

Toby glared furiously up at Sam. "Don't think you're going to get away with this, Sam!" he shouted. "You're not! This escape attempt is illegal! You are committing a serious crime by breaking out of the detention center! That's where you belong until your cases are brought up before the courts!"

Sam shook his head. "But, Toby—our cases are not *going* to be brought up, are they? Our cases are going to disappear from the books, aren't they? Because *we* are going to be made to disappear, aren't we? You see, Toby—we know everything."

Toby pulled a small silver whistle from his pocket. He stuck it into his mouth, took a deep breath and blew a piercing blast. Guards!" he screamed. "GUARDS! GUARDS!!!"

From far down the dark corridor came the crash of a door being hurled open. Out of the gloom, a group of black-uniformed figures came running toward them. All wore shiny black helmets on their heads, and all carried heavy truncheons. Their boots made a drumming sound on the stone floor as they raced along.

Measle turned his massive body to face them. As the guards drew near, they saw, for the first time, what was facing them—a human mountain that completely filled the great corridor. It had hands the size of coffee tables, feet the size of small cars—and suddenly, the guards' boots stopped drumming on the stone floor. The guards slowed their pace to a cautious walk. Their leader—a huge man who Measle thought looked very like the one who had chased Toby and himself up the spiral staircase on the night of the inquiry—took several more paces forward and then stopped dead. The rest of the guards bunched up behind him. Measle could see their eyes glittering behind the visors of their helmets. The big guard in the front smacked his truncheon down into the palm of his hand several times, as if by doing this, he could somehow give himself a little courage and authority.

"Guards, arrest these criminals!" yelled Toby. "Do your duty and arrest them immediately!"

The leader of the guards stepped forward and stared

a little fearfully up at Measle.

"You'd better come along with us, if you know what's good for you," he said, his voice shaky with nerves.

"And if you know what's good for *you*," said Sam, leaning forward out of Measle's front pocket and pointing his finger down at the guard, "you'll get out of our way."

The big guard took a step backward, treading heavily on the toes of several guards who were huddling behind him.

The guard watched through frightened eyes as Measle lumbered slowly by.

"Stop them!" roared Toby. "You *cowards*! Stop them!"

Measle ignored everything except his father's directions. He began to move fast now, thundering down the long dark passage, Toby's wild yells receding into the distance behind him.

"Good, Measle!" called Sam. "Keep going, son— now turn right here—around to the right, then the second left—good—now all the way to the end—"

Measle followed Sam's directions blindly—and he moved as fast as his huge bulk allowed. Long passages

331

were taken in five giant steps, shorter ones in two. Measle was moving so fast now that the wind he made as he rushed by rattled the doors in their frames.

Measle could hear faint sounds of pursuit far behind him, so he guessed that Toby had somehow managed to rally the guards and persuade them to give chase. But that didn't worry him too much, not now that he was the size of an elephant! He remembered being picked up by Basil Tramplebone's enormous tweezers and being deposited on the coal heap in the dirty railway yard . . . now the tables were turned and it was *his* turn to be huge. *Only please let Tilly's spell last a little longer. . . .*

They had just started down a corridor that was so long that the walls, the floor and the ceiling ran into a single point in the far distance. The corridor was lit by a series of harsh white fluorescent strips set in the ceiling, and there were doors, hundreds of doors, set into each wall.

I've been here before, Measle said to himself.

Then—

"Hey, it's getting a bit tight in here!" called Sam.

"We're being squished!" shouted Lee.

Measle looked down and saw that his father and

mother were now pressed uncomfortably close together in the pocket—and they were getting a lot heavier, too. Measle had hardly noticed their combined weight when he'd first lifted them into his top pocket; now, the pocket was bulging and pulling his whole leather jacket forward, making the collar cut into the back of his neck.

And there were other bulges, too, in the pair of side pockets in the jacket—and the bulges were getting heavy, as well. Matilda's wrathring suddenly slipped off Measle's little finger and clattered to the floor.

And the corridor was getting taller and wider. . . .

"Quick!" yelled Sam, "the spell's wearing off! Get us out of here before we all get squashed! Tilly first—get Tilly out first, Measle!"

Measle stopped and reached his shrinking hands into his shrinking pockets. He carefully pulled the still-sleeping Matilda out and lay her down on the floor. Tinker jumped out on his own and then watched with interest as the smelly kid extracted Iggy from his other pocket.

Sam and Lee had taken matters into their own hands and scrambled out of Measle's top pocket, hanging at first by their hands, their legs dangling in the air. But now the drop from the pocket to the floor was only a couple of yards, so Sam and Lee jumped for it, landing with two thumps onto the hard floor. Then they all stepped back and watched as Measle swiftly returned to his proper size.

Measle, now looking *up* at his family, said, "See? Tilly's spells don't last very long. And doing them puts her fast asleep. She won't do another one until she wakes up."

"Very interesting," said Sam. "Very interesting indeed. I wonder——"

Lee had hurried to Matilda's side and had lifted her into her arms. She turned her head and looked back down the long passage, then she cupped a hand behind one ear and listened.

"There's no time to be wondering about anything, Sam," she said quickly. "They're heading this way——and this time, we're helpless! Come on, everybody——we've got to move fast!"

Sam led the way, running ahead of them down the long corridor. He went at a steady, easy pace, making sure everybody could keep up with him——but, in doing so, he allowed their pursuers gradually to close the gap. It wasn't long before Measle heard the distant sounds of heavy boots pounding along far behind them. Sam threw a look over his shoulder and called, "Come on, everybody! It's not too far now!"

Too far to where? thought Measle as he trotted along behind his father. The corridor they were in seemed to be endless and featureless, apart from the regular succession of doors on either side.

On and on they ran, the sound of thudding boots behind them steadily getting louder and louder. Soon they could hear muffled shouts, that turned quickly into yells—

"Oy! You! Stop! Stop right there!"

And Sam did indeed appear to obey the distant command, because he suddenly skidded to a halt. In front of him was a pair of sliding doors, and next to them was a panel of buttons—

An elevator!

But the doors were closed and Sam was frantically punching buttons and muttering, "Come on! Come on!" under his breath. Measle, panting hard, looked fearfully back the way they had come.

In the distance, racing toward them, came the group of black-uniformed figures. Measle saw them all suddenly increase their pace as they realized that there was no longer an eight-yard-tall boy-mountain confronting them; now there was just a small group of helpless-looking people clustered together by the closed doors of an elevator. . . .

An elevator that wouldn't come!

"Come on! Come *on*!" barked Sam, still wildly punching the buttons.

And then, without warning, the doors hissed open.

"Quick! Inside, everybody!" yelled Sam. They all piled in together, all except Iggy. Iggy was staring with more fear at the inside of the elevator than he was at the approaching guards.

"Come on, Mr. Niggle!" shouted Sam, but Iggy didn't move.

"Is dat one of dose fings wot goes whooshy-whooshy up and down?" said Iggy, suspiciously.

"Yes!" yelled Sam impatiently. Immediately, Iggy took a step backward and shook his head. "I don't like dem fings," he announced firmly. "You can't sssee where you is goin'."

Measle stuck his head out of the elevator and looked down the corridor. The guards were only twenty yards away—and they were fast closing the gap.

"No, Iggy!" shouted Measle. "It's just a box! A big box to keep the rain out! Come on!"

Iggy's face brightened and he took a step forward—and Sam shot out one brawny hand, grabbed Iggy by the front of his jacket and yanked him into the elevator. Sam stabbed his free hand against a red button and the doors hissed shut at the very moment that the leading guard slammed his heavy body against them.

The elevator shot upward.

Iggy sniffed loudly.

"Dat was a bad fibby-dib you jussst told, Mumpsss," he said sadly. "Disss *is* a whooshy-whooshy fing. It'sss not a box to keep de rain out at all. I've ssstill got my rain cloud in 'ere wiv me, 'aven't I?"

There wasn't really anything that Measle could say about that because it was true. Iggy's fist-sized rain cloud was indeed still hovering over Iggy's head, dribbling gently down on the little Wrathmonk. Iggy sniffed disapprovingly once again, and then relapsed into a sulky silence.

Measle looked up at his father. Sam's face was grim, and so was Lee's.

"Dad . . . ?" said Measle, but Sam held up a hand and shook his head.

"Not right now, son," he said quietly. "There's one more obstacle before we're clear. Let's deal with that first, shall we?"

Ten seconds later the elevator hummed to a stop. The doors slid open and they all stepped out, Sam leading the way.

They were in a big lobby with a shiny marble floor. Ten yards away was a revolving glass door—and across the lobby, to the right, was a desk.

A big man stood behind the desk.

He had a red face and a droopy, walrus moustache.

The big man caught sight of the Stubbs family. He stepped out from behind the desk.

"Hello, Fred," said Sam.

20

RETRACING STEPS

With a shock that felt as if he'd jumped into an icy lake, Measle realized why everything had looked so familiar for the last few minutes; that final, long corridor, those lines of wooden doors, the elevator, this shiny marble lobby—

He'd been here before.

Just a couple of days ago, in fact, when he and Sam and Lee and Matilda and Nanny Flannel and Tinker had all trooped across this exact same floor. Only *then* they'd been going in the opposite direction—*away* from the revolving door of the Wizards' Guild Building and *toward* the elevator in its lobby.

But—but this isn't possible! thought Measle, trying desperately to sort it all out. His mind felt a bit like a pile of damp clothes in a tumble dryer. All the ideas were jumbled together and were tumbling, multicolored, around and around. *How can I be in Caltrop Castle one minute and in the lobby of the Wizards' Guild Building the next? The two places are miles and miles apart—maybe even hundreds of miles apart. We drove forever, Toby and me, all through the long night—and besides, Caltrop Castle is in the country, and the Wizards' Guild Building is in the city! None of this makes any sense!*

Measle's wild thoughts were interrupted by the sudden pressure of Sam's hand on his shoulder. They were halfway across the lobby, but the way ahead was barred by the stout figure of Fred the lobby guard.

Sam, his hand resting lightly on Measle's shoulder, stopped—and the rest of them stopped, as well. For a moment there was silence. Then Fred said, "'ello, Mr. Stubbs. Been keeping well, 'ave you?"

"Quite well, thank you Fred," said Sam.

"Good, good," said Fred, nodding amiably. Then he

frowned and said, "I 'eard about some sort of aggravation down there in the lower quarters. I couldn't quite get the sense of it, but somebody said that you were involved in it, sir. Something about you and Mrs. Stubbs being 'eld in the detention center—is that right, sir?"

Measle heard something behind him. He turned and saw the elevator doors sliding shut—then he heard the whine of the hydraulic mechanism starting up.

The elevator was going back down.

"Dad . . . ?" he said, tugging gently on Sam's sleeve.

Sam didn't take his eyes off Fred, but he nodded and said, "Yes, I know, son."

Fred was looking uneasily at each member of the party. Iggy was trying to hide himself at the rear, but Fred caught sight of him and took a hurried step backward.

"'Ere—is that a nasty little *Wrathmonk* you've got there, Mr. Stubbs?"

"Yes, Fred, it is," said Sam, in a very calm and collected voice. "Although it turns out that he's not really all *that* nasty—are you, Mr. Niggle?"

In the face of this difficult question, Iggy did his

face-twisting act again. Then Iggy's facial muscles settled down and he said, hesitantly, "I fink I'm *quite*
nasssty, actually."

Fred took another step backward.

"Sorry to mention this, Mr. Stubbs, sir," he said, "but
a Wrathmonk's got no business 'ere. Not up 'ere in the
lobby of Wizards' Guild, 'e 'asn't. 'E should be down
in the detention center, where 'e belongs."

Sam stepped forward, closer to Fred. He put both
hands on Fred's shoulders and looked the stout man
straight in the eye.

"Fred, we haven't much time," said Sam. His voice
was quiet but firm. "So I'll be honest with you. We're
on the run, my family and I. And Mr. Niggle, too. Any
second now, a bunch of uniformed guards is going to
burst out of that elevator over there and they're going
to arrest the lot of us. We haven't done anything
wrong, Fred. Not even Mr. Niggle. In fact, Mr. Niggle
has been very helpful to my family. But this Advisory
Board says we're to be arrested, and there's nothing we
can do about it. Unless you help us by letting us go on
our way, that is."

Fred's eyes widened with astonishment. He looked

long and hard at Sam—then he switched his gaze to Lee, then to Measle. He glared fiercely at Iggy, who was busy picking his nose. He looked back to Sam. And then, at last, Fred nodded slowly.

"I've known you a long time, Mr. Stubbs, sir—and you've always been straight with me. And Mrs. Stubbs is a fine lady, I've always thought that."

"Thank you, Fred," said Lee.

"And what I've 'eard of young Measle—well, it's all been good. And we can't be letting anybody arrest a little baby, now can we? And I'll tell you another thing—I don't like this Advisory Board and I *'specially* don't like these clumsy new guards they've got. I dunno where they come from and I don't want to know—but they've got no business clod-'opping around in the Guild Building, doing whatever they like."

Fred talks too much! thought Measle. *The elevator is going to be here any minute!* Measle started hopping anxiously from foot to foot, shooting desperate glances at Sam, hoping to catch his attention. Sam looked at him and then glanced over his shoulder toward the elevator doors.

"Fred, if you're going to let us go, perhaps now

343

might be a good time to do it. I think I hear the elevator coming back up—and it's going to be chock-full of those clod-hopping guards we don't like."

They all stood still, straining their ears—there was the distant whine of an elevator ascending at great speed—and the whine was getting louder and louder.

Fred turned on his heel and marched quickly back to his desk. At the same moment, Sam herded his family fast toward the revolving doors.

Out of the corner of his eye, Measle saw Fred reach under his desk. The big man fiddled with something under there—a switch, perhaps, or a button—then straightened up. At the exact same moment, there was a hissing sound as the elevator arrived.

But the doors didn't open.

Instead, after a short silence, there was a sudden hubbub of sound from inside. There were raised voices—then shouts—then the noise of heavy fists pounding against metal.

"Oh dear, Mr. Stubbs!" shouted Fred, "I'm terribly afraid something dreadful 'as 'appened! Oh dear, oh dear—whatever shall we do?"

Fred spoke in a sort of over-loud, high-pitched

singsong tone—the sort of voice that a very bad actor might use onstage when he's talking about something awful that has just taken place.

Sam paused, his hand on the revolving door.

"What's the matter, Fred?" he said loudly—sounding, to Measle's ears, a little artificial as well, as if he was reciting lines he'd just learned.

Fred shook his head dramatically. "A most unfortunate thing, Mr. Stubbs!" he exclaimed, waggling his eyebrows and pointing wildly toward the elevator. "Most unfortunate indeed! It would appear that the elevator is malfunctioning, sir!"

"Malfunctioning, Fred?"

"Yes, sir! It would appear that the elevator doors are, in fact, stuck, sir! Oh dear, oh dear, oh dear! Whatever shall we do, sir? All those poor people—trapped in the elevator, sir!"

Sam smiled. Then, in his normal voice, he said, "Thank you, Fred. I won't forget this."

"No, sir! Neither will I, sir!" shouted Fred at the top of his voice. "An elevator malfunction is not something one can easily forget, sir! All those poor, poor people! Now then, don't you worry about this—it's my problem, Mr. Stubbs! You be on your way, sir!"

"Thanks, Fred," Sam said. "Good night!"

Sam gave the revolving door a great shove and set it turning—and one by one the Stubbs family spilled out onto the dark and empty street.

Once outside, Sam gathered them all together.

"We'd better get a move on," he said urgently. "Those elevator doors won't hold the guards for long. Come on!"

Sam led them in a fast run down the dark street. There was nobody around at this time of night and few of the buildings that surrounded them showed any lights in their windows.

The Stubbs car was still where they had parked it. Sam yanked open the doors and everybody piled in— Measle and Sam and Tinker in front, Lee in the back holding tight to Matilda, and—

"Come on, Iggy!" yelled Measle. Iggy was still standing on the pavement. He was staring with admiration at the huge car, his fishy eyes wide with wonder.

"Iggy! Get in!"

Iggy shook his head. "Can't," he muttered.

"Why not, Iggy?"

"I'll make it all wet," said Iggy sadly. "Dose nice

ssseats—dey will smell all funny when I get off dem. Dey always do."

Sam reached under the dashboard and pulled a short lever—and the lid of the trunk clicked open and swung upward.

"How about in there, Mr. Niggle?" Sam shouted. "Nothing to spoil in there—and besides, it's too small for your rain cloud! The beastly thing will just have to stay outside!"

Iggy's face brightened. He said, "Coo—fanksss very much, Mr. Ssstubbs, sssir! Dat will do nicely, fanksss!"

He scurried to the rear of the car, hopped into the trunk and lay down, and Sam pushed the lever back and the lid of the trunk swung shut.

Sam punched the big red button and the car rumbled to life.

"Where are we going, Sam?" said Lee. "We can't go home—that's the first place they'll look for us."

"I know," said Sam. "Wait a minute—let me think."

Sam furrowed his brow and tapped the front of his teeth with his fingernail. Then, suddenly, he seemed to come to a decision. He reached forward and pushed the button marked A/P.

Yes? came the haughty voice of the car's autopilot.

"A destination," said Sam.

Where to?

"Lord Octavo's house, please."

Lord Octavo's house it is, sir.

The car pulled away from the curb and accelerated down the dark street

Iggy's muffled voice came drifting out of the back of the car. "We is goin' to Lord Octopusss'sss houssse? Coo, dat is good—I like Lord Octopusss. He gave me a cookie once. And I like it in 'ere, too. It is nice and dry in 'ere. I could live in 'ere, I could. I could live in 'ere, and I could sssleep in 'ere, and I could eat sss-weeties in 'ere, and I could—"

Iggy babbled on and on as the big green car roared through the night.

And Iggy's tiny black rain cloud—locked out of the trunk and thus separated from its master by a sheet of strong steel—tore frantically through the cold night air in pursuit of the speeding car.

348

21

THE COURT OF MAGISTRI

The hearing was going badly.

For the Stubbs family, that is.

The hearing was being held in the same great chamber as the original inquiry, and it was packed. Every Wizard and every Warlock who could manage to squeeze into the crowded space was there, and the court was hushed and expectant. Five elderly judges sat in a line on the platform, their long red robes cascading to the floor in folds. Behind them, on a taller platform, sat Justin Bucket, in a long blue robe with gold stripes on the sleeves. Justin looked pale and frightened, but nobody else did. In fact, Toby Jugg and the five Warlocks of the Advisory Board looked relaxed and thoroughly at ease.

"But can you *prove* all this, Mr. Stubbs?"

The judge who had asked the question was sitting next to Lord Octavo and was leaning forward on his elbows, looking hard at Sam with a disbelieving expression on his elderly face.

Sam and Lee were sitting in a small wooden enclosure, in front—and a little to the right—of the judges' platform. Sam opened his mouth to reply, but Tully Telford interrupted him.

"Of course they can't prove it, my lord," squeaked Tully Telford. "They can't prove it because none of it happened!"

Tully Telford was sitting on a plain bench inside another wooden enclosure. His pen was bigger than Sam and Lee's and was directly in front of the judges' platform. Toby Jugg and the rest of the Advisory Board were sitting just behind Tully. They all had faint smiles on their faces. Measle thought they looked as if they considered the entire proceedings a dreadful waste of time.

Nanny Flannel, Matilda Stubbs and Tinker weren't in the court. Nanny Flannel wasn't there because she hadn't been part of the adventure; Matilda wasn't there because Lord Octavo had said that she couldn't possibly be there, because everybody in the Wizards' Guild was terrified of her and they all dreaded the possibility that she might decide to use her powers again; and Tinker wasn't there because Lord Octavo had said that, while a silly little inquiry might encourage dogs to attend, the Court of Magistri most certainly didn't.

"All these extraordinary accusations!" squeaked Tully. "Such nonsense! The monstrous suggestion that Mr. Jugg somehow drugged the boy's drink in a freeway café and then simply drove him back to the Guild Building while he was unconscious! And the rest of it—pictures that come to life! Tiny cows! A murderous grimling! A suit of armor that attacks on sight! I ask you, my lords—how can we take these idiocies seriously? At best, these are mere figments of a lively imagination! Ridiculous, the whole thing!"

"Thank you, Mr. Telford," said Lord Octavo quietly. "Thank you for your opinion. Now, Mr. Stubbs— please continue."

Things had gone badly for the Stubbs family from the start—as Lord Octavo had warned them that they might.

Two days earlier a big green car with the skull of a baby dragon decorating the hood had rumbled up to Lord Octavo's front door just before dawn. Lord Octavo lived alone in a pretty little thatched cottage deep in the countryside. Sam and Lee had knocked on the front door, and soon there were the sounds of bolts being drawn back. The door cracked open, revealing Lord Octavo in his pajamas and dressing gown. He took one look at the bedraggled collection of people standing on his doorstep and, without a word, led them into his living room, sat them down and listened intently until Sam had finished speaking.

"You must understand," he had said, his clever old face wrinkled with concern, "that convening the Court of Magistri is a very serious business. It's hardly ever done—and only in matters of supreme importance. Also, remember I am not the only judge—there are five of us in total and not all will be friendly to your case. The accusations you're making are extraordinary—and the Warlocks you are accusing are all perfectly respectable people, most of them occupying positions of some power and influence. I am the senior judge, which helps you a little—but I can be outvoted, so you must not rely on me. Do you still want me to convene this court?"

"We most certainly do, Lord Octavo," said Sam. "Without the court, I don't see any future for us."

"And, if we should happen to lose," said Lord Octavo slowly, "I don't see any future for *any* of us."

From where Measle was sitting in the great room, the future looked bleak.

"I would like to propose to this court," squeaked Tully Telford, "that all so-called 'testimony' from these people be struck from the record, on the grounds that not a word of it can be proved! I further propose that any evidence from young Measle Stubbs and the Wrathmonk Ignatius Niggle be considered worthless—worthless, on the grounds that, as far as the boy is concerned, his mind is obviously seriously disturbed and, as far as Ignatius Niggle is concerned, no Wrathmonk has ever been allowed to testify before *any* court assembled by the Wizards' Guild, and now is not the time to change such customs. And, since the testimony of these two witnesses is therefore invalid, I propose that this court—and all the persons charged—be dismissed forthwith! Judges of the Court of Magistri— please raise your hands, those who concur with these proposals!"

To Measle's horror, four hands were lifted slowly in the still air. Only Lord Octavo's remained firmly resting on the desk in front of him.

"A case before the Court of Magistri does not require full agreement of the presiding judges!" shouted Tully triumphantly. "The Court of Magistri can rule by a clear majority! We *have* a clear majority—of four to one! The case *must* be dismissed!"

There was a general hubbub in the courtroom as every Wizard and Warlock there put their heads together and muttered their reactions to each other. Measle looked down at the faces of the six grinning Warlocks. Toby's smile was broader than anybody else's.

They're going to get away with it! thought Measle, *and there's nothing we can do about it! If only I could get them to tell what really happened! If only there was some way to reveal the truth, to lay bare their souls, to force them to stop lying, to open them up. . . .*

Open them up.

Open them.

Open . . .

And then the most peculiar idea that Measle had ever come up with dropped into his brain, like a single bead of water falling into a pond. A little drop of water that plopped silently into his thoughts, sending ripples of further thoughts rolling out across the surface of his mind.

It's crazy! thought Measle. *It's senseless! It doesn't even mean the same thing—but—but it's our only chance!*

Measle came to a momentous decision—and he came to it quickly, because the whole notion didn't bear examining too closely. He turned to Iggy and tapped him on the shoulder and Iggy twisted his head around quickly, spattering Measle's face with rain water.

"Wot?" he muttered, frowning at Measle.

"Iggy!" hissed Measle. "I want you to do your spell! I want you to do your spell right *now!*"

"Wot for?" whispered Iggy. "Dere's nuffing dat needs openin' right now, is dere?"

"Yes! Yes, there is, Iggy!"

"Wot, Mumpsss? Wot needs openin'?"

Measle raised his right hand and pointed straight down toward the wooden enclosure. "*He* does, Iggy! *Toby Jugg! He needs to be opened!*"

Iggy gaped at Measle, his jaw slack and his fishy eyes wide. "Missster Jugg ain't a *lock*, Mumpsss!" he muttered. "He's a *War*lock! Jussst 'coz it sssounds de sssame, dat don't mean it *is* de sssame! One is made of *perssson*, de uvver is made of *metal*. You can't open a *perssson*, sssee?"

Measle grabbed the front of Iggy's damp, mildewy coat, pulled Iggy's head next to his and whispered frantically into Iggy's ear.

"Maybe you can't, Iggy! But then again—*maybe you can*! It's worth a try, isn't it?"

Iggy's expression of dumb bewilderment didn't change. Slowly, sorrowfully, he shook his head. "You is potty, Mumpsss," he said.

Down below, the judges were settling back into their chairs. Lord Octavo rapped on the desk in front of him with a small silver hammer.

"Fellow Wizards, fellow Warlocks," he said, "I find myself in a minority of one in this case. Mr. Telford has pointed out, correctly, that the judgment of a case before the Court of Magistri does not require full agreement from the presiding judges. A majority vote is sufficient. Therefore—reluctantly I must add—it is my duty to close these proceedings, with the verdict that no fault, blame or guilt attaches to these persons here before us—"

Measle had one last trick up his sleeve. He pulled Iggy's ear close to his mouth and whispered into it. The whisper was hoarse and urgent and filled with panic, but the words still rang crystal clear in Iggy's head.

"If you try your spell on Mr. Jugg, Iggy—I'll give you two hundred red jelly beans—*every day for the rest of your life!*"

This time Iggy didn't even pause to think. Instead, his pale, thin little face lit up with greedy joy and, in the next instant, he turned away from Measle, leaned over the balcony of the gallery and, staring fixedly down at Toby Jugg, he screamed, *"Unkashhhriek gorgogashhh plurgholipsss!"*

Instantly a pair of lavender-colored beams shot from Iggy's eyes and sizzled down through the still air of the courtroom, smacking Toby cleanly on the back of his head.

For a moment there was a stunned silence. Toby himself slowly reached up a hand and stroked his long hair, as if he was smoothing it back into place. Other than this gesture, he seemed not to have noticed that anything at all had happened.

It obviously didn't work! thought Measle miserably.

There was a buzz of fear from those who had heard the spell and seen the lavender beams. Quite a few of the audience in the great room rose to their feet, and several Wizards pulled back their sleeves, getting themselves ready to hurl their own spells around—but Lord Octavo held up his hands and shouted over the mounting din.

"Calm yourselves, everybody! That was just the foolish little Wrathmonk, Ignatius Niggle, pointlessly performing his only spell! It does nothing other than open stubborn locks! It's quite harmless! There is nothing to fear! Why he did it is anybody's guess—but there's no harm done and now he's mana-less—so, please, all of you sit down again! You, too, Niggle. We shall deal with you later!"

Slowly the hubbub died away and everybody sat down—but there were a lot of suspicious looks directed at Measle and Iggy, and three of the four judges bent their heads together and began an urgent, whispered discussion.

Well, thought Measle, *it's now or never.*

Measle got to his feet and leaned over the balcony. His heart was thumping with nervousness and his tongue felt dry and rough, like a piece of sandpaper.

He gulped.

He licked his lips.

He took a deep breath.

And he knew—as sure as he knew *anything*—that this wasn't going to work.

"WHAT DID YOU PUT IN MY DRINK, TOBY?" he shouted, his voice echoing around the great chamber.

All eyes flicked up to the small boy with the peculiar haircut standing up in the front row of the gallery. Toby Jugg turned slowly, raising his eyes up to where Measle stood. He smiled an affable smile and then he said, quite simply and cheerfully, "Oh, a marvelous concoction, old son. Dunno what it's called. Got it out of the alchemy labs. I must say, it worked like a charm—knocked you out cold, didn't it?"

The silence that hung over the great courtroom was thick and heavy. Nothing stirred. Nobody moved. Breathing stopped. Even if a pin had dropped, it almost certainly wouldn't have made a sound.

And Measle was thinking, *I don't believe it! It—it's working! Toby Jugg has been opened up!*

"WHAT DID YOU DO NEXT, TOBY?"

"Popped you back into the car, old son, turned it around and drove straight back to the Wizards' Guild. Put you to bed in the basement labyrinth—when you woke up, I said you were hundreds of miles away, in Caltrop Castle. Then I left you to your own devices. Watched you, of course. Watched you cope with all the dangers I threw at you. Thought you did jolly well, too."

"ARE YOU THE PRIME MAGUS OF THE WIZARDS' GUILD, TOBY?"

"I certainly am, old son," said Toby, with a careless little laugh. "I wiped the floor with poor Bucket. He didn't have a chance against me. I got nearly twice as many votes as he did—"

"Shut up, Toby! *Shut up!*"

The scream came from Dorian Fescue, who was on his feet, his yellow face trembling with fear and fury. The other Warlocks were on their feet as well, all staring with furious and frightened eyes at Toby Jugg.

"Be quiet, Mr. Fescue," said Lord Octavo in a mild voice. "Be quiet and sit down, please."

"I will *not* sit down!" yelled Dorian, anger turning his yellow face an unpleasant shade of orange. "Everything Jugg is saying is a tissue of lies!"

"BE QUIET AND SIT DOWN! ALL OF YOU—BE QUIET AND SIT DOWN IMMEDIATELY!"

All five Warlocks sat down as if somebody had suddenly thumped them hard on the tops of their heads—and Measle sat down, too. He couldn't help it. There was something in Lord Octavo's new tone of voice that simply forced the listener to obey instantly.

Lord Octavo smiled and looked up at Measle.

"One of my more useful little vocal tricks, Master Stubbs," he said, using his normal voice again. "The last time I used it was on a charging water buffalo. It stopped him dead in his tracks. But that's another story. Now—you're doing extremely well, young man.

361

Perhaps you should think of pursuing a career in the law—when you're a bit older, that is. Meanwhile, would you object at all if we asked a few questions of our own?"

"N-no, sir."

"Thank you." Lord Octavo brought his gaze to bear on the six Warlocks, who were now sitting huddled together in their enclosure, nervous expressions on their faces. All, that is, except for Toby Jugg, who sat on his section of the bench with a relaxed and cheerful smile on his lips.

"Mr. Jugg," said Lord Octavo, in a cool, quiet voice, "we would like to know if Justin Bucket is involved in this affair?"

Toby laughed boisterously. "Justin? That idiot? No, of course he isn't! He's a dope—and a *Wizard* dope to boot! Only Warlocks need apply here!"

Lord Octavo nodded pleasantly. Behind him, Justin Bucket's face turned a deep crimson.

"And did you use the Guild Building's mana to further your own ends?" continued Lord Octavo. "And, in so doing, did you place young Measle Stubbs in extreme danger?"

"I can't deny that," said Toby with a broad smile.

"Did you give Officer Offal money, Mr. Jugg?"

"I certainly did," said Toby. "Rather more than I wanted to, actually!"

"Why did you give Officer Offal money, Mr. Jugg?"

"To get him to open Measle's cell door."

"And why would you want him to do that, Mr. Jugg?"

Toby laughed his careless, booming laugh. "Well, so that all the Wrathmonks could get at him, you see. I knew they would make short work of him if they could get at him."

"Short work, Mr. Jugg? Do you mean they would *kill* him?"

"I should say so! Well, that was the whole idea, wasn't it? Once we'd discovered the boy had no magic, there was no point keeping him alive, was there? He and his father were of no value to our schemes, you see. No—all we needed by then was the Mallockee and her mother!"

Lord Octavo leaned back in his chair, his eyes twinkling. Then he turned to the two judges sitting on either side of him and said, "Perhaps my colleagues might like to question Mr. Jugg—now that he seems ready to tell the truth?"

For the next hour, all five judges barked question after question at Toby Jugg, and Toby Jugg answered every question with the utter, exact and absolute truth. Lord Octavo only had to use his special voice twice more—once when Toby was telling the court about the worldwide search for more Manafounts (he repeated Ermintrude Bacon's plea for a specially *handsome* Manafount husband, and Ermintrude shrieked with embarrassment); and once again when Tully Telford tried desperately to take control of the court by using lots of complicated legal words and phrases that nobody could possibly understand. At the end of it all, when every question had been asked and when Toby had revealed the whole monstrously wicked plan, there was a long, deep silence in the courtroom.

Sam Stubbs broke the silence.

"Well," he said, getting to his feet and holding out his hand to Lee, "I seem to remember we've done this before. This time I hope we shall succeed. So, once again, with the court's permission, I would like to take my family home."

Lord Octavo smiled and then turned to the other judges. "I trust nobody has any objections?"

The four other judges shook their heads. They looked a little stunned.

Lord Octavo twisted further around in his seat and peered up at Justin Bucket. Justin's face was very pale and his lips were compressed in a thin line—and his eyes were wide with fear.

"Mr. Prime Magus," said Lord Octavo, his voice ringing out through the whole great courtroom. "Do *you* have any objection?"

Like the judges, Justin didn't speak. Instead, dumbly, he, too, simply shook his head.

"You are free to go, Mr. Stubbs," said Lord Octavo, turning back and looking gravely down at Sam and Lee. "But before you do so, I would like to say something. This has been a terrible ordeal for you all. On behalf of the Wizards' Guild, I would like to offer our apologies to you and you family. I would also like to express our profound gratitude for bringing this unfortunate matter to our attention. That is all. Go home now, Mr. and Mrs. Stubbs. Take young Measle with you—and trust us to handle the rest of this dreadful business."

"Thank you, Lord Octavo," said Sam. Then Sam and Lee looked up at Measle and grinned at him. Sam jerked his head toward the door and called, "Come on, Measle. Let's go home, eh?"

Measle got up—and, instantly, he felt his arm gripped in a small but powerful hand. Measle looked down into Iggy's face, which was doing its twisting, muscle-pulling, grimacing again.

"What, Iggy?"

"Er," said Iggy, his fishy eyes swiveling madly, "about dose red jelly beans, Mumpsss—"

"They'll be at my house, Iggy," Measle whispered. "So, if you still want them, you'd better come with us, hadn't you?"

22

LOOSE ENDS

Iggy Niggle came to live at Merlin Manor.

Not *in* Merlin Manor—just *at* Merlin Manor. Nanny Flannel wouldn't let him in the house.

"I don't *care* if it saved you all!" she exclaimed crossly. "I'm not having some wet little creature dripping all over my nice clean kitchen! It can live outside!"

Measle spent half a day trying to think of some argument that could change Nanny Flannel's mind—but he stopped trying once Iggy saw the kennel.

The kennel was supposed to belong to Tinker. When

Tinker had come to live at Merlin Manor, Sam had gone out and bought the biggest and the best (and certainly the most expensive) doghouse that money could buy.

Tinker had refused to use it. *What's the point of that?* he'd thought, firmly turning his back on the kennel and walking away from it with all the dignity that a small, fuzzy, black-and-white dog can muster. *What's the point of a little tiny house, when there is a socking great big house right next to it—and the socking great big house has got all the nice soft furniture in it, eh?*

So the kennel had stood empty, close beside the kitchen door—until Iggy Niggle saw it.

"Wot is disss, Mumpsss?" said Iggy, his eyes wide with wonder and longing as he stared down at the kennel. It was painted blue and white, with clapboard sides and a real shingled roof. It had a little arched doorway and, inside, a smooth, clean, wooden floor. Sam had put it right beside the kitchen door in the hope that Tinker—who used the kitchen door more than any other door in Merlin Manor—might get used to seeing it there and decide to give it a go. But that hadn't happened, because Tinker insisted on sleeping as close to the smelly kid as he could possibly get, which was certainly *not* just outside the kitchen door.

Measle saw the look of yearning in Iggy's eyes and did a bit of quick thinking.

"It's—it's a little house, Iggy. Do you like it?"

"Do I like it! *Do I like it?* It'sss—it'sss—*bee-yoo-tee-full!*"

"You think it's beautiful, Iggy?"

Iggy nodded so vigorously that raindrops flew off his head and spattered everywhere.

"Well, that's good," said Measle, "because it's *your* house, Iggy."

Iggy's jaw dropped. "Mine?" he whispered.

"Yours, Iggy."

The kennel was the perfect size for Iggy. He still had to lie curled up inside it, but it was a lot less cramped than his old box. And, since it had a proper roof with real shingles on it, the rain slid off it very efficiently and, once inside, Iggy stayed perfectly dry. It even had a little window and a pretend chimney, and when Measle painted "Iggy's House" on the front, just over the arched doorway, Iggy thought it was the finest and most desirable residence in the whole wide world.

And the Stubbs family found a use for the little Wrathmonk, too. Idle Wrathmonks are worse than busy ones, so there had to be something for Iggy to do—and Lee figured out what it should be. There was a wonderful collection of roses at Merlin Manor—thousands and thousands of them, in many different colors, planted in flower beds all over the vast gardens. And they were always being attacked by aphids. Aphids—those tiny green insects that suck the sap from the stems of roses and spoil the flowers. Iggy's new job was to visit, regularly, all the roses in the Merlin Manor garden and, one by one, gently breathe on them.

Quite soon the display of roses at Merlin Manor was one of the finest in the whole country.

The business of the two hundred red jelly beans that Measle had promised Iggy might have posed a bit of a problem, but Nanny Flannel solved it by declaring that, if the wet little thing gave her his word that he wouldn't try and come into her nice clean kitchen, then she would *make* him his two hundred red jelly beans fresh every day. And, since Nanny Flannel's red jelly beans tasted much better than the ones from the jar (they were made from real strawberry juice and didn't have even a milligram of magic in them), Iggy was about as happy as a Wrathmonk can be when he's not allowed to be unpleasant to anybody—which, in Iggy's case, was very happy indeed.

Having a Mallockee for a sister turned out to be not quite as disturbing as Measle had feared it might be.

They did several experiments with the little girl—measuring her abilities, testing her magical output, noting her extreme fatigue after performing even the simplest of spells—and the results made everybody in the Merlin Manor household sigh with relief. Matilda's spells were never hurtful, she always fell fast asleep after doing them and they never lasted longer than ten minutes.

"I bet I know why they're so harmless and don't last long," said Lee, peering fondly down at Matilda, who was once again fast asleep in her cot. Matilda had exhausted herself by turning Iggy's old black coat a luminous shade of orange. (Iggy was very pleased with it—at least, for the ten minutes that the color lasted.)

"Why don't they last, Mum?" said Measle.

"I think it's because we were swimming in dragon's blood that was mixed up with seawater," Lee said thoughtfully. "And there was *far* more water than there was blood—so Arcturion's mana was very heavily diluted, you see. I reckon it might have been something like one part of blood to a thousand parts of water—so Tilly and I were getting only a fraction of the mana that a *real* Mallockee should get."

"I think we might keep that information to ourselves," said Sam, who had just strolled into the nursery.

"Why, Sam?" said Lee.

"Well," said Sam, tapping the front of his teeth with his fingernail, "I think it might be quite a good idea if we let the Wizards' Guild go on thinking that Tilly's a really *powerful* Mallockee, don't you? It won't hurt them to be—well—a little *frightened* of the Stubbs family. We'll get a lot more respect, I should imagine. And if those two horrible office boys, Mr. Needle and Mr. Bland, ever come to visit us again, they might behave themselves a bit better if they know there's a powerful Mallockee in the house, don't you think?"

"I rather think I do," said Lee.

Several days later Lord Octavo came to visit.

Lee and Sam and Measle gathered around him, all

four of them sitting comfortably at the kitchen table. Iggy was allowed to peer in through the kitchen door—but Nanny, holding a floor mop at the ready, made sure he came no farther.

"I thought you might like to know the outcome of the trial," said Lord Octavo, sipping at a cup of tea. "After all the truth came out, it was decided that Toby Jugg should be sent to the detention center. He'll be down there for quite some time. Officer Offal is currently occupying the next-door cell, and *he'll* be down there for a fairly long time, too. The rest of the gang have been banished from the Wizards' Guild for life. They've been stripped of their magical powers and sent back out into the human world, where, no doubt, they'll continue to make dreadful nuisances of themselves. At least *we* won't be bothered with them."

Lord Octavo looked up from his cup of tea and peered at Iggy, who was craning his neck through the open kitchen door.

"Mr. Niggle," he called, "you'll be pleased to know that you've been given a full pardon and are to be allowed to stay here under the watchful eyes of the Stubbs family—just as long as you don't get yourself into any more trouble. Do you understand?"

"Coo—fanksss, Lord Octopusss," said Iggy.

Lord Octavo choked back a small laugh. Then he looked gravely around at every member of the Stubbs family and said quietly, "I'm not going to inquire about the Mallockee. As far as I am concerned, she is entirely your responsibility. And I am confident that it's a responsibility that you will all take very, *very* seriously."

"Oh, we will, Lord Octavo," said Sam. "Very, *very* seriously indeed."

A few days later, it was breakfast time once again at Merlin Manor.

Lee, Sam, Measle and Matilda were sitting at the big kitchen table. Sam, as usual, was buried behind his newspaper. Tinker was wandering from person to person, hoping for a treat to be dropped down into his open mouth. Nanny Flannel was at the stove, carefully pouring hot red sugar syrup into two hundred little oval molds. Iggy Niggle was standing at the open kitchen door, his fishy eyes staring greedily at the process.

Sam's newspaper started to shake.

"I don't *believe* it!" he muttered. "The *idiots*! The *cretins*! The stark, staring, barking *lunatics*!"

"What's happened now, Sam?" said Lee, putting down her cup of coffee and leaning forward on her elbows.

Sam lowered the newspaper to reveal a heavy frown of irritation creasing his forehead.

"They've done the stupidest thing you can imagine!" he said furiously.

"*What* have they done, Sam?" said Lee. "And, who are 'they,' may we ask?"

"*They* are the collective morons of the Wizards' Guild," barked Sam. "And they have done something so *unbelievably* silly—"

"*What* have they done, Sam?"

"Justin Bucket has resigned. He's no longer the Prime Magus."

"Well, that's good, isn't it?" said Lee.

Sam sighed heavily. "Oh, sure—*that* part is good," he said. "But it's who they've chosen to take his place, to be the new Prime Magus. Of all the brainless, dim-witted, senseless ideas, this takes the biscuit! How on earth could they have been so irresponsible to have picked such an *utterly*, *totally* and *completely* unsuitable candidate!"

Lee snorted with impatience. She rapped her knuckles on the table and said, "Well, who is it, Sam? Who is this dreadful person they've picked to be Prime Magus?"

"Me," said Sam sadly.